PRAISE FOR
WE PIERCE

"An unflinching and deeply moving look at how we respond when circumstances take a turn for the worse."

—*Time Out New York*

"A well-written, surprisingly straightforward account of a not-so-straightforward war."

—*Kirkus Reviews*

"Starkly realistic and timely. . . . The characters are richly individualized. Huebner's blunt and unvarnished prose lends impact to the questions he poses and morality of the Gulf War."

—*Publishers Weekly*

"[*We Pierce* is] about fighting for what you believe in."

—*Newsday*

PRAISE FOR
AMERICAN BY BLOOD

"A strong first novel, vividly evoking the shock of Custer's defeat at the Little Bighorn, as it would have been felt by the young soldiers who experienced it. Andrew Huebner has merged action and emotion well."

—Larry McMurtry

"I believe *American by Blood* is a small masterpiece—as perfectly constructed, beautifully written and affecting a story of the American West as has been told in our time."

—Charles Gaines, author of *A Family Place*

ALSO BY ANDREW HUEBNER

American by Blood

WE PIERCE

A NOVEL

ANDREW HUEBNER

SIMON & SCHUSTER
NEW YORK LONDON TORONTO SYDNEY

SIMON & SCHUSTER
Rockefeller Center
1230 Avenue of the Americas
New York, NY 10020

First Simon & Schuster trade paperback edition 2004

SIMON & SCHUSTER and colophon are registered trademarks
of Simon & Schuster, Inc.

For information about special discounts for bulk purchases,
please contact Simon & Schuster Special Sales at
1-800-456-6798 or business@simonandschuster.com

Designed by Jan Pisciotta

Manufactured in the United States of America

3   5   7   9   10   8   6   4   2

The Library of Congress has cataloged the hardcover edition as follows:

We Pierce : a novel / Andrew Huebner.
p. cm.
1. Persian Gulf War, 1991—Fiction. 2. Brothers—Fiction. I. Title.

PS3558.U3126W4 2003
813'.54—dc21   2003041618

ISBN 0-7432-1277-0
0-7432-1278-9 (Pbk)

I would like to dedicate the book to my brother Dave and my wife Sarah.

Soldier, your eyes shine like the sun.
I wonder why.

—Neil Young

Zero hour,
   a 767 jet plane,
   276 soldiers,
   an M-16 apiece,
   rucksack,
   full desert camouflage fatigues, the same boots, socks and
underwear, different smells, beliefs and mother's marks on their
foreheads.

   The second of August, 1990, Saddam Hussein's Iraqi forces,
three full divisions and one of special forces, one hundred thousand troops, tanks, trucks and armored personnel carriers
crossed the Kuwaiti border. The Iraqis took control of Kuwait
City and the country's oil wells in forty-eight hours. George
Herbert Walker Bush, the forty-first president of the United
States, condemned Iraq's act of naked aggression and called on
the United Nations to respond. By August 5, President Bush
drew a line in the sand and planted the Stars and Stripes at the
Saudi Arabian border.

   Sergeant E-5 Smith Huebner's tank company, D, the Dark

Lords, would be part of that line. Less than two weeks later as part of the 66th Infantry, 1st Battalion, 64th Armor, United States Army, Huebner boarded a plane for the Arabian desert. His mind was imprinted with Hollywood images, combat skills enhanced by computer simulation. He had never visited violence upon another man on command. In theory, he could kill with his weapon or his hands; Huebner was really good with his hands. Guys liked to have him around when they took on Marines or sailors in bar fights, trading battle techniques and drinking formations. They fought Marines on Hay Street in Fayetteville, North Carolina, near Camp Lejeune, and sailors on Virginia Beach at the base in Norfolk.

Years of indoctrination and relentless training shut away any doubts that might have lingered outside the vacuum-sealed windows of the brand-new plane, that they could lose, that they were just organisms of wingless flesh flying against the wishes of God in a gigantic piece of galvanized tin, a folly held together by a mathematical equation of physics they had never paid attention to in boring math classes, written by a nerd with horn-rimmed glasses they had outrun on the playground and only picked for the team because they felt sorry for him. It was part of their destiny to win any fight and bear any burden not because they were right or stronger of will or sent by God as other warriors of ages past, but because they were born in America from where the best machines of death were spawned, from the Gatling gun that eviscerated the Indians, to the mushroom cloud that burned the Japanese alive.

Most Americans had to watch the Special Reports on the news that interrupted their soap operas, ball games or the new fake real shows like *Current Affair* and *Cops* to learn exactly where Kuwait was. Smith's brother Sam called that Sunday when Bush made his speech. No one had cared about the Middle East since Reagan had gotten the hostages back from Iran. Hadn't Iraq been our friend then?

You're not going, are you?

We're the first to fight, Smith replied, his voice dropping a register.

The soldiers were given war manuals to read: entries on the human dimension of warfare, sign communication with the enemy, first aid for melted skin. They were offered pocket New Testaments and small American flags, the kind little boys wave at the old soldiers at Memorial Day parades. Conversations started and ended without anyone noticing.

Smith had a note his wife had written for his leaving and slipped into his hand the last morning he left for the post.

Don't read this until you're on the way, Meg had written. God, even her handwriting is sexy, he thought. His wife had kidded him about how horny he was since he'd gotten the call in the middle of the night from his immediate superior.

Hey, war is sexy, he teased back.

I ain't complaining.

Sergeant Huebner opened the fold and looked at her words:

It looks like you're going to be a daddy. I didn't know how to tell you. Don't worry. I'm very happy. I haven't been to the doctor yet, so cross your fingers. I love you and miss you. Don't be gone long.

Huebner hollered, then he remembered where he was. A couple soldiers looked around, but they took his enthusiasm for war excitement and pumped their fists.

He stared out the window or at the back of the soldier's head

in front. This soldier had a spot on his shirt. This consoled Huebner: he had a clean shirt. His wife had worn it to bed with him
and then washed it fresh. Things like a clean shirt mattered. The
other would die, certainly. Huebner walked to the bathroom,
past one soldier sleeping with his mouth wide open; another biting skin off his fingers; a third staring, inappropriately, in Smith's
direction. When Huebner raised his eyebrows, this soldier never
blinked.

No movie. Twelve hours, waking sleep and taut nerves. In another hemisphere they saw the first F-15 Eagles. Someone
shouted, the plane trembled, they actually felt them. Huebner
looked out his window at blips of streaking metal, bursts of pure
heat force that ate the air and obliterated gravity. The soldiers
counted aloud, one, two, three, four, five. The fighter jets made
everything, the black-blue night sky, the stars, a part of their
background shot. Huebner watched the trails disappear; the
same firepower that guarded his life could kill him in an instant.

He thought of what a captain he knew once told him at the
National Training Center. Huebner liked him; he was really
squared away.

You treat your weapon like she's your wife. Make sure she's
always with you and ready for war, son, Captain Anderson said.
Once he held up an envelope. Be careful, he said, check everything three times, or this is how you come home.

At the port of Dammam, the soldiers trooped off the plane into
an open-air oven, then bused to a dark warehouse that smelled
like a toilet. Flies hovered brazenly over the black filth on the
floor; soldiers batted with their hands, cursed, squashed vermin

with their boots and spread sleeping bags. Huebner spit a couple times, lay down, closed his eyes and wished for sleep.

A couple hours later, he jerked up, his brain reeling between time zones. He rubbed his eyes and looked around at the ranks of men trying to catch up on their sleep in the middle of the day. No protection, no aircraft carriers or destroyers. A single battalion of fifty-eight Sheridan tanks from the 82nd Airborne Division rumbled outside. These air-deployable reconnaissance vehicles had arrived ahead of the soldiers to secure the airport and escort them to the warehouses. The ADRs weren't heavily armored; they would lose a real firefight against Iraq's Soviet T-72s.

Half-asleep, Huebner was thinking of his wife. An alarm sounded, Whoop, whoop, whoop, an M-8 box with a chemical sensor. Shouts, groans, one soldier jumped up and ran across the waking others in his underwear. Yells of, Gas, gas, gas were muffled as masks were pulled over faces. Soldiers fumbled half-asleep for gear; they were living in their MOPP 2 suits. Mask first, in nine seconds flat. Huebner blew to clear, flipped the hood over his head, then cinched the straps secure under his arms. The gloves came last and his weapon. Huebner jumped to his feet, but someone had thrown up on the floor; he slipped, fell on his ass, and said, Goddamn.

Welcome to the war, boys, some hammy colonel called, laughing. It was only a drill. NBC, as in nuclear, biological and chemical. The colonel stood on a jerrybuilt wood platform, waving his pro-mask. He imitated the M-8 box, Whoop, whoop, whoop.

He's lucky he doesn't get himself shot, someone said.

Huebner almost tore off his ear when he removed the mask. It hurt, a lot, but he played it off like it was cool; all of them did.

Sleep disturbed, soldiers lay back down and waited for orders. A few talked shit and tried to chat up the few females, to cover up worries of home and the enemy, to try to create normalcy in all that man-made squalor and tension. As a target, the warehouse made them nervous. They all knew about Beirut, ten years before. Two hundred fifty soldiers blown to pieces. The enemy had driven a truck right up to the handicapped parking.

Huebner stowed his mask in his duffel bag and went toward the giant tin sliding doors. Soldiers traded off turns walking outside and down to the water. A breeze, hot and dry, rippled the clear blue seawater: the wind bent the tall grass down toward the earth, lapped the water at their feet in the shallows, turned over the whitecaps in the deep. The setting sun glittered off the surface and turned the blue to silver. His sweat dried on his skin, hot wind, harsh heat, a hammer and anvil squeezing all thought from his brain, turning consciousness itself into a lingering, lazy museful wish for coolness, and every wheezing breath into a reverent psalm for release, deliverance from the harsh, unforgiving heat.

Huebner looked back at an American flag already flying in front of the warehouse. He listened to the flap of the canvas in the strong wind.

You see how dirty that place is?

A soldier named Fredericksen had spoken. When he took off his helmet, his blond hair glowed in the waning dusk light. He'd been out in the sun or he had some dye in it, some L.A. thing. A radioman, he was skinny, his uniform billowed off his body in the wind.

Welcome to Kuwait, Huebner said.

I thought this was Saudi, the radioman said.

Saudi Arabia, a third said. We're in Dammam.

Huebner looked at the moon reflected on the calm bay water.

Whatever, he said.

You scared?

Me? Hell no, Huebner said.

Right, me neither, Fredericksen said. Both of them laughed, then cut it short and resumed their complaints. There was the food, the heat, the filth, better to talk about all that.

Never were the markings on the face of the moon so clear. Blown sand danced through the night sky and spiraled toward the earth in the hot, dry wind. The incandescent brilliance of the moon and the stars turned the drifting sand into a curtain of fluorescence that draped to the desert floor.

Huebner walked back to the warehouse, flinching at the clattering noise of Black Hawk takeoffs. From the elite Delta Company, they hovered overhead then shot out, graceful as hawks, headed for reconnaissance missions near the Iraqi-held Kuwait border. A truck thundered by; the driver smiled through the window and pointed at the helicopters. Huebner flashed a thumbs-up and scrambled out of the way. The trucks carried tanks as they were loaded off ships arriving each day in the Gulf. These fast surface ships, gray Navy cargo carriers that can run to thirty-three knots in open sea, left the Bay of Savannah the day after the invasion of Kuwait and sailed through the Suez Canal. The Army loaded them so heavily their hulls stuck in the shallow waters of the Savannah Harbor. The captains pitched their ships to starboard at full tilt to rock them out of the muck at the river bottom and out to sea.

Huebner wondered which load had his tank. He was trained to shoot the big gun and he felt sketchy, out of place, waiting on the ground. He felt anxious to climb inside his beast and roll.

Huebner stood by the door of the warehouse and watched new arrivals. For every two who would face combat three soldiers worked on support, checking engines and organizing supplies for anticipated troop movements. Army advance teams set up Bedouin-style tents in forward camps where their stronghold gave way at its perimeter to the true Arabian terrain, miles and miles of dry sand, dirt and dune. All makes of jets and cargo planes passed one after another, taxiing in and out of position. Giant flatbed K-loaders full of supplies and equipment, clumsy in the sand, shuttled between the planes and the dock areas. Huebner tried to get some air, mind his own business and stay out of the way. Captain Jobe found him there.

The captain laughed, spat a wad of tobacco on the ground, reached into his pocket and placed a fresh wad in his cheek. A big man, from Nebraska, at least six-four, a little overweight for a captain, he clapped his hands and pointed toward a Humvee.

Meet me there with your weapon and gear in five, Got it?

Yes, sir.

Thunder boomed and crackled, the heat lit up the night then echoed far off in the darkness. Sultry sea breezes blew the sand against their windshield with a rasp, as if the humid, heavy night air was suffocating the wind. The troops left some time after midnight. A single road linked the oil ports and ran alongside the main oil pipeline across Saudi Arabia all the way to Jordan. Captain Jobe and Sergeant Huebner took lead, the lonely vulnerable tip of the arrow. Their job was to take the first convoy of tanks into the desert. Crews loaded the tanks onto twelve flatbed heavy equipment transfer or HET trucks, manned by Saudi Army National Guard soldiers and Filipinos, not mercenaries—they were in a war zone with no visible weapons—just men looking for work far away from home. Captain Jobe had his sidearm, a .45-caliber pistol, and Huebner, an M-16. Yellow super-glow headlights beamed onto the asphalt highway. Sometime in the night the caravan drove past a van wrecked on the side of the road. Smoke billowed from the shoulder, thick and colored green in the phosphorescence of their headlights. Orange flames licked out of the broken windows of the wrecked Chevy. Had it been hit? Would they be next?

A flash of lightning lit up the sky for a moment. Huebner and the captain both flinched, but they drove on. At dawn the sky lightened to a glistening powder blue edged in gold and yellow. Some of the trucks behind them pulled off the road. Jobe said, Let's stop and see what's going on.

Huebner slowed down and pulled two of the Humvee's wheels carefully onto the soft grainy shoulder. A few trucks followed; others went speeding by down the highway. An Arab driver stopped his truck in the middle of the highway, hopped out, spread out a mat and kneeled to face the sun, just a hint of light in the distant purple horizon. They're praying, sir, Huebner said. No shit, Jobe said. Let me get a count. You stay here, Jobe said, and went off walking down the road. Sergeant Huebner stood and watched the silhouettes of the men kneeling beside shadowed trucks. He daydreamed as he watched. In church back home the parishioners would call them heathens. Was there a difference between these men and their enemies? To pray five times a day seemed pretty devout. Huebner was once a week, at best. He wondered if the prayers were just dogma. Maybe Arabs thought of it like breathing and maybe that was better. Or did they wish for things, to be back home, or some special place back in Iran or Yemen? Did they wish to be American? Huebner wondered, with extra money to spend at the 7-Eleven on Slurpees, or to have grown up doing bong hits or trying to make girls in the backseats of old Dodges listening to REM. Or did they frown on everything American and pray for their own version of the good life? They moved out and arrived in the initial assembly area two hours later. An Arab man ran out into the highway and waved their Humvee over to the side of the road. Huebner followed Jobe's gaze out the window. Already some green Army trucks and jeeps gathered around a makeshift scrap metal and chain link corral. Five camels trotted nervously in circles. The man on the ground was dressed in ragged, dirty cotton pull-string drawers, skinny, with rope sandals and a faded Adidas T-shirt. Must be his camels, Jobe said dryly.

A couple other officers waved at Jobe from a tent a hundred yards beyond the corral. The captain waved back then shuffled through the deep sand toward the tent, a hand to his face as the hot wind blew the sand in his eyes. As another truck rolled in, the Arab ran out into the highway, directing the truck to the side of his corral. Huebner yelled at him, held up his hands, pointed at his own chest. The Arab nodded thankfully then went inside the corral to tend his nervous camels. He pulled one by the reins and patted its flank. The tall, gawky animals almost hopped, on all four legs, without the fierce dignity and grace of a horse's trot, more like giant spiders.

Each truck or bus followed the next, filling up the great field of sand, scraggly weeds and coarse brown sticker bushes. Hot and dusty, soldiers trooped in line out of the buses, set down their packs to rest away from the road. The hired drivers lay down in the scant shade provided by their trucks. Huebner stood out in the road, waving the trucks in. He heard shouting and turned to see the Arab with a blue ceramic bowl filled with a bubbly white liquid and a dirty water glass. He poured a glassful for Huebner, laid the bowl down and pointed at the camels. You got to be kidding, Huebner said. The man smiled and bobbed his head. Thank you, Huebner nodded. The milk smelled like livestock, but he drank it anyway. It was warm and heavy. When the Arab walked away smiling, with his glass and ceramic bowl, Huebner hustled over the sand to their Hummer and grabbed a bottle of water. Thirty minutes later Jobe finally came over and told him, Get some shut-eye in the Hummer. I'll call you when I need you.

Yes sir, I'll do that.

Huebner woke to someone shouting, glanced quickly at his watch, 1200 hours, asleep since nine. A transport had run over the heads of two of the drivers, gone to sleep in the shadow of the trucks, a mess of blood, bone and brain. Huebner turned away then looked back again. Most of the soldiers had probably never seen anyone dead either. Huebner didn't want to seem soft. Something about the hollowed-out feeling it gave him felt cool, like when he was in high school, after he got the wind knocked out of him in a football game. Next to him a lieutenant named Schwartz had the dry heaves. Schwartz had evidently waved on the trucks. He was just a young man with a mop of short curly hair when his desert floppy hat blew off in the wind.

Shit, they look like their heads exploded, Schwartz said.

His face was pale; two soldiers had to pull him away. He got free, ran a couple steps in the deep sand toward the dead men like he thought he could help them. A little swirl of sand as fine as talcum powder, blown by the wind, had already begun to cover what was left of their faces. Captain Jobe was there.

You want me to call this in to command, another lieutenant said, walking up. But he cut himself off and backed away when he saw Schwartz's face.

Already called command, Jobe said. They're gonna send over some body bags. Gibson, he said to the lieutenant. See if you can find some ID on them. Bag 'em and send 'em back on next supply truck.

Yes, sir, Gibson said.

It wasn't your fault, Jobe said to Schwartz and patted the lieutenant's shoulder. It was the easy thing to say because everyone knew it was Schwartz's fault. He knew it himself.

2

When he packed his desert gear, Huebner had brought some pictures his new wife and he had taken in a photo booth in the Kmart in Savannah. He married Meg Johannson just a month before he was called to go. When Smith got his permanent assignment to Fort Stewart, her parents helped them buy a bungalow on a peninsula off the coast of Georgia in a town called Sunbury. Someday he wanted to have a real family of his own. He had missed out on that as a child.

Smith had always wanted to join the Army. He picked marketing and managing as his major because it seemed popular, but he didn't want to finish his degree and become another drone like the rest of his dorm buddies. When the girl he'd fallen in love with graduated, he felt like he needed to make a move. Smith wanted to do something extraordinary, something great. Smith's father, William Ezekial Huebner, was named after a soldier, a comrade of some long-forgotten ancestor. Zeke had been the first in his family not to join the armed forces and in Smith's eyes, he suffered for it. Instead, Zeke went to trade school to become a draftsman. His attitude toward the military was an upturned middle finger. He was a biker, not a soldier. At sixteen his father, Will, ordered Zeke to quit high school:

It's about time you all started supporting me, Will told Zeke and his little sister. Zeke got a job at a gas station and later as an apprentice engineer at the power plant. It didn't matter much to Zeke; he hated school anyway, but his sister quit studying for college to work the soda counter at McCrory's.

You're an asshole, Zeke told his father. She's a smart girl.

Will just laughed. You'll see. When Zeke brought some college books home, Will made fun of him.

Where's your cardigan? he said.

Zeke knew what his father meant. You're going to learn who runs things sooner or later, Will said.

You're just a scared old man, Zeke told him.

Zeke's mother, Betty, had to step between them. Betty said her husband started drinking hard liquor, because he couldn't handle the swells. Will yelled at people in traffic, and in his cups would talk of settling scores, smoke Pall Malls with the lights out and the kitchen smelling of open bottles. He had gotten a job as the county plumbing inspector when he came back from World War II, a political appointment for his service as a pilot.

Zeke made it to the university, but on a Saturday, to take the civil service exam. He said Smith and his brother Sam belonged at a good school, Emory or something up north like Princeton. He had wanted this for himself.

Those are private schools, Smith said. Who's got the money for that?

You got a chip on your shoulder, Zeke said.

It was passed down, Sam said, always the wise-ass.

Meg knew how to carry herself. She didn't slouch when she

walked, wore a necklace that was her grandmother's, and spoke with breeding. When she was ladylike, it brought out the man in Smith.

This must be what it's like to date Princeton girls, he thought. She was a debutante and an honors scholarship student. She told Smith her mother did not like him.

If you lie down in piss, Mrs. Johannson said, you can expect to come up muddy.

She could have said pigs. She often mixed a couple afternoon martinis with her Xanax. Smith always tried to be polite to her and she was like the iced tea she always had ready to serve in the refrigerator: a lot of honey and ice. She thought it was naïve and wrong that her daughter had chosen her mate for love alone. She came up in a different time. Getting drafted was respectable, but to join the Army was simple. Meg's father respected the uniform, but Smith could see he thought it was a little crazy or just plain stupid not to go in as an officer.

His uncle Pete had survived Vietnam, but was never the same. Something in Smith was scared the same would happen to him. Something else wanted to prove that it wouldn't. Smith was also fascinated by war, like he had been in training to be a soldier since he was young. And that day when Smith walked into the office at the shopping mall, the recruitment officer made it sound like joining the Army would be practical; his studies in business would not go to waste, but instead he would have a perspective most of his contemporaries did not.

When he left for the desert, Huebner also packed his brother's graduation tassel and a photo of Sam at fourteen, tousled out-of-control curls and a city league basketball jersey, skinny. Smith worried about Sam. Sam had come to the wedding with dark rings under his eyes; his tux looked like he'd slept in it. Smith had walked in on his brother and his friends in Sam's motel room. In high school when Smith hung out with his buddies, they took bong hits, but Sam and his friends had already graduated to white powders. Sam just sat at the desk, watching a fire burn in the wastebasket. Something smelled strange.

What the hell? Smith said as he put out the fire. But Sam hardly noticed. He looked sky-high.

Each of them felt the other had taken the easy route. Sam drifted in and out of college. He spent a summer working as a custodian at an outlet mall, smoking a lot of reefer and reading great books. A high school teacher who saw promise in his poetry had recommended *The Grapes of Wrath* and *Crime and Punishment*. When he finished Dostoyevsky, he decided he could not live at home anymore.

What do you think you're going to do? Zeke asked him.

I want to go to New York City to write, Sam said.

Good luck, Zeke said, and smiled. Whatever Zeke meant, Sam took it wrong. He stomped out of the house, got drunk and rowdy, threw up out the window of his friend Frank's Mustang. When Frank dropped him off at the end of the night, Sam didn't make it home. He never slept in his father's house again. That night Sam passed out in the leaf pile. Smith found him out front in the morning on his way home from Meg's place.

Zeke burst into Sam's room that afternoon as he was packing and nursing a king-hell hangover. Zeke handed Sam a newspaper ad for a writer's workshop in town.

I'll pay for it, Zeke offered.

Sam shook his head, fighting back hot, sudden tears.

You gotta go, don't ya? Zeke asked.

Wouldn't you? Sam said, looking away, out the window and then in his dad's eyes.

Yeah. Good luck, son.

Thanks, Pops, Sam said. He never felt close to his father, but he felt like they understood each other, that the world came to them somehow in the same way.

His father gone, Sam folded up the newspaper clipping and stuck it in his wallet. Then he ran to the bathroom and got sick. When he was done packing, Zeke made them sandwiches and soup and then Sam left.

Smith stayed at home in Athens, fell in love and joined the Army. Sam moved into a house full of anarchists, punks and hardcores. They were his friends, but he wasn't one of them. By the end of the year, he was in New York City. The weekend Sam was leaving, Smith came to the house in his uniform to see his brother and drank shots with the guys at the kitchen table. There was a TV on, a news report on rising gas prices and bad OPEC relations competed with REM on the stereo.

What album is this? somebody asked, a girl with bushy red hair and a tight green Fetchin Bones T-shirt.

It's called *Green,* Smith said.

Oh yeah, soldier boy, what's your favorite song?

I like "World Leader Pretend."

You would, the girl said, smiling, and disappeared behind a door.

I think she likes you, bro.

That's all right, Sam. I'm taken. I got a hot date tonight.

Sam's friends all thought the uniform was a joke, some kind of prop for a punk rock show or something.

I didn't know you played in a band, a kid with a safety pin in his ear said to Smith. That looks real.

It is, Smith said.

That's so cool, the kid said. His hair was colored red and yellow and peaked into a curl that fell over his eyes. They all called him Rooster. Hey, we're all doing acid. You want some?

Naw, maybe not, Smith said.

Smith, in his dress uniform, took Meg to a ball for her little sister's debut. Meg's mother belonged to the Daughters of the Confederacy. They walked over a swept smooth dirt path, the humid summer air perfumed by the gardenias, roses and wisteria. A big square frame house loomed, newly whitewashed, hung with lush ivy, adorned with cupolas, spires and scrolled balconies and shaded by ancient, gnarled white oaks. Servants dressed in white cotton shirts and pale khaki attended the grounds; one combed the edges of the path clean with a real wicker broom, another gently sprayed the rows of flowers with a hose until they glistened, then moved on to the path to keep the dust down.

I bet they still call them Negroes, here, Smith said.

Don't push it, Meg whispered in his ear, as she cooed and smiled at one of the older ladies.

Oh hello, Mrs. Grierson, she half-curtsied as Smith tipped his hat.

Men wore blue and white candy-striped seersucker suits, straw boaters with red, white and blue ribbons and carried ornately carved wood canes handed down to them by their fathers. Women wore flowing designer dresses from the season's trunk sales, wrist corsages of fresh flowers and received compliments with grace and poise.

The distinguished Senator Jesse Helms from North Carolina was there. Helms had two stars on his lapel that sparkled, and spit food on Smith's tie when he talked. The senator singled Smith out as an example of a fine young man. Meg's father was a big political contributor. Meg was the most beautiful young woman in the room that night—drew the eyes of all the men— and she was his. The men complimented Smith on his uniform.

That Uncle Sam is one fine tailor, said a tall man with a rakish wink and gap-toothed grin.

These folks are hard to read, Smith whispered to Meg.

Oh Smith, they love you, it's all right.

They love a man in a uniform. Smith and Meg whispered to each other as they stood with the crowd and they were indulged, and congratulated on her sparkling diamond engagement ring.

Do you think they can tell I was born a Yankee?

I imagine they can. Meg winked as he kissed her.

They look at us like a patriotic postcard, the Stars and Stripes forever.

Newly bloomed flowers of the Republic, Helms toasted the young couple. He offered young Meg a rose and she accepted a kiss on the cheek from him.

He's so sweet and courtly it leaves a taste in your mouth.

A bad one, Smith said.

You two young people are an example of what's right with America's young people today, Helms said when he took Smith aside for a drink.

You don't see me. You have absolutely no idea who you're

talking to, Smith thought as he nodded politely and said, Thank you, sir.

You fill out that uniform like a real soldier, son, the senator said.

Yeah, and I was hanging out with some punk rockers, today, sir. Smith wished he could tell him who he really was.

Smith smiled at Helms. Smith had been raised to respect the government. The intelligent young man with Fuck Life tattooed over the American flag on his chest he had discussed foreign policy with at Sam's house came from the same country as this man. So did his brother Sam. Smith really believed in the flag and all it represented, the promise of men who could bridge all the gaps, like Bobby Kennedy and Martin Luther King. Isn't that what they died for? That wasn't just pabulum written in his schoolbooks. And the power that even a man like this senator represented was part of it too. It was intoxicating.

So was the liquor they raised in their glasses. Smith looked at Helms's suit and saw old wood benches and lecterns of the old Senate Building. His father had taken them to see it when he was younger. He pictured the old man making a speech, his courtly drawl filling that great room.

When Senator Helms toasted Smith and slapped him on the back, Smith felt a welling of pride. He drank up and then they both had another.

When they shook hands, Helms held his for a moment and looked into his eyes, Penny for your thoughts, son?

Smith could not speak.

I guess you got a lot on your mind, the senator said.

What did you say to him? Meg asked, and poked Smith in the ribs as they walked away.

Nothing he hasn't heard before, baby.

He really is a nice man, Meg said. I've known him since I was a child.

Tell that to the help.

Shame on you, Smith.

Sam and Meg's cousin, Dorothy, had flown to the coast of Georgia when they heard the news that Smith's division was on call to defend Saudi Arabia, she from Wilmington, North Carolina, and Sam from New York. Late on Saturday, Smith and Meg drove them to Savannah and they spent the rest of the night in bars, drinking toasts to honor, love and country. The next day when Smith went out early to call the dogs in, he came across his brother Sam standing out in the woods smoking a joint.

You don't have to hide out here, Smith said.

Really? The New World Order doesn't extend this far?

Smith laughed. Don't be a wise-ass, he said. We already rule this country.

It's a nice country, isn't it? Sam said, sniffing the air, taking in the tart pine trees and the tall leafy oaks.

Yeah, it is, Smith said.

Sam laughed and held up a cicada skin. I found it hanging off a tree branch, he said.

How long did you watch it before you realized it was just the shell?

Ten minutes, Sam said, and giggled. Let's put it on the car for a hood ornament, he said. Sam offered his brother a hit off the joint, and Smith laughed it off.

Don't push it, he said.

Oh yeah, right, Sam said.

Smith had first turned Sam on to pot when they were teenagers, but the Army had instituted a strict drug policy in the post-Vietnam early eighties. Smith had no problem giving it up. You can walk away from anything. This was something Smith had learned.

The four had planned for a boat ride out to St. Catherine's Island, but the girls heard hurricane bulletins on the forecast.

Let's go anyway, Sam said.

Smith laughed. Maybe I'll get lucky and miss my plane.

That's the spirit, Dorothy said. She was a tall girl, thinner than Meg, with bright green eyes. She seemed more nervous than Meg, but maybe that had to do with Sam.

Sam made coffee and told stories about his apartment search (the girlfriend method seemed to be his most successful and treacherous) and his struggles to support himself, working first as a bicycle messenger and lately at a bookstore on Fifth Avenue. He had entered a program at City College where he could take graduate classes in English even as he finished the undergrad degree he'd started in Georgia.

That sounds like a pretty advanced program, Dorothy said.

Leave it to Sam, Smith said, and smiled proudly.

I also got a job teaching a couple of literacy classes at a community college, Sam told them.

You're a professor? asked Dorothy.

Sounds like they'll take anyone, Smith joked.

No, he's right, Sam said. They will. Sam made everyone laugh with his infectious, nervous energy. He talked so fast that he stuttered and then laughed at himself. It meant a lot to Smith that he came.

The brothers walked down the gravel road to the dock while the girls got things ready for a picnic. Smith had a little fifteen-foot fiberglass with an outboard pull-cord put-put engine. The breeze eddied the blue bay water in wavelets that slapped at the slime-green dock supports. A seagull skimmed over the surface, then hovered, picking at something dead floating in the bay.

Hey Sam, Smith said. There's something I been wondering about.

Shoot.

What happened to you at the wedding reception? Smith asked, trying not to look at his brother.

Hey, Sam said. You don't have to worry about me.

You were supposed to make a toast. You were the best man. Where did you go? What were you and your buddies doing?

Are you a soldier or a cop?

You know it's not like that.

Sam looked his brother down and tried to let the inference pass, but this didn't work. It was your wedding, he said.

Really Sam.

Did I embarrass you in front of the society people?

Go to hell, Smith said. The mosquitoes were still out and he slapped one on the back of his neck. He hadn't meant it to come out like this.

Sam said, I didn't tell you to marry a rich girl and join the Army.

She's not rich. I thought you liked Meg.

Richer than us. She's beautiful. What's not to like? Sam said. He lit the joint and took a hit.

Why do you always have to be stoned?

My brother is going to war tomorrow night.

So you should get wasted?

Sam turned away, squinting after the sun as it hid for a moment behind a bank of swollen purple clouds.

I went to a protest, he said, and made a funny face. Sam was guileless. He could always get his brother to laugh. And he did now.

Against what, Smith asked, smiling.

Against the war. This thing is about oil.

No, it's not. It's about America. We got to stick up for our friends.

Kuwait. That's not my America, Sam said.

A friend is a friend, brother.

You know what?

What?

We sound ridiculous, like a bad TV show.

Just because it's cheapened by them, doesn't make it any less real.

Hey, that's my line.

Sorry, Mr. Lefty.

Sam laughed. Not everybody up in New York is so gung ho about this.

Not everybody down here is either.

You don't have to go.

Wake up, Sam. I want to go. This isn't 1969. You watch the news. The Iraqis are holding a couple of thousand people in Kuwait. A lot of them are Americans. Hostages. I wish this was some TV show, but it's not. And y'know what, it's my duty, as stupid as that might sound to someone who is not part of this.

Sam finished the joint. The flit of fire disappeared into the water and he turned back. Y'know what? he said.

Tell me.

I don't want you to die. Part of me wishes I could go with you. To have your back.

You look a little skinny, but we could probably use you, Smith said.

But he couldn't tell if Sam heard. He had turned back to the clouds. The wind kicked up and they watched the sun break through the trembling trees.

3

They rode in the tank with all hatches open. The dry desert air choked attempts at speech in midsentence. The soldiers sat as still as they could, drifted into waking sleep, restless, fitful, sweating relentlessly. They drank from warm bottles of water, and for release emptied their bladders into the same water bottles or took turns balancing from the open hatch where the sun had baked the metal hot enough to evaporate their piss on contact.

As the tank crested a dune, something on Sergeant Huebner's daylight sight caught him by surprise. His heart jumped in his chest. They had gotten the beasts on the ground and were moving camp from one location on the map to the next. There had been no reports of enemy activity in their vicinity, but still they were careful and a little jumpy. They had been in Saudi Arabia for less than a week.

As the gunner in the M-1 Abrams, Huebner had a daylight and a heat sight. The viewer worked like a large rifle scope and came equipped with three or ten power. He looked through the viewer with both eyes, like binoculars.

Unidentified troops, Huebner said into his headset. He took a deep breath and pulled his forehead from the viewer for just a second to wipe the sweat from around his eyes.

Going higher to confirm any friendly activity, Captain Jobe replied.

Huebner nodded and adjusted his sight from three to ten power.

Rogue TOC, this is Dark Lord Six, Jobe said, switching his junction box to change radio frequencies. Huebner and the rest of the crew were able to hear this exchange through their headphones. We've acquired a number of dismounted individuals, identify friend or foe.

Wait One, going higher, came the reply from battalion.

Sergeant.

Sir?

What's the range?

Fifteen hundred meters.

Got that, Morrison? Captain Jobe asked.

Roger, sir, came the reply. Specialist James Morrison was the crew loader; he was twenty-four and like Huebner also from Georgia.

Jobe lowered his hatch to battle height and got his binoculars. He had a catch that allowed him to keep it about six inches open during an exchange with the enemy. Jobe stood on his seat looking through the space. To his left, the loader, Morrison, sat on another seat bolted to the opposite side of the turret. Smith's place was just in front of the commander's knees. Their crew-driver, Private Joe Maxwell, was cut off from the others in the front hull of the tank. Maxwell was just nineteen and taking a few semesters off from college.

Identification, Sergeant?

Negative, sir.

Smith's heat viewer showed small white dots.

Red Con One, Jobe commanded. Battle carry HEAT.

Sabot in tube, Morrison replied. Going to have to pull it out and replace with HEAT.

Roger, Jobe said. There was a pause, then he said, Oh for Chrissakes.

Sir? Huebner could see the forms on his sight, but he needed Jobe's command to open up the gun. He was ready for anything.

When he heard Captain Jobe laugh, he switched to the daylight sight.

Bedouins, Jobe said, and called back in to brigade. Rogue TOC, this is Dark Lord Six. Unidentified personnel near Target Reference Point 4, Bedouins.

Civilians?

Roger.

Keep an eye on them until they're safe, Dark Lord Six.

Let's set up a laager, Captain Jobe said to his crew. You fellows can go ahead and take a break, he said, and poked Huebner lightly with his boot. You look like you could use one, Sergeant.

Jobe got back on his radio to notify the rest of the company. Red, White, Blue, this Black Six. Perimeter secure.

After Maxwell stopped their vehicle, Huebner followed Morrison out of his hatch. Huebner had forgotten his sunglasses and the sun's glare hurt his eyes.

It's hard to say if it's hotter in the tank or out here, Huebner said, as Maxwell handed him a warm bottle of water from the Sponson utility box behind the turret. They had sixteen other tanks in their company, four platoons with four in each, as well as the executive officer's crew tank. As Captain Jobe called out the order to laager, a simple wedge defense formation, the rest of D Company spread out over thousands of yards.

Sergeant, Jobe called out. Keep an eye on them. Let me know when it's clear. These Bedouins don't have loyalty to any country. They play their own hand of cards, boys. Command said we should keep a wary eye on 'em.

Yes, sir.

Huebner, Maxwell and Morrison walked across the open sand to get a better look. They had gotten their helmets out of the Sponson along with the water. They wore their gas masks on their hips. Morrison had the tank's M-16, Huebner and Maxwell each carried a pistol.

The Bedouins walked in single file or rode camels attached in line by rope. There were at least fifty skinny, scraggly goats. A woman was drawn on some kind of sled over the sand. Her face was greasy with sweat and streaked from the constant blown dirt. They came over a hill, one by one, and passed right by where the three soldiers stood. At this time of day the intense heat and glittering sand had a kaleidoscope effect on the eyes. Currents of heat rippled across the expanse of day sky, eddied on slightly by the hot breeze. Just parched bare earth, no relief from the searing sun for miles and miles. *Sohool* is the Arabic word for these desert flatlands.

Why do you think they're dragging her like that? Huebner asked. They had walked to within twenty feet of the Bedouins.

I believe that woman is in labor, Morrison said, and cocked his head to the side.

The Bedouin woman screamed, and a boy, poking a stick in the sand, turned and stared back at his mother. The men did not look at the soldiers as they passed. The women showed their eyes briefly then looked away. The little ones stared.

The Bedouins were barefoot, with rags wound round their heads, their long shadows distorted by the heat. Their faces and hands matched the dried and cracked squares of the weathered earth, bare, worn down to some inner layer of crust by the sun's heat, swept clean by relentless wind.

Brothers look like they've been walking for generations, Morrison said. He removed his helmet and wiped his brow. The sun glared off his shaved head.

Man, Maxwell answered. They smell.

Maxwell, you are a piece of work, Morrison said. You are the pièce de résistance.

You can speak French all you want. I ain't falling for it. I wonder what happened to them, Maxwell said.

We did, Morrison said. We happened to them.

Us, the Iraqis, or something in between, Maxwell replied.

Maybe nothing happened to them, Huebner said. And this is just the way they live.

That ain't right, Maxwell said.

Should we do anything? Huebner asked.

Morrison shrugged his shoulders and smiled. She just broke water, he said. She's going to have a baby right here.

Man, this is cool, Maxwell said. Can we keep following them, he asked. Sir?

I don't know, Huebner said. This isn't the freaking Nature Channel.

Look, fellas, Maxwell exclaimed. This is so cool. I wish I had a fucking video camera, he said.

Huebner turned and saw a Hummer approaching. As it

neared he recognized Colonel Agard. He rode shotgun with his driver, Specialist Humphrey.

Huebner, Maxwell and Morrison saluted.

First to fight, sir! they said together.

Victory, the colonel replied with the division's special greeting. What are we doing here, fellas?

The Army doesn't tell you either, sir, Maxwell said. Huebner wanted to hit him, but the colonel laughed.

Good one, he said. Sergeant? Huebner nodded to the others and went to join Colonel Agard at his jeep.

What's going on over there? Colonel Agard asked.

Just some poor cousins, sir, Huebner reported.

The colonel nodded. Is there anything we can help them with? the colonel asked. Maybe some community relations? He chewed on a cigar and was known to hand them out to subordinates on occasion. He came from a military officer family, had brass in his bones, they said.

I don't think so, sir, Huebner said. He felt like gushing about the baby and the mother, but thought better of it.

You got a good look at them?

Yes, sir, we were watching them walk. They were dragging a woman. There was this old couple . . . Huebner trailed off when Agard shook his head, up and down three times.

Forget them, Colonel Agard said, and spat in the sand. They're not there.

Excuse me, sir?

What kind of ammo did you load for them?

We loaded the HEAT, sir.

What is that exactly?

Sir?

Agard waved his hand, impatiently, a fly hovering near his ear. He said, Humor me, Sergeant.

Sort of like liquid fire, I think.

The radio in the jeep squawked and the driver, said, Colonel, sir?

Agard waved him off. The driver listened for a moment and said, Colonel, maybe you should take this.

Agard held up his hand, Wait. They're just nervous. Every fucking blip is an Iraqi invasion, he said under his breath and turned back to Huebner. We expected them to press in Saudi Arabia. Three states in the north think the king is full of shit. They would welcome old Saddam with a wink and a smile, the colonel said, and winked. What were we talking about?

The HEAT rounds.

Oh yes, the HEAT. . . . Is that like napalm?

Better sir, more advanced.

Advanced, I like that word, son. You ever see what napalm can do? It takes the skin right off, peels it away. Imagine what it must feel like to be skinned alive, son.

Huebner nodded.

You said more advanced. What would that do to our Bedouin friends? the colonel asked.

Sir?

The HEAT. . . . what would it do to them?

Well, I-I've never seen . . .

You've seen the training films.

In practice they never used live rounds. However, on video-tape once Huebner saw the gas disintegrate an old tree in the desert in a split second. The tree's shadow hung in the air after impact, engulfed in orange gassy fire. The HEAT round gave off a trembling, surreal quality, as if the entire world as encompassed in that frame could at any moment, burst into flames. The HEAT rounds will penetrate or obliterate a target by injecting a three-thousand-degree jet of burning gas. This type of ammunition was developed to eliminate ground troops and/or nonarmored vehicles.

Huebner didn't say anything. He pawed at the sand with his boot and waited for the colonel to speak.

You're inside a tank. You're looking at a screen. They aren't people, just white dots on a green background. Targets. You won't see them, son. Then one day, they'll be in your head. Maybe you'll be sleeping, it'll be years later and you'll be talking to your kids and they'll be there, nodding their heads, listening, targets come to life.

Huebner shook his head. I don't really follow you, sir.

Agard laughed. Just remember war looks a hell of a lot different from here on the ground than it does from inside your tank. When you go to Kill formation the first time, we'll find out what kind of soldier you are, son.

Maxwell walked off a few hundred yards away with the boresight panel, a big sheet of cardboard with an X written on it, while Morrison and Huebner worked on the main gun. Morrison stood on a rock in front of the tank. He used a lens that can be attached to the main gun and hung down at a ninety-degree angle. This apparatus checks the line of the gun tube with the target.

Huebner sighted the bore-sight panel with a red laser to begin computation of the ballistic solution. A computer attached to the main gun took into account ammunition type, range to target, crosswind, lead and/or target movement. These calculations took a microsecond. Huebner pushed a button to lase, then pulled the triggers to shoot after employing the palm grips to activate the main gun. The fire control, manufactured by the Cadillac Gauge Company and commonly called the Caddy by tankers, was basically a handle with two hand grips, and went up and down and side to side to control the movement of the main gun. The gunner also controls a. 30-caliber machine gun. There is another mechanism to manually elevate and traverse the turret to better line up the aim of the main gun with the bore-sight panel.

The M-1 A-1 Abrams tank, named after a World War II hero, was developed by General Dynamics Land Systems and manufactured at a single production facility in Lima, Ohio. When the Army originally designed and built the M-1 Abrams in the 1970s, it weighed in at seventy-three tons. Cross-country, the beast can do thirty miles per hour, and forty-five on a paved road. In World War II a stationary American tank had to fire more than fifteen rounds to kill another at a distance of five hundred yards. The M-1 fires on the move and kills with one shot at a range of four times that. The gunner can track HEAT signature through smoke and haze at a range of two miles or more.

The sabot round is a small missile developed to penetrate heavy armor. These rounds hit the target with a thirty-six-inch dart of depleted uranium. This, as Huebner liked to paraphrase the official manual, brought to bear "the force of a 1968 Hemi-engine Barracuda street rod striking a concrete median at two hundred miles per hour, but with all of its energy compressed into an area smaller than a baseball." An M-1 sabot round enters its target and exits with a hole the same size, creating a vacuum strong enough to eviscerate anyone or anything inside. Despite its size, upon firing, the whole tank jumps and the concussion noise/force would deafen a man if he happened to be standing beside and lacked proper protection.

This was a drill they had gone over millions of times. Now they were in a foreign country; soon it would be for real. As Huebner looked through the viewer at Maxwell standing with the piece of cardboard in the middle of the open desert, he imagined what the gun at his fingertips could do to him if he wasn't on his side.

As night approached, the setting sun bled the color from the sky slowly, no trees, buildings or even tall hills. The sun's retreat emboldened the wind. When Jobe returned, he dismissed Morrison and Maxwell. Jobe and Huebner went over turret controls, friend or foe vehicle identification, fire commands and switchology, tank-speak for practicing enough to always press the right button at the right time, one of those ironic in-jokes for any Army man with half-enough brain to think about how silly it sounded. Others seemed to like the video-game technical quality of such jargon.

All of this was routine, but Jobe liked to keep his crew on edge. When his company went into battle, the tanks would form an arrow and the captain's crew would ride in the center and direct the movement of attack.

The sky turned gold as they got out, leaned on the tank, and watched night's blue curtain descend toward the desert floor.

The sunsets sure are beautiful here, Jobe commented. Huebner told the captain about the birth they'd witnessed with the Bedouins, and Jobe shook his head.

That's a trip, Jobe said, overtired and worried, drawn dark under his eyes.

The wind kicked up a little twister that covered them with a light blanket of sand. Jobe wiped the sweat from his forehead and left a black mark there.

It's going to be a month at least before our bodies are even assimilated to the heat, to this climate, Captain Jobe said. We wait for the Air Force. We wait for the Navy.

We're pretty exposed, aren't we, sir?

Pretty exposed? he said. He rubbed his eyes, tried to spit, but his mouth was too dry.

Do you know how many tanks the Pentagon estimates the Iraqis have in Kuwait?

A lot?

Three thousand, soldier. Do you know how many we have?

Three hundred?

That's right. What would the brass do if one thousand American soldiers were killed tomorrow?

Wouldn't play too well back home, would it?

No, it wouldn't, he said. A lot of flags for a lot of coffins, Jobe said, and brushed a smudge of wet sand off his chin. He looked at Huebner. Roger this, soldier. You hesitate, we die. When we go into Iraq, who do you think will be in the first tank?

You don't have to worry about me.

Let's hope not.

4 ―――――――――――――――――――――――――――――――――

The boys saw an American flag burned when Smith was six years old. This was 1974. In New Brunswick, New Jersey, the town fathers had a parade on the Fourth of July. Their great-grandfather was the grand marshal that year, for all of his years of service to the town fire department. He wore a blue blazer and a red cardigan, his hair combed back severely. He wore a flag pin on his lapel.

He showed Smith and his brother Sam how to march like real soldiers that morning in the long meadow in front of the town fire station. They waved the little American flags Great Grandpa had given to them as the parade went by. They marched in a circle around the maple tree and the wind blew the whirl-arounds down around them.

It was a big day for the family and hard on Grandma Betty because Grandpa, Old Will, spent it in the bar, as he usually did when it was a big day for somebody in the family.

The sun beat down hot and bright and hit off everything that was shiny. It was hard to keep your eyes open. Smith, Sam and Cousin Joe had stolen beebees and straws from the drugstore in town. They shot the beebees with the straws at the tubas. It made a great sound when they hit. Several times Grandma chased after the boys to get them to settle down, to show some respect for the occasion. The last time she fell. She was always such a strong woman; you would never have known that anything had happened to her. It was just the look on her face and the tone of her voice.

The band was marching by, so it was hard to hear what she was saying from the ground where she fell. Her mouth opened. What she said was lost in the noise. Smith felt Grandma's hand on his knee. She whispered in his ear that she needed some water, some ice, something. She took his hand and held it. All the color in her face drained out. She was so pale that his heart skipped. Smith grabbed Sam.

Go and get Grandma a drink! Smith yelled at them.

Sam and Joe looked at him, then her, and took off. Smith must have started crying. He felt embarrassed; someone in his family had fallen and needed help. His grandmother had reached out to him, but she was too big for him to lift.

It's gonna be all right, Grandma said.

Joe and Sam came back with a grape and a cherry ice.

We weren't sure what flavor she liked, Sam said.

A ripple came through the crowd. A man had grabbed a flag from someone's grasp.

People started to shout. Smith heard screaming; the power of that voice made Grandma jerk. Their view of the street was fragmentary and changed as the crowd moved back and forth. Smith was kneeling beside her; the grass and pebbles cut into his knees, making marks and stains. The pebbles hurt. At one point Grandma reached up with just her forefinger and wiped one of the tears from his eyes.

A man with a beard had grabbed the flag and doused it with lighter fluid, but he only got the corner set on fire. He was chased and caught by four men who beat him with their fists. Then the cops came in with billy sticks and finished it. Smith had only seen the fire for a second. The red, white and blue of the flag, the orange gasoline flames and the smell of it cut through the crowd.

Later the three boys sat up with their great-grandpa. His face looked ashen, in his chair beside the radio, listening to the Boston Pops Holiday Program. It was hot and humid as the dickens well into that Fourth of July. The warm and heavy breeze bent back the tall grass down by the slowly coursing river as crickets hissed in the heat. The old man had a catch in his breath that night. He couldn't cough it out. He still wanted a smoke though, but only allowed himself the occasional cigarette. He would have one tonight after the kids went to bed.

Since he was a boy Sam had followed his older brother, Smith. He rode on the back fender of his bicycle to play baseball and football with the big kids in the neighborhood back when they lived in New Jersey. After they moved down south, he finally beat his brother in one of their wiffle ball games. He remembered the score, 4–1, and that his brother had let him be the Yankees that day. Sam played basketball, baseball, track and football under the same coaches as his brother. When they were teenagers Sam and Smith had bought a Ford Pinto together for $175 and taken it with them to college. Sam had not made any specific plans for school, so he followed after Smith to the same state college in the mountains of Georgia. Sam's actual plan was to go for a year and a half because that was exactly the amount of time he had read that Bob Dylan had spent at his own state college in Minnesota before he set out for New York to change pop music history.

Smith had started a band with some friends and needed a singer. Sam was already writing song lyrics with a friend back in high school. When he got there he found out he couldn't sing, so he started writing. Sam actually spent almost three years in Athens, but he left exactly a year after Smith graduated and went to assume his duties at tank school in Fort Knox, Kentucky. Sam moved into the punk rock house in Athens with some friends from a rival band of his brother's and lived there for the summer. It was the first time he had ever done anything without following in the footsteps of his older brother.

When the summer was over, Sam got on a Greyhound bus and went to stay with his grandmother at the old family house in New Jersey. He got the Sunday *New York Times* and circled job prospects. After many fruitless interviews, Sam answered an ad for political activists he saw in *The Village Voice.* He was driven out to Queens in a station wagon and dropped off to go door to door and ask for money for a peace organization called SANE. Part of his rap was to say that the group was started by Eleanor Roosevelt. He got a lot of doors slammed in his face and found out that Forest Hills was a pretty old school conservative neighborhood.

But I like Ronald Reagan and George Bush, one kindly old man told him. He gave him a dollar and a drink of water. Keep the money for yourself, he said.

Sam stayed with his grandma for a couple of months, got a job at the Doubleday bookshop and soon after that the first place of his own to live. Moving to New York to try to become a writer meant the same thing to Sam as becoming a soldier and going to war meant to his older brother, Smith. Just as his brother Smith wanted to serve his country and distinguish himself in battle like Captain Joshua Chamberlain at Gettysburg in the Civil War and follow in the footsteps of great battle tacticians such as George Patton, Stonewall Jackson and the German tank genius Erwin Rommel, Sam wanted to write an important book about this time and his country. He wanted to move to New York from a faraway small town and become a writer like Thomas Wolfe, Ralph Ellison or Jack Kerouac. He read all their novels and when he first came to the big city, he sought out their haunts. He drank a beer and smoked a joint at the West End bar near Columbia College campus where Kerouac had described first meeting Allen Ginsberg. When Sam first went to Brooklyn on the subway, instead of a map, he brought his well-worn copy of *You Can't Go Home Again*.

He knew he was naïve and kind of a cliché. A girl he met in a bar had said this to him one night over beers. So what? Sam had asked her.

He spent a lot of time walking around the city. In Bryant Park he found out where to score weed and he went down to Greenwich Village to walk around on the streets that he learned the names of from Bob Dylan songs. This was his life, just another kid from somewhere else who wanted to be someone else. He saw a jazz band at the Lenox Lounge on 125th Street in Harlem, went dancing downtown at the Peppermint Lounge and saw a couple bands at CBGB's. He finally went back to school in the spring when he realized a college degree might come in handy after all.

He sent his first novel to Grove Press, one of Kerouac's publishers, and got it back with a form notice three months later. He was embarrassed when he looked at it again and thought he could do a lot better. He had to. He wrote and sent off two more books that year. He didn't revise them, like Kerouac, but just wrote five to ten pages every day until he was done. He wrote a book about a homeless man who thought he was Christ and put up a cross made of railroad ties on Coney Island and another about a young man who shows his older brother that he has learned to fly. It was a cross between a sexual orgasm and an epileptic seizure. It was set on the old West Side Highway and on the streets around Hell's Kitchen. He loved to walk around the old neighborhoods of New York. He knew no one however, and was usually on the outside looking in.

He made some friends at work and met some girls, but it was not until the next summer when things started to pick up. That was when he met Clayton at an Earth Day protest and then Eleanor at the party on the rooftop. It was at the end of that summer in early August when Iraq invaded Kuwait and he found out that his brother was going to war. He was at work in the bookstore. It was a slow Sunday afternoon when he found out. He had not even heard of Kuwait, but by the next day he went in to work to ask for a few days off to see his brother before he left. The manager was nice and everyone was swept up in the war fever. He told Sam to take a few days if he needed it and come back next week. He gave Sam an advance on his pay for that week. By the afternoon Sam was on a Greyhound bus headed for Savannah, Georgia. He was scared for his brother, but also excited for him. Smith's dreams were becoming a reality. Alone on a twenty-four-hour bus ride with a dime bag of weed, a pen, a notepad and a few books to read, Sam wondered about his own.

The heat of the desert never let up. Jobe took the company on numbing five-mile hikes in the middle of the day, "to keep their wind up." The soldiers kept moving in the hot, dry wind, breathing the heat, eating the time-swept sand, wrapped in scarves, do-rags and pieces of faded T-shirts that reminded them of back home under their helmets and the only solace was that there was none—that they were out there, soldiering on, rock-solid, hard enough to take it. The soldiers slept when they could, woke up with the sweats, and always felt vaguely sick. A month passed before they could bear the temperatures, which routinely topped 120 degrees Fahrenheit. In Saudi, the stages of assimilation went from elation to boredom and missing home with big swings back and forth.

The desert sand all looked the same from a distance: long flats rode out for miles, with constant slight rises and dips, clumps of green weed faded by the sun and dried in the heat, once in a while a single tree, something like a pine but with long needles sticking out from the spindly trunk; sand, scraggy clumps of brown weeds, sandstone boulders and cracked shelves.

But the sand came in many different sizes and textures. Sand as fine as talcum powder hung in the air all day long, blown by the wind in swirls and eddies. This fine sand invaded every orifice, got into the food and spoiled their machinery. The locals call this kind *rumuel.* The bigger pebbles of sand are called *teen.*

In the Old West, out on the high plains, the Indians lived off the buffalo for all their basic needs; in the Saudi the tankers lived off their tanks in much the same way. Up to ten soldiers could sleep on its surface; clothing and blankets dried on the back grille of the engine exhaust, which was also used to heat water and food.

The female soldiers were back in the support positions. Once in a while one of them would bring the mail. Otherwise it was just the guys and the flies, intolerable, little black flies everywhere. Green bottle flies and great big, black horseflies guarded the wooden three-hole latrine; dung beetles made dive-bombing raids. The flies swarmed whoever got the daily shit-burning detail and made everyone else just generally miserable most of the time.

Daily routine: at first light, stand to. They filled sandbags, then came shaving and personal hygiene. A few minutes passed before the body caught up to the shock of the heat, but once it did, sweat poured down. When they weren't on the move, they were taking care of the vehicles. Maxwell cranked the engines; Huebner checked his sights; Morrison lubricated and cleaned the tank weapons. He started with an oil-base at first then switched to graphite, because the light coat got covered with sand in moments. Eventually, Morrison had graphite lube sent from his family back home.

Captain Jobe lectured the company on navigating the desert, Iraqi Army weapons systems, capabilities and organization, Arabic customs and heat-coping techniques. They went over the Rules of Engagement, Conduct Rules and Rules of Combat and received official, laminated cards for each of these sets of rules. They were ordered to carry the cards in their breast pockets at all times.

What about the camels? Maxwell asked.

What about them?

Is there an official distance we should keep from them, sir?

Jobe cocked his head and spit on the ground. It was hard to tell if Maxwell was being serious or just plain stupid.

So they don't kick us or something. I thought the Army might have a directive or an order for that, sir.

Thank you, Private Maxwell, I must have overlooked it. It says here that if you get too close to a camel, you should wrestle it to the ground. If it's a female, you're allowed to fuck it. At the canteen, they have camel condoms.

Everyone broke out laughing and looked over at Maxwell.

He didn't crack a smile. Are they the rough and ready, sir? he asked.

Jobe turned red, then he laughed out loud.

They drilled on formations: company wedge for cruising long distances at battalion or company strength and the Kill-4 for platoon-level attack readiness.

For food there were MREs and T-rations. The first were Meals Ready to Eat and came in little brown bags. Lieutenant Holmes's Red Platoon nicknamed them Meals Rejected for Ethiopians. In tests conducted by the Army's NATIC labs they had been found to last five years "plus or minus," Jobe informed the men dryly. The Ts were not individual meals, but big tins that could be cooked up in large quantities. The first lettuce they got made everyone sick. They ate dehydrated pork patties, franks, spaghetti, ham and eggs, chicken with rice, tuna with noodles. Sometimes too there were Saudi-provided brown bag lunches. They took turns guessing the kind of meat in the sandwiches, but the fruit was edible and welcome.

Once a week, they got a good shower from a .50 ammo can. These are rectangular metal boxes about the size of a large shoe-box. They took turns holding these up over each other's heads. The tanks blocked the wind somewhat. Later, at a permanent camp outside the town of Al Sarrah, they built wooden showers, with black plastic tanks at the top of the stalls. An immersion heater from the kitchen warmed the water and a bilge pump from an M-113 pumped it up into the shower tank. Each platoon built its own latrine and decorated the walls with pages ripped out of their favorite skin mags, mailed from back home and passed through the Saudi censors in coffee cans and potato chip canisters.

After dinner, personal training. Pushups, situps. At night they jogged up and down bare ridges to the north over rocks that jutted out where the sand had drifted or fallen away. Jumping jacks, jogging in place and belly dives. They often played brutal games of tackle football with the other companies. D Company, the Dark Lords, held their own. Morrison was a damn good quarterback, while Maxwell and Huebner got their hits in at inside linebacker. They were the captain's crew and expected to be bad-ass. The men played a lot of Frisbee too, hard-hitting games of Ultimate. Frustrated and lonely, they took it out on each other.

The men listened to Armed Forces Radio, but the British Broadcasting was better. Maxwell and Huebner went to supply and grabbed a bunch of cassette tapes one day. Maxwell played Metallica and Huebner, AC/DC's *Back in Black* and The Clash. They had wired a Walkman to the 17-80 junction box for CVC. This was the combat vehicle crewman headset microphone, which the crew used to communicate with each other inside the tank. Their helmets were made of nylon with plastic shells with the headphones built in. Morrison liked the rap group N.W.A, which he played so much that they got to know all the words. The captain's favorite was the B-52's *Love Shack*.

At night the fine sand was there, flowing through the air. When the moon and stars were bright, iridescent specks glistened. At the end of each day, Huebner and Morrison cleaned their weapons for a second time and checked the NBC gear, especially the batteries in the chemical protection alarms. Once Huebner went for a walk and picked up four small stones. All of them were beautiful. The first was flat, like a fragment of an eggshell, the outside a dark ochre and pink quartz and the inside black like coal. He posted them to Meg, enclosed with a long letter where he tried to tell her what he felt about the war, and what it had done to their lives together and apart. He wrote to her about the future, about how proud he would be as a father.

At rest, they positioned the tanks in a large circle, facing out, with maybe fifty yards between tanks. Maxwell and Huebner hung a tarp off the side for a lean-to. Since Captain Jobe was the leader of the company, his tank sat in the middle of the circle. Next to them was the executive officer's tank and company trains, logistics, medics, engineers and mechanics. These totaled about twenty to twenty-five extra men. When they went to sleep, Maxwell turned the radio down real low and picked up on one of the Saudi stations. He had no idea what was going on, but he enjoyed it.

I'm starting to get this, he claimed.

Four companies, four platoons apiece, fifty-eight tanks strong: they spent the rest of the day checking gear and forming a hasty defense, with each of the companies, Alpha, Bronco, Charlie and Captain Jobe's Dark Lords gathered in circle formations. Jobe and his crew were too tired to set up their lean-to that night, just pulled out their sleeping bags and slept beside the tank under the stars.

Medics woke the soldiers sometime in the night for anthrax shots, and they were given PB pills in case of gas. Morrison got

sick from the medicine, but no one else did. The pills gave Huebner cottonmouth and nightmares of his family in bloody car
wrecks every night for a week. He had no idea what he was
putting into his body, but he took it anyway; scared not to.

You awake? Morrison asked Huebner.

Yeah, Huebner said.

Gassed, shot at or shelled? Morrison asked.

What? Hunh?

C'mon, what would you rather?

I'd rather not think about it.

Humor me.

I'd rather be shot, Maxwell piped up. Or gassed, Maxwell
went on. I'd like to think I'd have a chance.

Huebner said, You'd die slower if you were gassed.

Have a chance to take someone with me, Maxwell said.
Rather die crawling on the ground than never know what hit me.
He laughed, What I would like, he said, is to get laid.

You never been laid anyway, Huebner said.

Fuck you, Maxwell said.

Huebner got up to go for a piss and Maxwell followed after
him. Six months before Max's college football coach had told
him he needed a little more size and if he took a year or two off
to join the Army his scholarship would be waiting for him. So he
agreed the Army would be a good choice for him. He'd joined
up as a buck private, gone through six weeks of basic training at
Fort Bragg in Fayetteville, North Carolina. Maxwell had just
been awarded his private stripes, or skeeter wings as they were
called.

Maxwell said, Hey, do you want any of these? He held out his
hand.

What the hell is that?

Cool out, dude. Got them from the captain. Some kind of uppers, I guess. He said he got them from some fliers back in Dammam.

No thanks, Huebner told him. Maybe later on, he said. He didn't want Maxwell to think he judged him.

Suit yourself, Maxwell said, and smiled. He looked around, sort of nervously. Hey, remember the other day when I went to supply and got the macaroni snacks?

Huebner smiled.

Captain Jobe was there and Morrison, too. They were set up ten miles back behind the lines. Maxwell got antsy. He got a new symptom of stress every day. The dry air gave him nosebleeds. This time he said his cock was chafed.

Probably from jerking off too much, Morrison said.

What if it is? Maxwell said.

We need some camouflage netting, Captain Jobe said. Feel like going over to the Forward Support Battalion? Take Maxwell with you. Bring us back something to eat to, hunh? Captain Jobe said, and rubbed his stomach.

Thanks, Chief.

Maxwell drove the truck and Huebner rode shotgun. No one was allowed to take off by himself. Three hours later they came back with a box of "lunch bucket" macaroni and cheese snacks.

What the hell are those? Morrison asked.

These are precooked, Maxwell said proudly. Made to be popped into a microwave oven.

Let's do that, Huebner said, and laid a couple in on the tank's turret out in the hot sun. In a few minutes they were sizzling, hot enough to eat.

They told Maxwell, Good score, and ate them until the box was gone. Thirty-two count, eight apiece.

So listen, Maxwell was saying now, There's this girl in supply that wants me to fuck her.

Don't they all? said Huebner.

If I get her knocked up then she can go home.

And?

Well, what do you think I should do? You're married.

Huebner laughed out loud.

She said she doesn't have to keep it. She can abort it when she gets home. But I don't believe in abortion, Maxwell said.

We've hardly been here a week, Maxwell. For heaven's sake. You're nineteen years old, man.

So? I can't have beliefs?

One minute you're stealing mac and cheese, the next, this.

I didn't start this war.

Hey, Max, get it while you can, I guess. And if at first you don't succeed, try it again.

Thanks.

Huebner looked back, but Maxwell wasn't joking. That's all right, Huebner said.

When everything was quiet, Sergeant Huebner lay down on his sleeping bag under the immense desert sky and slowly tried to picture every moment of the last weekend he had spent together with Meg. He thought back to that Saturday at St. Catherine's Island. The voices of his brother, Meg and Dorothy bounced off the water into the dense silver of the rain-charged sky. A breeze came off St. Catherine's Sound strong and warm, and brought along the bracing smell of the ocean. Hard laughter pitched off the surface of the water toward distant blue.

The transistor radio in the boat trailed weather reports into the gaining wind. The hurricane had gone out to sea off the eastern coast of Florida. Sam switched it to an oldies station and Smith heard them singing along with a song by Three Dog Night. He was out in the bay, guiding his little boat back to land. Sam and the girls had jumped out and swum to a small shallow at the island beach. Seagulls squawked loudly overhead. Thunder rolling in the distance reminded Huebner of infantry practice on the scrap grass desert fields in California.

Waves broke over the normally placid shoreline, chasing the fiddler crabs back into their pinprick holes. Flocks of birds crisscrossed, twisted and banked, then headed to the trees for shelter from the coming storm. A curtain of clouds opened for the sun. Sheets of mist blew off the surf, projecting rainbows that glistened in the humid air.

After Smith pulled the boat on land he went back into the water for a swim. Meg came out to meet him; her skin was warm in the cool blue water and he forgot where he was and where he was going. She kissed him and Smith tasted the briny sea.

5

The week after her husband left for the desert, Meg went to the bathroom with the small stapled-shut paper bag from the drugstore. While she sat there waiting, a fly buzzed, stuck between the window and the screen. The sea smelled of salt, astringent almost, an agent of cleanliness on the breeze against the smell of the smoke pile she'd lit in the yard for the sand gnats. Meg . waited with the little plastic indicator in her hand, looking for the red heart.

At two o'clock in the afternoon she got into her car. She drove to the doctor and sat down in the waiting room.

No appointment?

The woman at the desk bulged out of her white polyester uniform, not unattractively. Meg held her breath until the temptation to judge went away.

The receptionist got Meg's look. Meg just blushed and raised her eyebrows.

The receptionist said, Sit down, honey.

Everyone was "honey" or "dear" as long as they didn't smell

and shopped at the right stores in the air-conditioned malls or the old downtown shops and not at Kmart.

Meg thought of her husband: she had liked Smith the first time she met him. He wasn't a part of her world, nor the world outside it. They met in the student union in a study group. He had brought a copy of *Steppenwolf* by Hesse but forgotten his textbook. Meg let him look on with her. His nearness tickled her spine and quickened her breath in a way she could not control. When he asked her out, she said, Sure. Meg liked Smith because he was polite. He knew to walk on the outside, to follow her up the stairs and lead her down. He knew how to make her feel like a woman. She thought he had character and was dashing. And there was precious little of that among the boys she had grown up around. She was used to boys who sat a little too easily in their chairs, who would never think to get up when a girl entered the room; boys who laughed about wrecking cars they'd been given by their fathers as if they didn't know the value of a dollar. She fell for him and she didn't regret it, but—good Lord—look where it had gotten her now.

You're from the Fort? the receptionist asked, We'll fit you in.

They all knew that the man responsible for her condition was thousands of miles away. In a week she would go to see her mother for a while. For now she could talk to Cecily, Specialist Morrison's wife. She would understand.

Meg waited for the lady doctor, as Smith called her in his charming tease of a way, the only female gynecologist in the lower Savannah region. Meg took her flipflops off there in the waiting room and touched the tight industrial carpeting with her bare feet. She felt the rug with her toes and blinked tears from her eyes.

A couple of hours later she was home, had drawn a cool bath, alone with the now very tired buzzing fly, the smoke pile in the yard. Before she got into the tub, she got out the fly swatter, opened the screen and gently guided the big old horsefly out.

As Huebner lay awake on his sleeping bag that night, a big black horsefly landed on his hand. He had saved his letter from his wife and just sat down to read it. He stared at the fly for a moment by the light of the moon. It reflected off the sand and cast light all around. The fly bit Huebner's hand. He cursed, swatted, left a big red splotch of his own blood on his wife's letter. He would keep the letter and someday Meg herself might see it. How could he explain to her the blood, the absurdity of him being here at all? He could never explain it. It was a job and an adventure. The old television ad had not lied.

Well, it's for sure now, Meg wrote. We're having a baby.

She told him it had rained solid for the week after he left for the Gulf. One day she was out driving, the rain got so bad she had to pull off the highway. She saw a dog in its pen by the side of the road. It had gotten up on the roof of its house, and now the poor dog was stranded. It barked and looked around at the rising muddy water. She could not do anything for it.

Meg said he shouldn't worry, but since he had left, she felt like that dog. Both of them would just have to wait until the water went down and things were back to normal.

She said she loved him and she had beautiful memories of their last nights together.

In a postscript she wrote that Sam had called and she had wired him one hundred dollars Western Union. He told some story about the messed-up paperwork on his job. She wasn't sure she believed him, but she sent the money. Huebner had walked off to the perimeter of the encampment. He still had tears in his eyes when Morrison walked up.

Good news from home? he asked. Of the crew, Morrison was his closest friend. Maxwell was just a young recruit. Captain Jobe, of course, was another matter.

Huebner had met Morrison at the Georgia State Fair when they were in high school. They competed in a race, tied for first, and then never saw each other again until the Army. One of them had gotten a little homesick, asked the other about his accent and realized the connection. Morrison was the first black quarterback to win all-conference in his county down-east. They had been in the same company for weeks. When they were assigned, it was to the same tank.

We're having a baby, he told Morrison.

Isn't that good news?

Yeah, it is, Huebner said. He wiped his eyes and looked around.

Well, if anyone asks, Morrison said, I'm as happy as hell for you.

The battalion moved deeper into Saudi Arabia and closer to Iraq all through September and October. They had to refuel twice a day when they ran full bore. For a tank, riding in an M-1 Abrams is like riding in a limousine. The shock absorber torsion bars are huge and the wide tracks make contact with a great deal of the ground. This is why the tankers call it a "pig."

The treads came up to the middle of Smith's chest and he

was six feet tall. Whenever Huebner saw tanks all lined up in formation, revved, waiting for the signal to move on, he thought of what it would be like to ride through the streets of an invaded town. That kind of weaponry makes dissent, discussion, all the finer points of politics and diplomacy irrelevant.

As they rode behind the point in the middle of the arrow-shaped formation, they felt pretty invincible. The Army had given out lorans to find their way in the desert. Captain Jobe mounted the little black box on the inside of the main turret and ran it off the tank's power. The loran picked up signals from transmitters stationed along the coast of the Persian Gulf and told them their position.

In the desert the topography was fluid; maps had to be updated and even then were often useless. Morrison's sailing experience came in handy whenever Maxwell got lost. Morrison navigated the desert as if it were the open sea, by converting latitude and longitude to the Military Grid Reference System on the maps. Eventually, he taught this method to Maxwell, who learned to ride the angles and make no sudden turns. Huebner never really quite got it and Morrison and Maxwell would make fun of him. To him, they always seemed likely to get lost.

You know what they say?

What's that?

In the land of the blind, the one-eyed man is king.

Ha, ha, ha, Huebner said.

I'm just glad you're the gunner, Maxwell told him.

So am I, Huebner said. In the land of Iraq, the man with the biggest gun is king.

His first two weeks in New York City, Sam lived with a five-foot-tall man named Benny Bing who suggested he'd share his bed with Sam if he were cold on the couch.

Suit yourself, he said.

I will.

The tiny man bragged he had understudied for Mickey Rooney on Broadway.

He was all reputation, he told Sam, hung like a soprano. Benny Bing was a vitamin fanatic who talked about life extension like a preacher and kept a Magnum pistol beside his bed. It's the biggest gun a man can hold in one hand, he said. Something about his smile was so sleazy it made Sam cringe.

Sam found work, first as a bike messenger and then at the Doubleday bookshop on Fifth Avenue across from the Trump Tower. Everyone wanted to be something or somewhere else, an opera singer, a stockbroker, a writer. A lot of celebrities and hordes of rude tourists shopped there. The showroom was clean, but behind the scenes, it was shabby and depressing. Sam held Steven Spielberg's credit card at the desk while the director picked out all the books he wanted. He gaped at how tall Johnny Cash was in person, laughed with his coworkers at Andy Warhol's ridiculous alabaster wig and nearly knocked over Diana Ross, when he didn't see her behind an armload of books.

Sam made $112 take-home pay for forty hours work and moved into a railroad flat in the Bronx with two others from the bookstore. One was an opera singer who had worked there for seven years. He had two "wrinkle-free" outfits and wore one, while he washed the other in the sink each night and hung it to dry out on the fire escape. He smelled like mildew from five feet away. He lived in a dream world all his own.

That apartment was in a truly desperate neighborhood, Burnside Avenue, near 183rd. It's right by the old New York University campus, Mildew Mike told him. It was built for the university's divinity school.

Sam nodded and said, Oh, of course.

Mike liked to tell the story of how this uptown campus was designed by the great New York architect, the scandalous Stanford White. The downtown Greenwich Village neighborhood was considered too full of temptations and many of the pledges were being waylaid. This story meant a lot to Mike.

He insisted on taking Sam for a tour of the neighborhood, capping it off by leading him to the Beaux Arts library and a bronze bust collection in a trash-strewn garden with rusted iron archways. The whole place was a ruin. The library, once the crown jewel, had been gutted by fire and partially destroyed by a Molotov cocktail during student riots in the 1960s in demonstrations against Nixon's bombing of Hanoi in 1968.

When Sam told a cute Australian girl from the store named Sandy about the tour, she said, Augh, Mildew Mike! Tut, tut, we have to get you out of there.

She was interviewing at publishing houses and eventually landed a job as an editorial assistant. To celebrate Sandy threw a party at a friend's apartment on Central Park South that she had invited Sam to, and that's where he met Eleanor Perkins. She was tall, with dark hair and blue eyes that drew him across the room to her side. He suggested they go to the roof for a look. He stuck a bottle of champagne in his jacket pocket.

Look at that, she said to him and pointed. In the distance was what looked like flames coming off the roof of an apartment building.

Maybe someone's having a barbecue up there, Sam said.

There's too much smoke for that.

Maybe they're cooking steaks.

You're funny, Eleanor said. I wish there was something we could do.

Even if we could call we would never know the address.

Wow, she said. That's certainly a fire. She pointed again and Sam kissed her for the first time. They stood up there in the wind, as sirens sounded in the busy streets below.

Now, we'll never forget this, Sam said.

You know something, you're pretty romantic. Eleanor smiled and kissed him back.

Later when Eleanor asked him what he was doing in the city, Sam blurted that he was going back to school to study writing.

Really?

I dropped out of school when I left Georgia to get out on my own. But you don't want to hear all that, Sam said, and kissed her again.

Not so fast, she said. Why don't you tell me a little about yourself? Tell me a story, Mr. Writer.

Sam was a little buzzed from the champagne. He told Eleanor that his brother Smith was five when their mom left home, and he was barely three and a half, still eating from a high-chair. They had moved to their grandparents' house on the grounds of the Buccleuch Mansion in New Brunswick, New Jersey. Zeke lived there too, but he was not always around. He was out drinking and would come home with his shirt ripped from fighting. Then he was gone for a year. He came back, quit drinking and moved the boys down to Georgia with him. He had a succession of girlfriends. One tried to talk to them about their mom. Zeke wouldn't have this.

He hit her once and raged, Don't try to talk to my kids.

She stuck around anyway. Sam remembered this woman wore T-shirts with pockets on the front. She never wore a bra, and this gave Smith and Sam something to talk about as teenagers.

Sam asked questions and watched television with her; Smith would go to the ball field or the mall during the day.

You must have missed your mother, Eleanor suggested.

Sam got quiet and thought. I guess, he said.

The boys played sports. Sam was as good as Smith, but he would always tell someone to go to hell and get kicked off the team. Sam never made it easy for Smith with the coaches; when they asked Smith, What's up with your brother? Smith shook his head. Sam dyed his hair blue and then jet black. He got a leather jacket, said he didn't believe in God. That's classic, Zeke said.

Sam started hanging out with the local punk rockers. He wrote songs, sang with a hardcore band and toured the South with them the summer after high school. Sam liked the out-of-control feeling of being onstage. He would do stage dives and surf through the crowd. Smith made all-state in football and enrolled in an ROTC program to help pay for college. He told Sam he liked the discipline. Smith was sensible.

What do you think of his being in the army now? Eleanor asked.

I disagree with war, he said. I disagree with the killing. Smith believes in what he's doing. He wrote me a postcard and said he was fighting so that his brother could protest.

That's a pretty large view to take, Eleanor said to Sam. He really loves you.

He's naïve, Sam said.

Some people are, Eleanor said, smiling.

Thanks a lot.

I didn't mean . . .

That's all right. Maybe I am naïve. I think he didn't like college and he wanted to grow up fast. He fell in love and wanted to get married, but he had no way of supporting himself, let alone a family. The Army works for him.

You've got a tradition of military service in your family?

You could say that. No one ever went to West Point, though we've had someone in every war since the Revolution. My grandma likes to tell those stories. But my father hates all of it.

You take after your father?

No, that's not right. Not by design anyway. Sam laughed. The Army is something Smith's really good at. But going to war is different.

You must be scared for him.

I am, I guess, Sam said. Scared for what he will have to do and what that's going to do to him. I thought after Vietnam we wouldn't have to fight any more wars. Didn't that prove it was stupid enough?

He stayed at her place on Third Street in Brooklyn as often as he could over the next few weeks without actually ever spending the night.

I'll sleep on the balcony, he said. I will sleep out in the hallway, to protect not only your reputation but your apartment from intruders as well. He kept his place with Mildew Mike; the other room turned over as people from the store moved in, stayed a week or a couple months and moved out.

Sam took Eleanor to see the campus and she loved it. She took photos of the ruins and combined the images with text in paintings of how she imagined the neighborhood in its prime at the beginning of the twentieth century when the lushly landscaped campus had first opened. Her series of paintings won an art competition at the Cooper Union that year.

When Sam told his brother over the phone about his new girl up in New York, Sam said, Y'know, she reminds me a little bit of Meg.

You mean, she's a free spirit and more together than you, Smith replied.

Right. Sam laughed.

Sam went back to school. The year before he had quit the University of Georgia with about forty credits, majoring vaguely in political science and switching to the honors English program when he showed some writing to a professor. She took him under her wing until he disappointed her.

I can tell by your comments in class that you've read the books, but you have not turned in a single essay. You talk a lot in class, but my guess is you stay in school because you like the girls.

Sam blushed. I have been doing some writing, he said, and handed her a short story he had been working on.

The professor sat down right there, under an oak tree, and read the story from beginning to end. Sam stood next to her, shifting from foot to foot as embarrassment warmed him from head to toe.

You have talent, she said. And you're charming, she said, and smiled ruefully. But talent and charm don't add up to a degree. Maybe you don't belong here.

Sam walked into a science exam, then right back out when he looked at the paper and realized he didn't know a single answer.

Smith was leaving for basic training and Sam had moved in with the punk rockers. Their dad had asked Smith what to do with the dog. Years ago, their dad had gotten drunk at a party and traded a gerbil Smith had for it, and since then Old Blue had been his responsibility.

What about Old Blue? Zeke asked him.

Blue he's a good old dog. I'm sure going to miss him, Smith said, and gave the dog a pat before he left.

Later when he learned his dad had put him to sleep, he said, What the hell did you do that for?

When Jane and I moved in, there just wasn't room. I asked you about him, son. You didn't say anything.

I thought you would feed him, not kill him. You could have found another home for him or something.

Zeke shook his head and bit his lip as Smith stewed in anger. If the boy wanted to show his ass, he would keep his covered. Children were always like that with their parents sometimes, no matter how big they got. That's how Zeke saw it. Blue was a good dog, but he was just a dog.

Smith wondered if his dad had a heart. He didn't know how someone could be that callous. It was like something in him just didn't work, or had been broken long ago.

When their mother had passed away in an institution in Boston, Sam went up for the memorial service. Eleanor insisted that he go.

I can't believe your dad and your brother won't come, she said. Where are they?

Zeke had to go hunting and Smith's learning to drive a tank out in California.

California?

The Mojave Desert. They practice there. Anyway, Dad and Smith can't make it.

You're not kidding, are you?

No.

Do you always call your dad Zeke?

That's his name.

There was a photograph at the memorial service that Sam had never seen of his mother from when she was young.

She looks like you, Sam said. I never even knew she looked anything like that. I'm surprised.

I'm not, Eleanor said.

Eleanor wore all black and was almost six feet tall, with a short crop of black hair. She had hazel, green-blue eyes.

They change depending on how nice you are, she said to Sam.

Sam took her for long walks all over the city. They would get a cheap bottle of wine and he always had some pot, but in those days that was all. They went to the Cloisters, to Coney Island, to Central Park at least once a week; there was a lovely place at about 106th Street. They would get a little drunk and sit in the grass. She would lie down and look up at the sky and he would read to her from whatever he was working on in his writing. She loved the deep, melodic sound of his voice. Sam loved to make love to her in the open air. That summer she fell in love with him. Whenever they went into the city, it was theirs.

He applied to different schools. NYU and Columbia were too expensive and out of the question, so he ended up at City College. They had a program for a BA/MA degree in English. He took the graduate courses as his electives. He discovered Melville and Ezra Pound. He took a class in Boswell and Johnson with an esteemed professor who was writing a book on their letters to each other. The old man with the flyaway white hair termed Sam's first paper "determined" and "sweet," but Sam was not really prepared for the work. He spent a day reading the City College catalog when he realized that a lot of his classes would not be transferred from Georgia. He went into advisors' offices and boldly explained how certain vaguely worded courses he had taken in Georgia should pass for the ones he needed in his current curriculum. He was able to wipe out an entire semester of undergraduate work this way.

You're not going to quit talking until I see things your way, are you? an advisor asked Sam.

No, sir, he said.

6

On a Saturday in early November, Maxwell got use of a Humvee and Morrison and Huebner hitched a ride with him into the closest town, Al Sarrah. In a sun-scorched pale sand field outside of the town limits, there was a livestock disposal field soldiers had nicknamed the Pet Sematary. Carcasses of goats, camels and dogs, putrid and decayed, lay in piles, bodies splayed in odd positions, rotting into one another. Carrion birds and shiny green flies hovered overhead. Sergeant Huebner could not help but look at first, but had to turn away when the wind shifted. He turned back when he heard the shots. A gun sounded once, then again.

That sounds like a shotgun, Morrison yelled.

Nonmilitary? Huebner asked.

Well, yeah . . .

Stop the freaking jeep, Huebner yelled at Maxwell. Stop!

Maxwell skidded into a dune and pulled up the brake.

The Humvee was equipped with a hand-mike radio. Dark Lord Six to Rogue TOC, got a situation report, Huebner called in.

Okay, send it, came the reply.

Couple of local nationals, Huebner said, reaching for his bandanna to hold up over his nose. They have weapons, but don't pose a threat? At Grid 1-2-4-5-7-8.

What are they doing?

Disposing of some local livestock.

Roger. Got it. Logging it. Let me know if anything changes.

A couple of men stood out in the sand fields. Wind billowed their thoabs. The men had already shot three animals, two goats and a camel. They had one more goat to go.

The black and white shaggy goat jumped and the first man missed the shot. The other laughed and shot the goat himself, matter of fact. Bang! The animal had been hit in the leg. It made an awful bleating squall, with a foamy sort of white pus leaking from its mouth. The men jumped back and hollered something in their language. Sordid, playful fun.

They're torturing the poor thing, Maxwell said. Should we take away their guns?

We're not the only ones who get to have weapons, Huebner told him.

C'mon, Maxwell said. Let's fuck with them a little. He grabbed the M-16 from the back compartment of the Humvee and started off running toward the men.

What's he going to do? Morrison asked Huebner.

Something stupid! Huebner said. He hollered and went after Maxwell. The private got off one good shot into the goat's neck before Huebner tackled him. The Arabs laughed at the American soldiers as Huebner and Maxwell got up cursing, rubbing sand off their uniform pants.

That was the worst tackle I ever saw, Morrison said, walking up. He smiled at the Arabs, took Huebner by the arm and started walking him back to the Humvee. Maxwell went over and picked up his gun. He looked at Morrison and Huebner, then at the Arabs.

C'mon, Maxwell, Morrison said quickly. Let's go. Let's go back to the jeep.

Maxwell checked the M-16 over and scuffed the sand with his boot. He kicked back his head and hollered, did a little dance in the sand.

Look at that fucker, Huebner said. He thinks he's in the goddamn NFL.

I don't know. I thought it was a good shot, Morrison said. Lighten up, dude.

Huebner reddened and shook his head. Maxwell said, Hey, wait up, fellas. That's the first time that rifle's ever been shot, in a war, I mean. That was fun, right, Sarge? He was still breathing hard.

Ahh, it was bullshit, Huebner said. I can't believe you took the gun off safety, Huebner hissed at Maxwell. I should fill out a report and have you sent to fucking parts and maintenance. Don't you know anything about protocol, soldier?

I kinda prefer to do things by feel, sir, Maxwell said, and grabbed his crotch with his hand. Huebner had to laugh at this, finally.

The Humvee was stuck. Huebner got in and turned the key, but the back wheels spun and kicked up sand in his face. The Arabs came over and pitched in. Maxwell introduced himself to them. The men were actually Syrian.

Those Saudis are some tight-ass bastards, right? Maxwell said.

When the Syrians looked at him quizzically, he pantomimed it for them and everyone laughed.

Saudis all think they kings are, one of them said.

Everyone was wary friends when the soldiers waved good-bye to the Syrians.

Al Sarrah was a crossroads in the middle of the desert. The roads were not paved; they were dusty gravel and dirt. Just outside of town, the land changed to pale green where the constant windswept sands cut the grass short. Soldiers were given fifty dollars to spend. Shacks served nonalcoholic San Miguel beer and nasty hamburgers. Everybody kidded about the rotting animals at the end of the road, but ate the burgers eventually. Next door a cardboard sign boasted of "American-style pizza," but served tomatoes and cheese wrapped up in flat Arab bread. These were actually very tasty as tomatoes and onions were grown on farms throughout the region. Ma Bell had also set up a phone bank and a shop with primitive video games: ones they knew as teenagers, Pac-Man and Space Invaders.

The locals had fashioned the makeshift buildings out of leftovers dropped off passing oil trucks: corrugated steel, truck tires and rims, piles of tires on fire, wooden boards, pallets. The arcade was made entirely of tin roofing. It got hot in there. Morrison and Maxwell wrapped wet towels around their heads and disappeared inside to play video games for a half-hour.

Huebner waited outside. Looking around at the locals, Huebner couldn't help but believe that the average Saudi appreciated the United States. They could certainly use America's help with Saddam Hussein, and they liked the dollar. But, the soldiers had been warned by command, the Saudis didn't really like U.S. culture and would just as soon Americans didn't hang around too much. As he stood there waiting for the others to finish with the games, a woman dressed head to toe in a black aba'ya flashed him a peace sign.

For a couple of weeks after Meg wrote about the baby, he had called, but had not gotten her on the phone. Huebner left her messages and told her he loved her.

This time he let the phone ring ten times, but there was no answer. He banged the receiver so hard that it cracked apart in his hand. His thumb was bleeding when Morrison walked up.

Look, man, Morrison said. You know the deal, because of the logistics in the theater, Jobe said mail could get delayed up to a month.

Great.

Smith, I talked to my girl Cecily back home. She went over there and checked on your wife. I hope you don't mind.

I feel like kissing you, Huebner said.

Not in this Army. Cecily said that Meg had gone to Atlanta for a while. She went to stay with her folks. Cecily says to tell you she's fine.

During the fall the temperature dropped to between eighty and one hundred degrees. It started to get awful cold at night. Behind the great red rock that made a cragged cathedral entrance to their bivouac site, there was a solid rock floor surrounded on three sides by gradated walls of sandstone. The walls were ridged and cut with caves. Colonel Agard's tank battalion set up command quarters on the valley floor and many of the platoons took places in the caves. It was like a great prehistoric stadium. The dimensions reminded Sergeant Huebner of an old brick football field where he had once played in high school. An eerie, magic light descended when the sun dropped behind the big rock and turned the puffed blanket of clouds over the desert red. At night, when Sergeant Huebner stood on the desert floor and looked around at the lights of each platoon winking on along the valley wall, it was an awesome place to be.

Jobe came up with the name Graceland for the camp, marked by the bones of a dead camel someone had called Elvis. The soldiers settled into some kind of routine. Most of the time, Huebner believed any moment that they could be under attack without notice. He attended mandatory training sessions in common task testing. His crew had AFV, or armored fighting vehicle drills. Captain Jobe drilled the company on first aid, buddy aid, rules of combat, rules of engagement, Geneva Convention, individual tasks. Maxwell and another driver from Charlie Company named Martinez pretended they were drunk, told the captain they'd mixed up some kind of home brew from engine fluid. Not in the mood for pranks, Jobe let them walk back from the drill site a couple miles outside camp. The two of them came back four hours later at sunset trailing a caravan of Bedouins in a dented Toyota pickup truck.

The soldiers trained in concert with the fuel trucks and eventually could refuel an entire tank company in thirty minutes. They practiced battle drills by walking around in the desert with hand-held radios and worked on the standard operating procedure for breaching obstacles, such as Saddam's infamous fire trenches.

The 66th Division participated in training drills with the Marines, and an engineering regiment of the French Foreign Legion. When the Legionnaires went out to jog in the morning, a truck followed directly behind their unit ready to distribute NBC suits in the event of a surprise chemical attack.

Halloween, Thanksgiving, Christmas on the way. By December there would be over half a million troops from the United Nations coalition in the desert. Huebner's unit had been there for more than four months. Originally the United States secretary of defense made a statement that the Desert Shield troops would be replaced in four months. This rotation was delayed and then canceled. The chairman of the Joint Chiefs of Staff Colin Powell said the next troop movement might not come for two years.

Who's going to fuck my wife while I'm gone? Captain Jobe complained.

Huebner looked at Maxwell with a stare that said, Keep your mouth shut. He wasn't sure if the captain was joking or not.

Anyway it wasn't a joking matter. Morrison got a letter from home about his son's discipline problems in school. A lot of the soldiers were bitter. They wanted to fight or go home.

After the United Nations voted to authorize "all necessary means" to liberate Kuwait, President Bush offered to exchange envoys with Iraq. Most of the Dark Lord Company got up at 0500 hours in the dark of one cold desert morning and listened to the BBC report as Secretary of State Baker met for seven hours of meetings with Tariq Aziz, Iraq's foreign minister, in Geneva on January 9, 1991.

I believe they're going to work this out, Morrison said, as ever, hopeful.

No way, Huebner said. Hussein is never going to give up Kuwait.

He would if we let him.

In a three-page letter presented by Baker from President Bush to Saddam Hussein, Bush warned, "There can be no reward for aggression. Iraq must join the civilized world." He offered no negotiations or compromises.

Aziz refused to accept the letter. Iraq would not leave Kuwait. A few days later in the United States Congress the House of Representatives authorized use of force to expel Iraq by a vote of 250 to 183, and following equally passionate debate, the Senate concurred, 52 to 47.

Every day on his way to work Sam saw the same homeless man. His right foot was missing at the ankle, he never wore a shirt and he had a large wooden cross draped around his neck. He would senselessly scream obscenities at the young, well-heeled lawyers and brokers who passed by each morning and afternoon on their way to and from work. Sam taught a composition class four days a week at the Borough of Manhattan Community College in Tribeca. He wrote on the campus lab computers after class in the afternoon. He would see the poor man on the sidewalk yelling at the financial crowd. One afternoon Sam bought a cheap bottle of wine, sat down with this man and tried to talk with him.

Thanks for the wine, the man said. He got angry, yelled at the passersby and lost track of what he was saying.

Sam asked the man if he had a place to live, if he could help him with anything.

The man laughed. I like the wine, he said.

That's cool, Sam said.

He stared at Sam, took a long drink and wiped the dark red drops off his chin. Wait a minute, he said. Who are you? What do you do? The man went through his pockets and tried to pull himself up onto his one good foot.

It's all right, Sam said. I'm a teacher.

The man nodded blindly. His glasses had fallen off and Sam retrieved them for him. Some man in a really nice suit, sunglasses and briefcase, tripped over the man's leg and cursed. This sent the man into another loud fit of cursing and yelling.

Have some more wine, Sam told him.

More wine. The man drank and grinned. He stared at Sam again and nodded after a moment and offered Sam the bottle.

Sam took a drink and frowned. The wine was pretty bad. Peach-flavored Cool Breeze, it said when he looked more closely at the label, $1.51 a pint including tax, 12 percent alcohol by law.

The man laughed at Sam. What do you teach? he asked.

Sam looked at him, surprised.

Didn't you think I was listening?

I teach English, Sam said. But I'm really trying to write a book.

What's your book about? the man asked. He still sounded too angry and agitated for casual conversation, but he had stopped yelling and cursing. For a moment he forgot the passersby who tormented him and was able to focus on Sam.

It's about a young Native American who comes to New York to be a writer, Sam said.

The man nodded, drinking.

He feels like he's betraying his heritage. He has a high-powered agent and feels like a whore.

Sounds more like a thesis than a story, the bum said, and winked at Sam. Does he make a lot of money? the man asked. He started turning red and his voice rose with each word.

He grabbed the bottle from a stunned Sam and threw it back against the brick wall. The bottle shattered and wine splattered all over him and Sam.

What the fuck! Sam shouted.

The homeless man laughed. Put that in your book! he shouted over and over. Sam brushed the glass off his book bag and walked away.

Sam decided he would write this man into his book. His hero, the one-named Indian novelist Barefoot, had not written anything in a year. He hung out in clubs, did too much coke and fucked models. Sam knew about as much of this as he knew about getting a book published. One night outside a club called Area, the author meets this man begging outside, drinks with him and spills his guts. Barefoot mentions his hatred for his agent to this homeless man and the homeless man stalks and then axe-murders the agent.

Sam thought the story showed how the commercialism of the late eighties and the oil greed of the war in the desert were corrupting young artists. This was how he pitched it to an editor at Atlantic Monthly Press. He got an encouraging note back. The editor wrote to keep working on it. The editor said this to a lot of people, but he had picked the proposal out of a slush pile. Sam was thrilled.

Sam had based his character on a young writer named Alex Alright. A gossip column reported that Alright was throwing a party at a club called MK for another writer who was publishing his first novel with Atlantic Monthly Press. He told Eleanor to get dressed up and meet him at Twenty-sixth Street and Fifth Avenue after work. They smoked a little reefer together in Madison Square Park. It was a windy early fall night. The wind picked up the leaves and danced with them across the streets.

She wore a black slip of a dress and as dusk fell, they smoked, giggled and made out on a bench. The lights in the buildings on the square and of the early evening taxi traffic gently passing by the park glowed.

Someone passing by said, Excuse me, Eleanor Perkins, is that you?

Eleanor looked up and shouted, Thomas!

She jumped to her feet and gave the speaker a great big hug. He was dressed in a nice jacket, a black T-shirt and tight jeans.

Sam, meet Tommy, Eleanor said. He was one of my best friends at RISD.

What's up? Sam said and shook hands.

Tommy told them his band was playing that night at MK.

That's a coincidence, Eleanor said. We wanted to go, we heard it's hard to get in.

No problem, Thomas said. I'll leave your name at the door.

You know him from school? Sam asked when he left.

Don't be jealous.

He seemed like half a mo, anyway.

Why do you say things like that? Eleanor asked.

I was kidding.

Sure you were.

Eleanor shook her head and led Sam by the hand out of the park. They went to see the band at the club and met the emcee. He told Sam that the Alex Alright party would be having dinner on the second floor.

I wouldn't try to crash the dinner, he said. Wait until after that and then come to the party afterward. I can get you in.

They watched the young writers finish their dinner from the second-floor landing and then went to join the party: a lot of drinking, people disappearing into the bathroom in pairs, loud music, talk, no dancing.

I'm looking for Hans, Sam said to a man waiting for the bathroom.

I am Hans. He took off his tortoiseshell glasses and wiped them, brushed some lint from his suit.

Sam Huebner.

I don't think I know you.

I sent you a manuscript. You wrote me back.

Really? Sometimes my assistant signs my name, he said.

Oh. I guess they're taking turns in there, Sam said, pointing to the bathroom. Three slim blond model types had slipped in just ahead of the editor.

You're kidding, right?

Sam smiled.

They're getting high in there. Honestly, I'm working on a book, too, Hans said. We're all working on books, man. In my opinion, it's a lot easier to get a drug habit than a publishing deal.

Sam found Eleanor in conversation with the host of the party and she introduced Sam to him. Alright was really nice and then later, after a few polite but persistent phone calls, he read Sam's work and bought him lunch a number of times at a New York hot spot called Coffee Shop. Sam always had a beer and cream of mushroom soup with bread. They talked about writing and Alright tried to be helpful. Sam showed him what he was working on. Eventually he edited some of Sam's work. Alright cut out

more than half of what Sam had shown him. He offered a lot of
encouragement, but he was honest.

It's a business, he said, you have to meet them halfway. This
East Village artist shit is pretentious and pointless.

You mean they're afraid of something edgy.

No, just the opposite. You need a selling point. Besides, let's
be real, you're as East Village as I am.

Sam got defensive. He knew Alright had a point.

I don't know if this Indian stuff is your story.

I want to write something topical, Sam told him. I grew up in
a suburb in Georgia—who cares about that—I wanted to do
something cool, he said. Sam was crushed when he looked at the
red marks Alright had made all over his manuscript. He rode the
train downtown and went to a dive bar on Fifth Street called Sophie's. He bought some coke off someone in the bathroom and
drank dollar beers until after midnight. He decided he would go
to Alright's apartment and tell him what he thought of his advice.
The author had mentioned he was having some friends over and
invited Sam to drop by.

Alright buzzed Sam up. Sam did the rest of the coke in the el-
evator on the way up and knocked on the door. Alright did not
invite Sam in. He opened the door, looked Sam over and
stepped out into the hallway.

Sam, he said, are you all right?

Of course I am, Sam said. I wanted to ask about all these ed-
its you suggested.

Oh, of course, Alright smiled. But now's a bad time. Why
don't you call me tomorrow?

Sam did not remember this when Eleanor asked him about it

the next day. Alright had called Eleanor to ask if he should be physically scared of Sam.

Sam wouldn't hurt a fly, she said. You don't have to worry about that.

Alright suggested that Sam needed to learn to edit his work and Sam told Eleanor he was just jealous.

I don't try to figure out what the hell I want to get across and tell a story to do it. I just write as fast as I can. It's like an athletic feat.

It shows, Eleanor said, and winked.

Thanks, Sam said. He never finished *Barefoot in Hell.* Instead he started a new novel about Times Square. Some homeless people and squatter artists living in the square go from building to building as they are torn down by developers. He wrote the story from the point of view of a soldier returned from a foreign war. He imagined the narrator as his brother.

This is by far the best thing you've shown me, Alright said. Keep writing.

Sam attended an open poetry reading at an artist's space on Rivington Street, ABC No Rio, on Sunday afternoons. He met a man named Clayton Brooks, a poet and playwright, who became a good friend. Sam hadn't become acquainted with the downtown scene. With Clayton and an actor named Delancey both habitués of lower Manhattan, he did. He would sit through three hours of earnest, punky, sometimes even good work. Smoking a nickel of pot on his one-hit pipe in the bathroom and drinking tallboys of Schlitz Malt Liquor. Sam always read near the end.

He sat, listened and drank until the emcee, a fellow named Jim Thorne, asked him if he had anything. This Sunday, after the reading was over, Sam got a standing ovation. He smiled wide and forgot his manuscript on the makeshift plywood podium.

It was dark when he went outside. After the emcee locked the door and walked off, Sam realized what he'd done. He kicked the door a few times then ran around the corner. He scaled a fifteen-foot chain link fence, went through the high, overgrown grass of a vacant lot, past people sleeping in cardboard, a guy getting a blow job from a crack whore and a couple of junkies shooting up. He cut his hand on broken bottles cemented into the top of a wall, found the back window, and saw his manuscript on the podium. He got the window open but not the gate. He sat down there on the back porch. Lights came on in the adjoining buildings; someone was playing a Spanish radio station, someone else, Iggy Pop. Sam sat down and smoked the rest of his pot.

Back out front, he bought a tallboy at a bodega and wandered several blocks over to the Williamsburg Bridge. He climbed the stairway onto the walk path over the Lower East Side and the East River. The bridge was quite a hangout. It wasn't safe, really, and working people avoided it, but Sam always dug that kind of edge. A Spanish guy waved to him. Sam thought he might be selling and walked over.

Weed, no mas, he said to Sam. Headline, he said. Headline.

What's that? Sam asked.

Dope, he said. Manteca.

He was skinny, talking fast, sweating in the cool evening breeze, gesticulating wildly with his hands.

Dope, he said. Manteca . . .

Sam shrugged his shoulders, hands to the side.

The dealer smiled and said, No problemo. He mimed a sniff with his nose, rabbitlike.

How much? Sam asked.

The dealer flashed five fingers twice. Cinco, cinco, he said.

Sam sniffed the bag right there on the bridge and looked at the shimmering reflections the streetlights made on the green water. He watched the men down in the park by the river. They were gathering what they could find to shelter them for the night, cardboard boxes, discarded circus posters, soiled black plastic bags, a cushion of matted leaves on the hard cement sidewalk. He saw one man lose everything, all the scraps he had gotten together, as the wind kicked up and blew it all into the river.

7

The week before Christmas the 66th Infantry Division received tents from supply for the first time. At that point, they had been in the desert for more than four months. A few Hefty bags full of mail arrived, letters from women with photographs of them in bathing suits, cards from high school classmates. Kmart sent nets and volleyballs. The town of Jacksonville, Florida, sent footballs, Frisbees and hard candy.

Sergeant Huebner got a weekend pass and went to a party boat the Army had docked in the bay off of Bahrain. He and some other soldiers rode a bus eight hours each way for about four hours of hanging out and drinking. In Bahrain the laws were not as strict and alcohol was tolerated. Morrison got the same deal as Huebner, although he went first, during the week of the Thanksgiving Day holiday. Morrison was in Dhahran on the day that President George Bush visited the troops there.

Did you see him? Huebner asked.

I did, Morrison said. He sat in an F-15. There were a lot of photographers around.

Was a pilot himself, Maxwell said.

That's right, Morrison said. He gave a thumbs-up. We all wanted to hear what was going on. Would there be a war? When? One soldier held up a sign. We've been here since August. Do we fight or go home?

What did he say?

He didn't say a damn thing.

Maxwell was sent to a private home. An employee of the American Oil Company took soldiers in for a night at a time. He got wined and dined. Morrison tried to tease him about it, asked if they had a daughter. Maxwell said the whole experience was like spending the night at your uncle John's house. It would have been a complete waste, he said, if he hadn't stopped off and spent the last night with his girlfriend in supply.

Smith had talked to Meg the week before. The baby was due in two and half months, but all that felt far away.

Sam sent him a tape of music: "Death or Glory," he had written on it. That Clash song was Smith's favorite too. He remembered when Sam had turned him on to the album. Ten years ago, on Smith's fifteenth birthday the record, *London Calling,* first came out in the United States. They had sat together in Sam's room with their heads against the speakers and played it all the way through, trading the lyric sheet back and forth.

Sam did not include a letter this time. He had just included a note with the tape and said, Happy birthday, brother! I made a copy of this for myself too. If you get lonely over there, listen to this and think of me. Don't worry, I'm fine.

Smith did worry, and he wondered how Sam was doing.

A drop of rain fell from the sky and wet his skin; in moments sheets of it were glancing against the walls of the canyon. A changing of seasons had come to the desert just when the harshness of the heat had become a welcome rival in the macho rite of vigilance, suffering and pride; here came the icy rains, drops so cold that they felt like they must have fallen from someplace higher than the sky. As he hid from the rain and wrote to his brother, this was how Sergeant Smith Huebner would remember the growing certainty of the war bearing down, as icy rain that raised goose pimples from his flesh and chilled his spine.

Hey Brother,

Guess who got shit detail this morning?! Imagine dousing a platoon's worth every morning in diesel fuel and setting it aflame. I don't have to, I can smell it. And you thought Zeke's chores were bad . . .

Seriously, Are you OK? Meg said you called to borrow money last month. We are glad we could help. And don't get mad at me for asking. S'what big brothers are for, even when they're halfway across the world.

Don't let this war stuff get inside your head too much. We can each only fight the enemy that's in front of us. Our government made a promise and now we soldiers have to keep it. Staying home and doing the right thing, I imagine, is hard too. At least I can keep busy over here. I trust that you are keeping your head straight.

Love,

Your big bro Smith

At Eleanor's design office Sam watched the TV with her as the jets streaked over the dark Iraqi sky. When they walked downstairs, night had fallen over the city. Horns blared. People streamed into the streets and shouted news to each other. Strangers stopped on corners to pass rumors. People crowded grocery stores to buy canned goods and milk just in case.

Thousands had gathered at Times Square to protest, march or just watch the revolving news headlines that lit up the Times Building. The police barricaded the streets; mounted officers kept the crowds in check with billy clubs and bullhorns. People spilled out onto Broadway and all the side streets.

Sam and Eleanor met up with Clayton and joined the crowds marching across town to the United Nations. It got to be late. Eleanor went home; she had to get up and go to work in the morning.

A reporter from Channel 11 asked to interview Sam.

Times Square makes me feel closer to the war and my brother, he told the newswoman.

Your brother is over there?

That's right. I just got a letter from him today.

Is there a conflict there?

I'm not against the soldiers, Sam said. I am against the war.

The news clip was picked up by CNN and broadcast all over the world. Their father and his wife saw it in Georgia while looking for news about Smith. Some of the soldiers in the backup supply unit in the desert watched it too.

Another protester came up to Sam as he walked away from the interviewer.

He had long hair, a sloppy mustache and a Che Guevara T-shirt. He frowned as they watched the interviewer walk along the edges of the crowd.

She has a nice ass. But look, now she's looking for someone else to exploit, the man said.

To tell you the truth, Sam said, it was kind of intense. He was still breathing hard, looking around at the crowds and the flashing police lights.

You could have been an advertisement for the war.

What the fuck are you talking about? Sam said, and took a step forward.

The longhair didn't back off either. You didn't say anything about corporate greed. Big oil. That's what's going to kill your brother.

You know what, Sam spat out, I don't say slogans for either side. I'm kind of hoping he doesn't die, Sam said, and took a step closer.

We're here to tell people what the war's about. It's a protest, the longhair said, and took a step back. You don't have to get angry.

Sam pushed the man hard in the chest. Fuck you, he said. Protest that, asshole!

Clayton Brooks, his friend from ABC No Rio, caught up with Sam. It was on a side street on the East Side. He had run down that way after taunting a line of policemen. At the United Nations people had gathered in small groups and sung "We Shall Overcome."

This is getting boring, Clayton said to Sam. They always sing the same fucking songs.

"That's Entertainment" by the Jam would work.

That's funny, Clayton said. We should start our own organization.

One that never joins in.

And no slogans. We could just say stupid stuff.

Call it Jerks Against the War. Make fun of the whole thing.

I like that, Clayton said. J-A-W. JAW. Hey, do you get high?

I don't have any reefer.

Not pot. Pot makes you stupid. I want to go downtown and cop.

The cops? I don't get it.

Cop dope, man.

You mean . . .

Right, man. The white knight, y'know. That old ragtime.

I never heard those.

Have you ever copped?

Once, sort of by accident, Sam said. But you probably know better.

Let's try yours. Then we can go to a bar I heard of where we can get some coke.

They took the F train downtown, got off at Delancey and walked east on Rivington.

I bought some around here once, Sam said.

Out in the street? I never bought in the street. Aren't you afraid of getting ripped off? Clayton asked.

I've been buying pot in Bryant Park for years. I'm just used to it.

We need coke too, Clayton said. We can go to my bar. Find some D here so we can do a couple speedballs later.

Come again?

C'mon man, you never heard that? Where are you from?

Georgia.

They don't have William Burroughs novels down there?

Is he a Baptist preacher?

They laughed together, high-stepping over a man lying passed out on the sidewalk, a mangy dog smelling round the newspaper laid over his head. An older olive-skinned woman pushed a shopping cart along and kicked at the man on the sidewalk in her way. He just groaned and she stepped around.

A thin Puerto Rican, his rag shirt hanging off his skinny chest, ribs showing through the skin, appeared from around the corner of Norfolk.

Need something? he asked. He talked herky-jerky and flashed a plastic bag.

Maybe, Clayton said, What's up?

What up? The skinny man said. Flaco's up, white boy.

Hey, don't call us that, Clayton said.

Flaco laughed out loud. What the fuck I'm supposed to call you? This ain't the Village, bro, he said, and laughed at his own joke, doing a little dance on the sidewalk.

What the fuck are you on, man? Sam asked.

I just shot a load of coke, man. I'm a little tweaked, y'know. Hey, c'mon, Get your money out.

Let's see the dope, Sam said harshly.

Flaco gave Sam the once-over. Now, that's a proper attitude, he said, talking so fast he was hard to follow. He pulled out a tiny rectangle of wax paper. It said "Blast" with a little picture of a rocket ship stamped on it.

This any good? Sam asked. Don't try to burn us.

Him maybe, Flaco said, and nodded at Clayton. You, never, he said. He winked five times in less than a second.

Yeah, right, Sam said, and looked at the little bag in the faint glow from the only streetlight that worked, half a block away. Looks all right to me. Clay, you got twenty bucks?

Clayton nodded and fished the money out.

We'll take two apiece, Sam said. He checked them all as Flaco turned them over.

C'mon, Flaco said. This is a dope deal, not a wine tasting. Hurry up!

That was funny, Clayton said.

You think so? Flaco said, and flashed his teeth, his palm out, trembling.

Yeah.

Good, fuck you and gimme the money.

Thanks, man, Sam said, and the man was gone down the street.

Let's go get a little tweaked, yo, Clayton said.

Yeah, right. What a trip he was.

It was the coke, Clayton said. You ever shot coke?

No, have you?

I hear it's quite intense.

Looks a little too intense for me.

They walked to a dark stoop halfway down the block. Clayton took out a pack of matches. Let's do a little now.

Here? Sam said. Right out in the street? People live here.

In Alphabet City?

We're not even there. We're below that.

Right, Clayton said, and laughed. He held up one of the bags toward the moon, shook it slightly until it was even. He folded the bag in half, rolled up a torn-off end of the matchbook and stuck it in the bag. He sniffed and took a deep breath.

Then Sam inhaled and snorted.

Whoo!

Right, that's some kicking shit, Sam said, and a cool and warm feeling went all the way through his body.

This is why they invented the word "cool," right?

I hear you, man, Clayton said, and sat down. You want a cigarette?

I don't smoke them.

Aww, man, try one. It's the best.

What the hell? Sam joined him on the stoop. Clayton lit him up and they sat and smoked.

See what I mean? Clayton said after a minute.

Yeah, I do.

It will keep you awake too.

This is better than the last time I did . . . Sam said, cutting himself off. He didn't want Clayton to think he was a total rookie.

That's all right, Clayton said, and laughed. I'm just getting started with this too.

I thought you . . .

Really, man, you got to be careful with this sort of thing. No one wants to become a junkie.

Clayton took him to the coke-spot bar and they spent half the night in the bathroom doing the drugs, the other half putting quarters in the jukebox and playing pool in the back. Later Clayton took Sam around the corner to an abandoned building where people had taken over the apartments.

They don't pay rent? Sam asked.

No, it's a squat. They can pursue their art and shit, y'know.

Sounds great to me. How do you sign up?

Well, you always have to worry about the cops. It's a little sketchy. You still got any dope left?

Maybe half a bag.

Let's do it and crash here.

No one'll mind?

Naw, no one gives a fuck here. I know them. I'll introduce you around tomorrow.

Cool. When he heard *London Calling* playing on a stereo in the next room, he thought of his brother and wondered what he was doing right now.

8

Sergeant Huebner lay down on the back hood of the tank and tried to sleep. Captain Jobe came walking back with Maxwell and Morrison close at his heels. Jobe tapped the turret and yelled down to Huebner, who was lightly dozing.

Desert Storm has begun, the captain said. The Navy just launched one hundred Tomahawk missiles at targets in Iraq.

January 16, 1991, was Huebner's twenty-fifth birthday.

We're going to war, Captain Jobe said. Our word might come tomorrow or it might not come for a couple of weeks.

What are we supposed to do in the meantime? Huebner asked, still half-asleep.

We're supposed to stay ready, cool and wait for orders.

Stay cool, my ass, Maxwell said, and that became their new catchphrase.

As in,

Hey, what's up?

Trying to keep my ass cool.

Hey, Cap, Maxwell complained. I thought we would go in first.

Fat chance, Jobe said, tapping his fingers on the tank. The Navy had to go first.

They all felt giddy. Captain Jobe showed off a nine-millimeter pistol he'd gotten from another platoon leader. He's my replacement, Jobe said.

Come again?

They expect a lot of us to get killed, Captain Jobe said. They've got replacements for all of us.

That's nice to know, Huebner said.

Ten F-117 Stealth fighters targeted power plants throughout the country. Within hours B-52s began raids on Iraqi strongholds in the Euphrates Valley. More than one hundred tons of high explosives, loaded on eight B-52s taking off from an Air Force base in Michigan's Upper Peninsula, were dropped on the Republican Guard's Tawalkana Division. After their mission the B-52s landed at a base newly established on the coast of Saudi Arabia on the Red Sea. The Saudis had waited until the war began to allow an air base so close to Mecca. In all, more than seven hundred planes from the air forces of America, Britain, France and Saudi Arabia made strikes.

ALCMs, or Air Launched Cruise Missiles, were fired on hydroelectric and geothermal plants in Mosul and on a telephone exchange in Basra, as well as other similar targets. These hits would shut down communications and turn out the lights in Iraq. The United States had never disclosed the development of these missiles to avoid potentially uncomfortable arms control issues.

A-6 fighters took off from the American flagship USS *Kennedy* and roared up the western border of Iraq. A volley of TALD drones and HARM missiles preceded a wave of jet fighters as they targeted a base in the southern Iraqi desert.

There would also be hits by the U.S. Navy Air Corps and the Royal British Air Force. Tomahawk missiles were fired on the border port on the Persian Gulf and assaults by F-16s and F-111s pinpointed areas of the Iraqi-occupied Kuwait City.

The air war conducted by the United States in a coalition with twenty-five other countries was the most extensive in history. The first objective would be to sever all communications from Baghdad to Iraqi troops in the field and cut off reinforcements by taking out railroads and bridges and crippling Iraq's transportation infrastructure. Phase two would undertake to knock out Iraq's air power to control the skies and prevent forces on the ground from calling in air cover. Initial strikes would be followed with weeks of heavy bombing to destroy equipment and troops. The final assault would be a massive ground attack.

As the next week passed, all of their drills on tactics and conditioning gained intensity. There were a lot more fights between the men, but they ended quickly. The commander of their battalion, Colonel Agard, fired the operations officer. He called Major Slade to his camp while the soldiers were all out on the ground in Graceland, doing calisthenics. All of them watched as ten minutes later Major Slade, red in the face, got into a Hummer and drove off the grounds of the compound. They never saw him again. The major had lied to Agard about the fitness of an assembly area, and passed on a false report. It involved only a square mile of land. Colonel Agard saw that what was reported was not true, and the major was sent away to division headquarters to push paper for the duration of the conflict.

The army shipped in all new M-1 tanks, a special New Year's present from Uncle Sam, fresh out of storage in Germany. They were supposed to be used if there was ever an invasion by the

Russians. They were like cars right out of the showroom. They even smelled clean. The M-1 A-1 Heavy Armor edition had an added layer of armor up front and a nuclear biological and chemical warfare over pressure air system designed to protect against contamination by blowing air out of the tank's compartment. The new tanks had the 105-mm rifled main gun upgraded to a 120-mm smoothbore cannon.

When the Scout platoons saw the new tanks, some complained that they needed new Bradley armored personnel carriers, but Jobe said, Guess y'all gonna have to go with what you got. The Bradleys will do fine, he said.

Colonel Agard called a meeting of all the officers and first sergeants crowded into a small general purpose tent. Jobe and Huebner, as well as the other platoon leaders, Holmes, Creighton, Garcia and Major Andoe, the executive officer, all had to show their IDs to armed guards to be admitted. The guards also collected all personal weapons, leaning M-16s against each other in teepee clusters outside.

It's not like there's a freaking door, Lieutenant Holmes tried to joke, but no one really laughed.

Colonel Agard got up and said it was his decision to wait until the last possible moment to show the plan. He waited, like someone might question him, but nobody did. That would be begging trouble.

The VII Corps will attack Kuwait and chase the Iraqis to the north. It's our job to get up there, to block their exit and then crush them in the Euphrates Valley. Any questions?

When he finished, Agard stood with his hands on his hips and stuck his chest out.

After a few seconds, no one had said anything, and Agard

laughed, brazen and loud, but nervous too. It showed in his eyes, the way they blazed blue, and by the jitter in his hands. He had made his point. He didn't expect his men to fail, the message was to do whatever they had to execute the plan.

I'll leave the details to y'all subordinates, he said. Captain Jobe, ya got your map? Looks like these men got a lot of questions they'd rather ask you than me.

Jobe stood up and sketched out the plan. They would become part of a massive left-hook maneuver, head out into the Saudi desert, then turn north for Iraq. The initial stage of the operation would take four days of constant movement.

On his way back from the battle objective meeting, Huebner found Morrison sitting by the tank. He had his helmet on his lap and all his gear spread around him on the sand. Morrison sat with his head leaned against the tank's tread. His dark, piercing eyes looked off into the distance.

Good morning, Huebner said.

Morrison looked back at him, but didn't say anything. By his feet lay his protective gas mask and next to that, his LCE, or load carrying equipment, a web belt and suspenders that hung over the shoulders and tied slung low on the waist. First aid kit, two M-16 ammo pouches, and two one-quart canteens. He had his leather shoulder holster and .45-caliber pistol along with two boxes of ammo. A few of the bullets had fallen out of the boxes and were on the ground. Morrison rolled a couple bullets in his fingers.

He had made a wall of his sleeping bag, his chemical protection overgarments, or CPOG suit, a charcoal-lined jacket and pants that attached at the waist. Next to that was his No-Max, a one-piece flameproof suit, used exclusively by race-car drivers, pilots and tankers.

I cleaned out the tank, Morrison said.

Without me? Huebner said, and tried a wry smile, but Morrison didn't bite.

All the duffel bags we filled with our personal gear last night got loaded on the truck.

Maxwell's Walkman, our skin mags, everything?

No more showers, everything in the camp is broken down. No more special care food boxes from back home. Everything except the good luck charms, Morrison said, and shaded his eyes with his hand. In place of duffel bags we're gonna get some good stuff: small-arms ammo, antitank weapons, claymores, extra track blocks and engine oil. He wasn't smiling. What's new and different? Morrison asked.

You look pretty well-protected.

Captain says we're supposed to wear the CPOG over the No-Max, he said.

Doesn't leave much room to move.

They just want to keep us alive, I guess. But let me ask you something.

Shoot.

Morrison laughed now. We wear the No-Max to stop flashes from the breech catching us on fire . . .

You know that's what it's for.

And the chemical suit is made of charcoal and we're supposed to wear it over the No-Max?

That's the order, Huebner said, and showed his teeth.

Last I heard charcoal burned pretty good. Every night we watch the planes going over. A lot of folks are dying out here, he said, and shook his head.

Not U.S. soldiers, son.

I heard one of the White platoon, one of Garcia's boys, got to go home for crotch rot.

If they let folks go home for brain rot, you'd be home by now.

So that's just a rumor?

He went home. You could go to. All you have to do is ask to see the chaplain.

They're being extra careful.

Don't want anyone to freak out.

Only kill who you're supposed to, I get it. So I guess all of us left really want to go.

Or we're too scared to admit we're scared.

Put me down for that, Morrison said, and laughed. What about you, Sarge? Mr. Stoneface killer.

Huebner only smiled a little. I have faith in you fellows. I know why we're here and we're the best-trained army in the world.

You really do believe all that.

I have to. Besides, this is a ride, man. I'm strapped in. Part of me is scared, but I like scared. Part of me has never had more fun in my life. I feel like I'm alive every moment of every day.

Amidst high winds and blowing sand, they loaded onto their tanks and headed up to the Tap-Line road. Captain Jobe handed out his little white pills and Huebner took two like everyone else. The 66th Infantry Division would join a large movement to the north and push east after reaching the Euphrates River. Intelligence placed most of the Republican Guard stronghold south of the river. CINC believed that Saddam Hussein had enemies in Basra. If the Allied forces could take control of this city, the opposition to Hussein's regime in his own country might explode. Joining the 66th in the XVIII Airborne Corps attack and moving into position now were the 101st Airborne and Cobra units, the 82nd Airborne, the 6th French Division and the 3rd Armored Cavalry Regiment.

On the afternoon of February 21, 1991, the Marine 1st and 2nd divisions mounted an amphibious assault on Kuwait City from the south, moving across two lines of minefields and up through the Burgan oil fields to retake the capital city. On the twenty-sixth another wave of ground troops, the VII Corps, after making an about-face in the Saudi Arabian desert, would head north through Iraq, then east across Highway 8, the Basra Highway, toward Kuwait City in a wave that north to south was as long as the country itself. These included the 1st and 3rd Armored divisions, the 2nd Armored Cavalry, the 1st Infantry and Cavalry, and the British 1st Armored.

The troops passed United States and allied trucks and equipment wrecked and abandoned in the haste to get into position. They saw the British 7th Armoured Brigade, nicknamed the "Desert Rats" and gave the victory sign to each other. A British Tornado flying at "nap of the earth" altitude came right over their wing man's tank; the force of the plane took the camouflage net right off.

Captain Jobe, from his hatch, saw the pilot's head in the cockpit like a snapshot. He seemed that close. Then whoosh and he was just a speck in the far-off night sky. They listened to the A-10s on the radio pick out enemy tanks and other targets. The A-10, or Warthog, is a heavily armored jet used for ground support. It flies low and slow, and is outfitted with a 30-mm cannon strong enough to take out an enemy tank.

That first night as a blue dawn crept over the desert horizon, Huebner talked to a Lieutenant Colavito on a break. Colavito had field glasses out. Huebner saw his silhouette on the sand in the glare off the moon. His shadow was giant, beyond that there was just a gray void. The two of them stood and watched the planes zip by overhead. The flashes in the dark were like a summer thunderstorm.

There would be the fireworks and then a big boom when the F-16s broke the sound barrier. A feeling in the air pricked the skin on the back of Huebner's neck, a shaking in the atmosphere that wasn't really there, then the blue streak of another jet's approach and the red fire out the back. As it passed, there was a feeling like something had sucked all the oxygen out of the air.

There they are.

They'd be pretty, Colavito said, if they weren't so deadly.

They're still pretty.

Huebner would probably never see him again. Headed into combat, he felt like everyone he met was his best friend. He wished his brother were here for this.

At dawn a master sergeant called an assembly of the entire tank battalion. Over 250 soldiers stood out in the open desert after sprinting double-time from their stations. He stepped aside and Colonel Agard stepped out from the wings.

Gentleman, he called out, this won't be a walk in the woods. Iraq has the fourth-largest army in the world. Expect 10 percent casualties in the first week. I want you to protect yourselves out there. If you're driving through a village and someone throws a rock, shoot them! If you're shot at, turn the main gun on them. If they have anything more than small arms, call for artillery. We want to win and we want y'all to come home. Remember what General George S. Patton said: The object of war is to let the other poor bastard die for his country! Now, listen up, the sergeant has an important announcement to make.

Agard raised both his arms to stop the swelling cheers from the crowd and stepped aside again for the sergeant.

My name is Joseph Standing Bear, the sergeant said. I come from Pine Ridge, South Dakota. I am fighting for the land my fathers died for. I am fighting for the waters of the great Missouri River.

He moved to the first soldier in the front line. Tell us where you're from, he said.

Corporal Leroy Gilchrist. New Jersey, sir.

Tell us what you're fighting for.

Beautiful downtown Newark, Gilchrist said, and broke into a wide smile. New Jersey, sir. For my daughter, RaShawna, at Robert F. Kennedy Grade School.

Sergeant Standing Bear moved to the next soldier.

Private Brantley Mann, sir. Barstow, California. For the highway, Route 66, sir. For my buddies from back home.

Private Ricky Dixon, sir. Asheboro, North Carolina. Corn liquor and dirt-track racing.

Private Ronald R. Jefferson, sir. Mobile, Alabama. Gulf Creek crawfish, sir.

Private Larry O' Connors, sir. Nodaway, Missouri. For my mother and father's farm.

Crawford, Nebraska. Rush Springs, Oklahoma. Fort Lauderdale, Florida.

Wolfeboro, New Hampshire. Utica, New York. Gorham, Maine. Boone, North Carolina.

Berlin, New Hampshire. East Springfield, Ohio. Independence, West Virginia.

Brownsville, Texas. East Los Angeles, California. Brooklyn, New York.

Garcia, Martinez, Pickens, Georgiades and Claus.

The names, places and pledges filled the air.

It was cool by the canyon wall. The colonel nodded hello and sniffed the air. Under a crag of rock blasted to the gray core by sand and wind, the colonel had swept the cracked-earth desert floor perfectly clean. He was pouring a bottle of water over his head when Captain Jobe and Huebner walked up.

Jobe, he said, you haven't come to the morning conferences for the last three days.

I sent my executive officer.

Do you think I care?

Sir?

That you're angry. Do you think I care? You got angry because I let another platoon get some practice they sorely needed.

No, sir.

You are a better man than that, Captain Jobe.

The captain shook his head. It was just practice, sir.

The colonel stomped his boot on the packed sand. A vein popped out on his forehead.

It's goddamned insubordination! he yelled.

Jobe took a step back, cringing. Agard stepped with him and stayed in his face.

If we were not going to war tomorrow, Captain, he yelled, you would be relieved of your command! You got that?

Jobe's lower lip trembled as he stood suddenly at attention and looked directly at the colonel. You could not put a pin between them. Huebner, watching, wished he was not there and as far as the two men before him were concerned, he might as well have disappeared.

Yes, sir, Jobe managed.

Anything else like this and your ass goes to sit with Major Slade back at supply!

Colonel Agard took a step back. He had risen to a parade stance and now he relaxed slightly. Jobe took this cue to breathe. This was what command was all about.

Agard looked around, at a loss for a moment. It was as if he was awaking from a trance. He reached to his feet for another bottle of water. He poured half of it over his head and the rest over Jobe's. Then he laughed and Jobe, after a long moment, joined him.

Jobe, he said, you better stay in line, son. You are the best man I got and I'd hate to have to go after them without you. You got that, soldier?

Yes, sir, Jobe answered, in full command voice.

Agard laughed again. To Huebner he looked really happy, a man in his element, shaking the water off his head as a dog would.

By the way, Sergeant . . .

Yes, sir?

I took the liberty of sending your wife a card of congratulations.

Sir?

Agard smiled, the lines creasing his face. His cheekbones stood out. He was gaunt from the heat too and the effect was unsettling.

I hear you will be a father, son. And don't worry, it's a very formal card, Agard said, and winked.

Thank you, sir. Huebner was genuinely touched and surprised. He just stood there for a second, waiting for the next thing.

I've chosen y'all to lead the way tomorrow. Your company will be the first Americans to cross the border into Iraq.

It's an honor, sir, Jobe said.

Agard nodded, and cocked his head. We finally get to use the depleted uranium rounds. You got an opinion on that, Jobe?

I am not sure what you mean, Colonel.

Do you think it's safe?

For us or for the Iraqis?

Agard laughed low, and winked. His eyes were shining. For Huebner it was hard to tell how ironic he meant to be. It was a sensitive subject to bring up. Some of the guys had been concerned, especially the loaders seemed vulnerable. They were the ones who directly handled the ammo. It certainly promised to be effective against the enemy. He guessed the colonel was making a point about resolve in battle, about no second thoughts, about what their job was. It wasn't something you could think about. He could have asked for a clarification, but that would be stupid. He was too scared to anyway.

I would not imagine the Army is concerned, sir.

Agard clicked his tongue and looked to the sky, again with an ambivalent, partly sardonic, partly philosophical tone to his voice.

He went on: Whether or not say ten years later your stomach comes out your ass or your child has two arms, what the hell. This cannot concern the Army. Agard mocked the way Jobe had used the word "concerned." He spat in the sand and cocked his head to the side again.

Depleted uranium, he said. It sounds safer than, say, undepleted uranium. The colonel laughed and shook his head. He finished what was left of his water. Combat is about winning. What could kill us tomorrow will save our lives today.

He looked at Jobe and Huebner but neither knew what to say.

That's all, boys. I guess I'm worried about my men. That's my job. Yours is to kick ass. I make the decisions, I take the heat. You remember that, Captain. I got your back. So let's get ready to go to war. What do you say, boys?

First to fight! Sir!

Victory, boys, Agard mouthed the company salute back to them, but he was drowned out. A warm breeze rose from the desert floor. It came up and took away the surface level of sand and danced with it, pulling a veil over the horizon. Jobe and Huebner slit their eyes, wiped the sand grit from the corners, and started walking back to their tank. Sergeant Smith Huebner looked up at the wall of the valley. The moon reflected off the glass fragments in the sandstone and sparkled in his eyes.

9

Dear Smith,

I received your letter yesterday. Please don't worry about me. I was just a little low on cash. My girlfriend and I thought about moving in together, then decided to wait for now. I guess we might take some time apart.

I moved into a squat. This is an abandoned building we've taken over. It's a pretty radical thing, if you get my drift. And the cops leave us alone. I went to a big demonstration the other night. Things are hot down here because of the war. Remember what the Clash said:

"Black man got a lot of problems, but he don't mind throwing a brick. White people go to school, where they teach you how to be thick."

There was a riot in Tompkins Square Park here the summer before last. And now there's a tent city in the park. The whole thing's really pretty intense and interesting.

You'll never guess what happened here. A guy overdosed. I didn't know him well, but I found him. He had crawled up on the roof and been dead for three days. He was stupid about the way he did the dope. I've tried it, but don't worry, not like that. I didn't like it. It made me sick.

Reading this over, I guess it might seem a little worrisome, but please don't. I can take care of myself. Thanks again for the money, I will send it back to Meg when I can.

And hey watch your back, would you. The Yankees are going to need you in one piece. Everything about politics and protesting aside, I hope you know I'm on your side.

Love, Your brother

Sam

P.S. I went on the bus to Jersey to mom's grave and left some flowers there from us.

10

Smith still remembered things Sam could not. Once, Zeke came home drunk. He lifted up the couch cushion like it was the toilet seat and took a piss. Smith laughed, but Daddy didn't find anything funny. Zeke called out for their mother but she ran, hid in the kids' room and quickly locked the door.

Come out! Zeke called.

Mama said, Tell your father you won't let him in.

Smith stood at the door and did as he was told. When their father broke open the door, Smith was right there. He took the brunt of the blow. Their mother screamed as Sam scrambled off the bed onto the floor. Zeke picked his wife up by her neck and shoulders. He was a strong man. Smith pulled his father's pants and bit his hand. Their father came out of a blackout with his hands around their mother's neck. Her back was up against the wall, her feet raised almost six inches off the floor. Later Smith had to coax his brother out from under the bed, but he was hidden behind some boxes with their cat, Buster.

Sergeant Huebner had gone off to the edge of the circle of tanks to read his letter. This would be their last mail call for a while. He stood under the stars; the desert night was so clear and bright, he could make out the words easily. When he was done, his buddy Specialist James Morrison called out to him.

Where you at, Sarge? I got some news.

Right here, Huebner called. What's up?

Hussein is willing to release the hostages, Morrison said.

What hostages? Huebner asked.

The ones in Kuwait, the foreign diplomats, y'know, one of the main rationales for us being here.

Sounds like the same old Kabuki dance to me.

I don't know much about Arab dancing, Sarge. This is good news. Less reasons for us to have to go into Iraq.

Haven't you noticed? We're almost there.

That a letter from your brother?

Yep.

What's old Sam up to?

Nothing big, Huebner said, smiled, and spat on the ground.

He's getting along all right?

Yeah, Huebner said, and stared off into the distance.

Morrison's uncle had mailed him some airline liquor bottles. He handed Smith a warm one of gin. They toasted each other's health, then threw the bottles into the desert night.

Eleanor spotted Sam first. She had walked down Broadway, taken a late lunch to look at some artwork in Soho. He was behind a table with another guy and a lot of books laid out.

Sam, she said. What are you doing?

Sam almost dropped the bottle of gin he was sipping from. He stashed it under the table, looked up and smiled, shading his eyes from the sun with one hand.

Oh hey, Ellie, he said. What are you doing? He tried to sound casual but his eyes looked weird to her, kind of shiny.

Sam, she said, you smell like a distillery!

That's just my cologne, baby. Bay rum, do you like it? Sam said, and smiled, wise-ass. There was something furtive about him that put Eleanor off.

Eleanor winced and looked down at the books on the table. Are these your books? Why are you selling them?

These aren't mine. I just have some of the same titles.

Eleanor picked one up and opened it. You're lying, Sam. I bought this one for you. Look, here's the note I wrote in it for you.

Yo Sammy, the guy behind the table with Sam said. I told you to tear those pages out. He thought Eleanor wanted to buy something. He had Bootsy-style star-shaped oversized sunglasses and a fake Afro wig. It's still a nice edition of Kerouac, he said. Grove Press. Notice the Henry Miller introduction.

I know, I know, Eleanor said, laughing through her teeth and at the same time casting a glance at Sam.

He had his mouth open and was trying to speak but nothing was coming out.

I'll take this one, Eleanor said. How much do you get for these, Sam? she asked.

Uh, I get most of it, if they're mine.

Anything else? the Bootsy guy asked. We have lots of good books here.

Yeah, Eleanor said. She went down the line and picked all the books she recognized from Sam's collection. I'll take all of these, she said.

Eleanor, don't. You don't have to.

How much is that?

Well, uh, Sam stuttered.

Tell the lady, man.

Fifty-five dollars, Sam said.

Eleanor handed over the money.

Do you have a bag? she asked.

She looked at Sam, her eyes welling up, started to speak then didn't. She took the bag and turned to leave, starting to walk away into the crowd of people passing the last of the mild winter afternoon on Broadway.

You know that chick?

She used to be my girlfriend.

That's hot, man. You still got her number?

Fuck you.

Hey, she's looking back.

Sam went after her and asked Eleanor to please meet him later. She hesitated, trying to find his eyes, then said that she would meet him after work.

There's a restaurant across the street from Tompkins Square Park?

Fine, she said. Don't be late.

He kept Eleanor waiting for twenty minutes. She sat at the bar and had a sex on the beach. The drink reminded her of college and made her feel safe. She had the bag of books with her. Eleanor sipped her drink and watched the war on the television with one eye on the sidewalk outside for Sam.

He swept in a few minutes later, wearing the star sunglasses, and kissed her on the cheek.

Sam, take off those glasses. You look ridiculous.

Willie gave them to me. I think they're funny.

Let's sit down, Eleanor said. I'm hungry.

They both ordered burgers, but Sam hardly touched his.

You're not hungry? she asked.

What? Sam said and took a big bite. I'm eating. What do you mean?

Sweetie, what's wrong with your eyes?

Oh, nothing. I did a little dope a little while ago.

You did a little . . .

Heroin, don't act so surprised. If you weren't so uptight, maybe we could have some fun later.

Sam, this isn't you, Eleanor said. She frowned and then caught it. She didn't want to sound like a nag. She mimicked talking on a phone. Earth to Sam, she said.

I've just tried it a few times, Sam said.

Then why are you selling your books?

Traveling light, Sam said, but Ellie did not laugh. Sam looked sullen, turned away to the window, toward Tompkins Square Park. Someone was shouting, and flames flashed in a trash can.

You'd rather be out there, hanging around?

Maybe.

Eleanor took a deep breath. Sam, I want to give these books back to you.

You bought them, he said. I've already read them all.

But Sam, they're yours.

Ahh, they're just possessions, fuck it.

What are you talking about? You loved these books.

Ellie, there are a lot of things you don't understand.

Try me.

Sam exhaled and scratched a place on his arm. I don't know, he said. With the war, with everything else that's going on.

Sam, you're not making sense. Have you heard from your brother? How is he?

Oh, you know. Sam laughed and affected a voice. Having a good time, killing off some sand niggers. All in a day's work.

You never talked that way before. Sam, you don't really feel that way.

Things have changed, Ellie.

You keep saying that. What? What has changed?

Ahh, don't get that hurt look again. You already got me on that once today.

Sam, that's mean. You've never been mean to me before.

You embarrassed me today. If I want to sell my shit, I will.

Eleanor exhaled and reached for her purse. She couldn't find any tissues there, so she put it down and walked quickly back to the bathroom.

Sam watched her go then reached under the table for her purse. He took out a couple of twenties and put them in his pocket. He looked at the bathroom door, then took a deep breath, grabbed the bag of books at his feet and headed for the door.

Eleanor didn't really let go and cry until she was out of the restaurant. Sam had left the star-shaped sunglasses on the table. Eleanor started to pick them up, then she just couldn't. She looked out the window, toward the park. Since the riots of the year before there was trouble in Tompkins Square Park. People had set up tents and were living there. Eleanor guessed it was to protest the rising rents in the neighborhood. Tonight some rabble-rousers had set up a blockade of wood pallets and garbage cans across the entrance. The police were breaking it up now and dark shadows scattered. Eleanor wondered if Sam was one of them. She went to the register, bit her lip when she counted the money in her wallet. She paid the bill and walked out into the cold; then she let go.

At the Iraqi border, Captain Jobe sent out a patrol of three Bradleys and two Humvees to identify and attempt to find a bypass around any obstacles. Reports detailed a six- to eight-foot-high sand berm.

A walk in the park, someone said over the company net.

What, no wires, no mines, no flaming tank ditches? Maxwell said over the tank intercom. We have been hearing about this shit for three months.

Just some trash cans and some scrap wood. I guess they just wanted to scare you, Captain Jobe replied.

Who? Maxwell said, and let loose a high-pitched laugh. The Iraqis or our own command?

Quit chattering and clear the line, Jobe commanded. Just keep the course, Maxwell.

There was a line of fifty-five-gallon barrels the Iraqis had set up haphazardly, the same large plastic barrels a highway crew use when they're working on an interstate. On the highway they might be filled with concrete. This would mess up a new Honda

Accord, but it did not concern Jobe. Their concern was the possibility the barrels might be filled with something else. Rumors had Saddam waiting for the Army to expose itself in the open desert, before releasing . . . what? Poison gas? A nuke?

The captain told them that an infantry colonel had ordered a biological squad—dressed in MOPP IV chemical suits with masks, rubber boots and gloves—to check it out.

I heard a Saudi border patrol unit saw them in their moon suits all cautious, kicking at the things and asked what the hell was going on.

When our men told the Saudis what they were doing, they had a good laugh.

What was so funny? Maxwell asked.

The Saudis had put the barrels there themselves, just to mark the border.

Earlier on the end run up the desert, Lieutenant Holmes's Scout platoon had run into stray trailers, one ancient Air Stream and other nondescript mobile homes. Colonel Agard ordered them designated by laser, then blown away with Hellfire missiles. If there was anyone in there, too bad.

At the border the Scout platoon blew a couple rounds into the berm to clear a path.

We don't want to have to stick our noses in the air, the lieutenant communicated to Jobe over the radio. Black Six, this is White One, Sabers ready.

Jobe said, This is Black Six, roger. Execute.

The Dark Lords crossed the border in a sandstorm. The land changed visibly once the company moved into Iraq. There was green vegetation as they got closer to the Euphrates River, now little more than a couple hundred miles to the north. There were trees the Arabs called *athal* with the long clumps of hairy pinelike needles, and shorter bushy ones with sweet-tasting leaves called the *sideal.* Ancient roads cut through the great open lands. The hard-packed sand was orange and flecked with stones.

Bullets pinged off the commander's weapons station. Captain Jobe returned fire. He dropped down to his seat in his turret and looked through the .50-caliber machine-gun sight. He pulled down on his machine gun's red elevation handle, connected by wire to his .50 caliber's butterfly trigger and a burst of bullets sounded over Sergeant Huebner's head.

Fifty! Jobe yelled into his mouthpiece. Now that they were moving, it was too loud for their voices to be heard otherwise. Jobe got on the radio and screamed, Contact troops north. Going higher, out, Jobe said, and flipped his radio switch, calling their company first and then announcing the same on the battalion command net.

What do you see? he asked Specialist Morrison.

Got troops, Morrison said hurriedly.

Battle carry HEAT, Captain Jobe commanded.

Roger, sir, Morrison said, as he reached to hit the knee switch to open the ammunition door. He pulled a HEAT round out of the honeycomb, rotated it 180 degrees and laid it on the breech. Morrison pushed the round forward with his closed fist. The breech closed with a "thunk," as Morrison grabbed the arming handle and shouted, Up. Then he stepped out of the way of the recoil and crossed his arms over his chest.

Sergeant, Jobe said, co-ax troops, hold your fire.

Huebner sighed deeply. When he saw the tank on the thermal sight, he bit his tongue so hard he tasted blood.

Enemy tanks! Huebner screamed to Captain Jobe. To Huebner it felt like someone else was speaking. He didn't recognize his own voice. On his thermal sight the outline of the enemy tank was black and its engine was clearly outlined darker from the heat it emitted.

Platoon, go to Kill-4. Switch ammo to sabot, Captain Jobe commanded.

Target identified two thousand meters direct front, Huebner said.

Shot up, Morrison called out.

Captain Jobe looked into his periscope to verify and said calmly, Fire.

Huebner switched to daylight sight, ten power. Their first shot was just slightly off target.

Goddammit! Captain Jobe hissed over the net. A flit of fire disappeared into blue. Tighten that line up. Do that fucker!

Huebner could actually see the torso of the T-72's Iraqi commander sticking out of the turret. He felt a sudden red-hot flash of anger at Captain Jobe.

Shut the fuck up, sir, he whispered under his breath into his own mike-piece, if I need your fucking encouragement I'll ask for it. He felt embarrassed too. He knew the captain was just doing his job, trying to encourage him, and he must be scared too, but he could not show it. Still, something in Huebner felt like it was personal. It wasn't anyone else's fault but his. He was the one with his finger on the fire control. In training they were drilled to feel part of a great big well-oiled machine. In that hot flash of anger he felt Why, so he would not think or feel what he was doing? He felt like he could see the line between emotion and training. He didn't dare cross it.

What was that? Sergeant!

Nothing, sir.

You got him lased?

Yes, sir.

This time he's ours.

The platoon in front of their tank had disappeared into a wadi. Jobe's crew was alone, but the American tanks had a significant advantage in main gun range compared to the Iraqis' Soviet-made T-72s. Time slowed down for Huebner. For a split second, the sandstorm blocked his daylight sight.

The world cracked open and all was clear. There was the Iraqi commander, his thighs, his waist, shoulders, helmeted head sticking out of the T-72's turret. This was the image that would stick in his head when he dreamed about the war for the rest of his life.

Gunner, sabot tank, Captain Jobe called out.

Huebner called out, IDENTIFIED!

Sabot up, Captain.

Jobe looked into his commander's extension and saw that Huebner had a good lase and an arm box in his sight.

Identified, Huebner repeated.

Fire.

The second sabot round went straight through the enemy commander's chest. It made a hole there, with ragged edges from his seared clothing. Huebner swore he saw the Iraqi commander, a green phantom in his daylight sight, held there for one breath, a millisecond. Then, the force-wind of the depleted uranium penetrator almost sucked the Iraqi soldier out of the turret.

His helmet blew off and tumbled away in a shower of sand. The sergeant watched as the perfect shot vaporized the Iraqi into nothingness.

They had been on a rise when Huebner fired, so the round followed a downward trajectory to the target; the round continued on its slight downward trajectory into the back of the T-72's turret; the tank exploded into a fireball.

Everyone in the crew, Morrison, Maxwell and Captain Jobe, went, Aww, like at the fireworks on the Fourth of July. They had seen it too.

Fuck . . . , Huebner said to himself as he watched on the daylight sight.

That was a beautiful damn shot, Maxwell said into his mouthpiece.

I was not aiming for *him!* Huebner yelled.

You sure got him, Captain Jobe said. Then Jobe switched his radio and reported. Rogue TOC, this is Dark Lord Six. Engaged and destroyed one enemy tank, he said. Grid 529175 continuing mission, over.

Roger, came the reply from battalion. Do you have any other contact?

Negative, Jobe said. He flipped the switch on his J box to the company net. Red, White and Blue, this is Black Six, any contact?

Black Six, this is White One, Contact negative. Repeat: contact negative.

Okay, Jobe addressed his crew again. Must have been left behind. Red, White and Blue, he called again to the other platoons in the company, go ahead and set out observation points. Be on the lookout for any ground troop stragglers. We're going to laager here for a little while. Wait for orders, Black Six acknowledge.

As the other platoons set up the OPs, it was starting to get dark and a half-moon was coming out. The four of them got down from the tank and checked the wreckage. Maxwell found a belt on the ground, maybe twenty steps from the still-smoking hulk. He bent down and cut off the buckle with his nonreg buck knife and offered it to Huebner.

This is yours, Maxwell said.

Huebner said, No thanks, and looked down at the sand. I don't want it, he said.

Why not? Jobe said, walking up. It's a cool souvenir. You're the gun man.

Frankly, sir, I think it's gross. It's his. Let it lie with him.

Frankly, sir, Jobe mocked Huebner and shook his head. Take the fucking thing, Jobe said, and held out the buckle. America has gone to war. This is history, Sarge. Don't gimme that just a part of the job, shit.

It's not that. I guess, I'm just numb.

Well, feel this. Look here, Jobe said. It's got something written on it. Some raghead letters.

Huebner looked at Captain Jobe and took the belt buckle. It's probably cursed, he said, trying to joke.

He didn't have anything against Jobe. He just didn't agree with him. And he thought he was overbearing sometimes. Still, he had the rank. Huebner looked Jobe straight in the eye and said, Thanks, sir.

Jobe beamed.

Maxwell hollered again and he and the captain exchanged a few high-fives. They walked back within a few yards of their tank and all sat down to eat where they could still see the destroyed tank. There was some smoke coming from the hole where the turret had been, but it did not pose the threat of fire or explosion.

A great wind came up and blew the sand in a cyclone over their heads. Huebner took his helmet off and the bandanna he had tied under it. He poured some water over the rag and wiped his face with it. He watched Jobe and Maxwell hollering back and forth to each other. Maxwell was miming an explosion with his hands and Jobe laughed, opened his eyes wide and they slapped hands again. Maxwell opened up an MRE and ate the food with great gusto, stuffing the spaghetti and meatballs into his mouth with his fingers, wiping with his hand when he was done. Morrison stood by, shaking his head. He ate peaches from a can and when he was done drank from it, letting the juice run down his neck.

Maxwell said, When you said, Do that fucker, sir, I felt his neck in my hands.

Did you, Max, did you feel it! Jobe shouted, and they slapped hands again.

Huebner slapped them both on the back, then sat down on the tread a few feet away from the others to eat his own lunch.

Sergeant, when we're done with dinner, Jobe called over to him, let's work on crew drills and check our bore sight, then do an MRS update to make sure there wasn't a reason we missed that first sabot.

You got it, sir, Huebner called back. Whatever you say, sir.

Jobe jerked his head up, gave Huebner the once-over and Huebner shot the captain a quick thumbs-up.

Huebner ate his food quickly, without tasting it. Two minutes later he had to look at the package, see the white sauce to remember he had the tuna with noodles. His mouth felt dry, filled with paste. The wind stopped for a moment and he slit his eyes. In the distance he saw the tank their platoon had just destroyed, smoke gently pouring forth from the place where the turret had been. Then he shook his head and went to climb back inside and check the fire controls.

You think there's something wrong with the computer? Morrison asked, peering down into the turret. He offered Huebner a drink from a bottle of water.

Don't think so. She hit good the second time.

We just missed?

Yeah, we did. We'll check it, though.

Huebner wiped his mouth with his sleeve and climbed back into the hole.

Man, it smells awful in here, he called out in Morrison's direction.

We were doing some sweating, sir.

Smells like a latrine, smells like someone shit his pants.

Morrison laughed. Wasn't me, but I'm sure we're going to have to hose this fucker out before this is over.

Roger that, Huebner said.

Huebner executed a computer self-test to check the system's ballistic solution capabilities.

He felt a tap on his shoulder, flinched and grabbed tight to one of the steel rungs of the crew ladder.

It was just Morrison, climbing down the turret. Whoa, he said, and pulled away from Huebner.

You're still wrapped tight, aren't you?

I never killed anyone before.

Roger that, Morrison said.

You ever see that movie *The Deer Hunter?*

That one of those Vietnam ones?

Three men go. One gets all shot to pieces. Another goes completely crazy.

I remember. Morrison nodded. With De Niro. He's the one who holds it all together, right? He's the Deer Hunter.

Right, Huebner said, that's it. And when each of us watch that movie, we all imagine we're De Niro.

Everything all right, fellas? Captain Jobe asked a few minutes later when he climbed back into the tank.

Sam met a poet at the readings at ABC No Rio. His work gave off the vibe that he had done drugs, lots of them, and had quit that life and gone on to something better. He wore a lot of black and went by the name K.

K played guitar in a band, dyed his hair bright blue or orange or silver. People like K always intimidated Sam. For years he had been going to CBGB's and Max's Kansas City and making the scene Sam read about in the punk rock magazines he bought off the 7-Eleven store rack back home in Athens. He would see K on his way to cop dope, Sam walking as fast as he could to the D'Lite spot on Second Street between Avenues A and B at the Building, Good Stuff on Ludlow above Delancey or Double A below. K would look calm and serene, working on his motorcycle or walking home from the train.

Sam would give a rushed greeting and keep on. K would nod and smile, the picture of indulgence and understanding.

Sam got his stuff and got high, then made it a point to walk a different way afterward. One night he ran into K on the subway uptown. Sam asked if they could get together to talk sometime. K said to meet him the next week at the Washington Square coffee shop on Fourth Street at Sixth Avenue. Sam didn't know any really cool or connected people, or even those who acted like they were. K had the longest, sharpest sideburns that Sam had ever seen and his writing had a lot of references to Burroughs, Lou Reed and the Marquis de Sade.

I really like your stuff, Sam told him the next day when they sat down at a booth in the coffee shop.

Thanks, man.

Someone was saying you publish a magazine. I was thinking about submitting something.

We only publish established writers.

Oh. Sam blushed.

K smiled and winked behind his yellow tinted glasses. What's on your mind? he asked.

Too much blow, Sam said. Sam thought this was funny, but K didn't laugh.

I think I need to quit doing drugs, or find a better way or something.

Which is it?

I got into a little trouble last week, you know . . . what do you do?

What do I do? K said, and raised his eyebrows.

I mean to stay clean.

I meet with friends and we talk.

Come on. How could that work?

It does.

I don't know. I wanted to meet you, but I'm a little disappointed. It can't be that simple. What do you and your friends do? he asked.

We talk, K said. He wrote down an address and handed it to Sam. Come on a Tuesday or a Thursday, K told Sam.

Sam was picked up in a drug sweep and spent the night in jail. A fellow saw him shivering in the corner of the bullpen cell.

Need some dope? he asked.

You don't have any, do ya?

The man laughed. You got a chippie, he said. He had frizzy gray hair, a faded bandanna.

What should I do? Sam asked.

I been doing dope since the sixties, the man said. Whenever it gets too heavy for me, I switch to coke for a few days.

Now, that sounds practical, Sam said, and the old man showed a gap-toothed smile. They watched then as someone at the other end of the cell stuck a finger down his throat and vomited on the floor. The sick man picked a couple plastic sealed bags of dope out of the mess, ripped them open and snorted them down.

Now that's fucking gross, Sam said.

I would give him twenty bucks for each bag, the old man next to Sam said.

Not me, I'm never gonna end up like that, an addict.

Give it time, youngblood.

When Sam got home he saw the slip of paper that K had given to him. Maybe there's something to it, he thought. He still thought what the old man in jail had said about switching to coke made more sense, but he could check it out.

What do you have to lose? K had said.

On a cold day in December Sam set out for his first twelve-step meeting. Sam made sure he copped some coke on his way. At least it was at a cool address, Sam thought, on Second Street between First and A. Sam figured it would be sort of like one of the poetry readings at ABC No Rio.

The meeting was not until half-past-seven; he had a few hours to kill after he copped. Sam wandered all the way across town to a dock out over the Hudson River, doing blow like the old-timer had advised and looking out toward Jersey City. He checked his watch, walked back to Eighth Avenue and got on the L train. When he got off at the First Avenue station, he did more blow behind a pillar and decided to get on the train again and ride back to the West Side. He did this a couple more times, then went up to the street, bought a bottle of Cool Breeze and said, Fuck it.

He didn't make it to the Cardinal Spellman Center until after K's meeting was over. He walked up to a man who looked friendly. He had a suit on, talked fast and stuttered a little. He came up real close and Sam backed off.

Do you know K? Sam asked.

Sure, but he left a while ago. There's another meeting here on Thursday.

The same time?

Sure.

That day was also freezing cold and windy. Sam was still holding on to his three teaching gigs at that time and had gotten paid.

If I'm late, he told his classes, I'm on my way.

He felt like he was burning from the inside out, like sparks were shooting from his fingertips. He chewed the inside of his cheeks and bit them until they hurt, ground his teeth and babbled to strangers.

On Thursday, Sam made it to K's meeting halfway through. It was in the basement of the community center. He pushed a button and was buzzed in by a guard. A pretty young woman sat at a table in front of the room and spoke about how she had gotten off drugs. Behind her something was written on a roll of paper that hung from the wall. Sam looked around and saw people dressed in leather and shades of black who, when it was their turn, talked about what kind of art they were doing and what bands they were in.

Sam stood at the edge of the crowd, listening to a woman with pink leather pants who seemed to be talking about God. Sam found the bathroom, went in the stall and did a couple more bumps of coke. When he came back out, he found a seat. Sam couldn't quit shaking his leg and sniffing loudly to try to clear his nasal passages of the coke he had just done in the bathroom. When people looked at him, he stared back.

Sam raised his hand and was called upon. Everyone who had spoken had said their name and identified themselves as an addict. When Sam did it, he didn't think he would start to cry. But he couldn't help it.

Some of the people before him had shared with the group about whatever everyday problems they were facing.

At least y'all are clean, Sam said.

Fifteen people came up to him and wrote down their phone numbers. Someone handed him a list of meetings. A skinny man with glittery hair took Sam's hand.

Hey, I'm Fly, he said. You want to join us for dinner?

I can't, Sam said. I got something to do.

Fly gave him the name of the restaurant and Sam said, I'll meet you there. The woman with the pink leather pants came up and took Sam's hand in hers.

We'll be there all night, she said.

Sam pulled away awkwardly, went straight to a coke spot on Fourth Street, a florist with no flowers and a couple of plastic plants. He walked to a bar called Sophie's on Fifth Street, sat there in a daze, drinking dollar drafts, going back and forth to the bathroom until the joint closed. Every hour he asked the bartender the time, planning to make it back to the coffee shop to meet his new friends.

A half-hour later Dark Lord Company refueled and rumbled on. Jobe positioned the Red Platoon in the rear left flank; the White and Blue platoons took the lead in echelon left formation. The company was supplemented by a Bradley platoon from Alpha Company 3-15 Infantry by task organization.

Dark Lord Six, this is Rogue Scout One, came over the company net. Be advised enemy force in a hasty defense to your right.

Roger, Captain Jobe said, got it. He thumped the metal turret casing with his knuckles for luck.

The small black dots that signified foot soldiers danced across Smith's thermal sight first, and he was exhaling slowly when he registered the larger rectangles that stood for armored personnel carriers and tanks. Tanks and troops identified, he said into his headset.

Since dawn the Dark Lords had been in the middle of the *shamal,* the Arab word for storm. The sun had not risen at all, some windblown pockets of rain, but mostly just the flying sand, from which derived the name. Visibility was limited. After two of the three platoons crested a tall ridge, the American tanks took heavy small-arms fire across their bows.

Red, White and Blue, this is Black Six, Jobe said. Enemy appears to be screening to our front.

Captain Jobe latched his turret in the open protected position for battle. More bullets pinged off the metal of the tank. Jobe flinched and cursed. Morrison closed his own turret and sank into a loading-ready position. Green and blue tracers flashed in the air and rainbowed over the desert sands, the tank and Captain Jobe's face.

Never knew scary could be so pretty, Jobe commented to his crew over the intercom, then opened up the radio to hear from the rest of the company.

Black Six, this is White One, came the call from the lead platoon, contact troops and tanks north.

Engage, Jobe replied.

Almost instantly there was a cacophony of tank fire, then it became part of the white noise of battle.

Going higher, Jobe said. He flipped the radio switch and reported, Rogue TOC, this is Dark Lord Six, contact troops north.

Dark Lord Six, I need a situation report.

We have spotted a group of enemy vehicles and are engaging the enemy in company size strength! Jobe said, his voice rising to a shout.

How many?

At least ten!

Roger, Dark Lord Six.

Maxwell.

Sir?

Let's close in.

Roger, sir. His voice sounded kind of faint.

Maxwell, you with us! Jobe yelled into his mouthpiece.

Yes, sir.

Well, give me a holler.

Yes, sir, Maxwell yelled, and then whooped once, twice and a third time.

There you go, Jobe hollered back. Sergeant?!

Target identified, Huebner said. He felt like all the icy tension he had expressed to Morrison had melted away into a smooth liquid. His motions on the controls flowed through him, straight and easy.

Sabot loaded, Morrison said.

Shot up, sir.

Fire.

Huebner squeezed the fire button. When the tank jumped, Smith's forehead jarred against his sight.

In his viewer the enemy tank was a green box with a darker place where the engine was. The darker spot denoted heat intensity. When the shot connected, the heat box grew until it covered the entire square. Huebner pumped his fist and pounded the metal casing of his instrument panel.

Frankly speaking . . . Jobe mocked, giddy.

Huebner flashed a thumbs-up to his captain behind him, but kept his eyes glued to the viewer.

That was some nice shooting, Sarge, Jobe said. Then he whooped and Maxwell and Morrison echoed after him. Huebner bit his lip and looked for more targets, flexing his finger at the ready on the fire control.

Time disappeared in the concussion of the main guns, the larger concussion of vehicle explosions, the noise of machine guns, the crackle of fire, the stench of gunpowder in the turret. It was like someone had a switch and was turning the sounds on and off. Huebner might hear them or not. He might also hear Morrison whispering rote procedure to himself as he loaded the next round, or his own fingers tapping on his sight, Maxwell breathing into the mouthpiece of his headset, the constant radio chatter:

Black Six, this is White One, engaged and destroyed three enemy vehicles.

Roger, White One.

Black Six, this is Blue One, engaged and destroyed two enemy vehicles.

Then a screamed epithet and, Black Six, this is White One, Twenty-three's been hit! Repeat, Twenty-three's been hit!

Fucking shit, all goddamn to hell, Jobe called out over the net.

Maxwell hollered once in response.

Maxwell, Jobe hollered. You with me?

Yes, sir, Maxwell said.

We'll get through this, Max, Jobe hollered once more. Answer me, Max.

Maxwell hollered back his yell, but his voice sounded like it was cracking up around the edges.

White One, this is Black Six, continue to engage!

Black Six, opposition eliminated. Repeat, Bradley disabled, friendly casualties.

Got it, Jobe said over the company net. Red, White and Blue, this is Black Six. Let's set up a hasty defense. Company wedge. White, lay out visual panels.

White, roger.

Red?

Red, roger.

Captain Jobe flipped the radio switch. Band-Aid, he said, this is Black Six. Casualties reported. Grid location 397621.

Black Six, this is Band-Aid. We are en route.

Battalion command, Dark Lord. Give me your sit rep.

Engaged and destroyed eight enemy vehicles. One of ours is hit, trying to assess the damage/casualties. Opposition eliminated.

Black Six, this is Rogue Six, got it.

We'll meet you there, Jobe said to himself. Driver, Jobe said over the intercom, get us close now.

En route, sir, Maxwell said, and coughed.

Sarge, Jobe said. Go down and check on Max, would you?

Roger, sir.

Huebner nodded to Morrison, who slid down into his place in front of the gun controls. Huebner crawled on his knees down to where Maxwell was in the front of the tank. Maxwell gave a holler when he saw Huebner. Tears ran down his face.

Hot fucking damn! Maxwell shouted into Huebner's face.

Huebner slapped him twice, right across the chin.

Maxwell flinched, all kinds of snot came out of his nose, mixing with the spit from his mouth and the tears from his eyes. He looked up at Huebner. His eyes were red.

Maxwell! Huebner shouted at him.

He didn't know whether to apologize or hit him again. He had acted out of instinct. He wondered if he had done the wrong thing. He suddenly saw the wisdom in Jobe's handling of their driver.

Maxwell, you all right?

Yes, sir! Maxwell said, shouting back at Huebner and wiping his face with one hand. What the fuck you hitting me for? Maxwell asked, his voice rising, sounding a desperate note. He kept his hand on the steering control and with him Huebner watched their course.

You're gonna be all right. You're going to be fucking fine, Huebner said, barely an inch from Maxwell's face. He could feel the heat of the private's breath.

I just lost it, I lost it completely when they hit ours. I was just going along and I felt, I felt sweat and suddenly I was crying. I didn't realize it.

It's a shock, Huebner said. We just got to keep moving through it. He saw how Maxwell's chest was heaving and realized he was breathing just as hard. Huebner had the sensation that he could not control his tongue; for a moment he felt like he was choking.

You all right, sir? Maxwell asked, and spat on the dirty floor of the tank.

Neither said anything. They were in the dark nether world of the tank, steel all around. Something, some understanding of their new reality and what it really meant passed between them. They could have been hit themselves. At any moment they could be ripped apart by ordnance under whose force their bodies would be nothing, like rag dolls pulled apart; they could be hit with a shell and melted into puddles of goo, blood and shit and worse, maybe disintegrated, vaporized like they weren't even there and never had been. Each saw it in the other's eyes and felt between them an intensity of shared feeling that was almost sexual, deeper than any other kind of brotherhood they had ever felt before. They felt it that instant; it passed between them from one to the other with a sureness that felt as close to death as they would ever know in this life. It only took the flash of a second.

Yeah, Maxwell said. I'm good, he said. I'm good to go, sir.

All right then, Huebner said. Each of his words felt barely ahead of the breaths that made them possible. His heart pounded in his chest. He felt in his lungs the pressure it took to breathe. He needed to get out of this space. He felt like he wanted to run.

When they were within a few hundred yards of the Bradley, Sergeant Huebner asked Captain Jobe to let him assist Medevac.

Those men are dying in there. Let me meet the Medevac on the ground.

You think you can take them over there? Jobe asked.

If you cover me, what's the problem?

All right, Jobe said, and got back on the radio. Band-Aid, this is Black Six. The area's still hot. We'll meet you halfway and take you over there. Coordinates 345965.

Black Six, this is Band-Aid. Got it.

Huebner took Jobe's place in the turret. When he saw the Medevac, he hollered as loud as he could and jumped down from the tank. Sand whipped in his face and scratched against the metal of the tank's treads. He caught his boot on something and tumbled, landing on his knees in the soft sand.

Arthur James Bowers was the medic on the scene.

Cover me with your M-16, the medic said to Huebner, and pointed at his small armored vehicle with the white cross painted on its hull. The ground Medevac vehicle, an M-113, was fitted for a .50-caliber machine gun, but not equipped with one. The M-113 was between the tank and the Bradley at a distance of less than one hundred yards. Huebner and Bowers sprinted over the sand and crouched for cover behind the Medevac vehicle.

Huebner tapped Bowers's helmet and shouted, Let's count one, two, three, then head for the Bradley. Ready? Go!

When Huebner heard the weapons fire, he ducked and rolled in heavy sand as bullets ricocheted in the air. Bowers followed his lead. They got up together and ran in front of the searing orange glow of the fire. Waves of heat from the smoking Bradley distorted Huebner's vision. The vehicle was tipped on its side, the main gun pointed off in a cockeyed direction. He felt a pounding behind his eyes. Two enemy ground troops came out of a berm at a distance of fifty yards. They were headed toward the smoking Bradley. Huebner squeezed the trigger and two quick bursts of fire dropped them. Bowers kept running, past the enemy soldiers now writhing on the ground.

Bowers shot a red star cluster flare to signal their position. Huebner felt his heart in his chest and heard his own breath in his ears. He had to piss so bad, he just hung it out his pants, his rifle at his shoulder; the medic was five feet away attending to the downed soldiers. He felt the heat of the flames on his bare flesh and was still fumbling with the buttons of his fatigues as he watched the M-1 Abrams coming over a rise, just twenty-five yards from the smoking vehicle. Huebner could see shadows dashing away into the open darkness as the tank neared. Captain Jobe in the turret opened up with his .30 cal, shooting round after round into the berm.

Thank you, Huebner whispered to himself.

The Iraqi shell had entered into the Bradley under its main gun: it tore into the stomach of the gunner, burned a hole through the turret, taking off the arm of the Bradley's commander on the way out. The gunner slumped in the turret. Bowers jumped up and dragged the commander down to the ground.

His face was white. Some of the skin had burned away. He was breathing, his eyes closed. When Bowers pulled his helmet off, part of the soldier's head seemed to go with it and the man gasped. His eyes opened, but they were not focused.

As Huebner covered him with occasional fire toward the berm, Bowers reached into the bloody and burned black hole where the wounded soldier's arm should have been, found the artery and clipped it.

Ugh, fucking hell. Bowers turned his head to the side and took a deep breath.

Huebner smelled sweet burning flesh, cordite, piss and blood. Together they laid this man on the sand and went back for the second one. At this point the other Medevac unit had arrived. When Huebner looked up again, their tank was grinding to a loud stop just a few yards away.

The second casualty was also badly burned. His lips and face were charred black and his eyes were white where he'd worn his sunglasses. They were now broken in half and dangling from his neck. He had a large bloody hole in his midsection, from upper thigh to his belly his fatigues were darkened with blood. Bowers clipped them away, swallowed back a second surge of bile, then wrapped the bloody hole with few feet of heavy-duty bandage. Then he got on his radio.

Medevac air, this is Band-Aid One. We have two walking wounded, one KIA and two for the chopper. Repeat, two for the chopper.

When the Black Hawk Medevac bird touched down, Huebner helped the medics carry the men through the blowing sand onto the chopper. The injured man suddenly grabbed Huebner's arm. Huebner thought it was the medic at first. The soldier tried to speak, started to say something, but Huebner couldn't get it. Huebner just nodded like he understood and turned away as he handed the soldier up to the chopper. He grabbed the legs of the next one and helped the medic get him on. This man was in shock, but Huebner could see his eyes following the medic's movements. Huebner took a deep breath; the smoke seared his lungs and he coughed.

When the chopper took off into the blue night sky, Huebner and the medic stood there, silently catching their breath. They were still just standing there watching the sand in the wind when Jobe and Morrison came walking up to them.

One man was hit bad, the medic, Bowers said. Another was too, but he'll live. Captain Jobe winced. Two walked away, Bowers added.

Jobe nodded.

Maxwell held up his hand for a high-five, but Jobe just glared at him.

Huebner caught a half-hour's catnap before they set out again. He fell asleep picturing the Bradley survivors and wondering what must have happened to the men the Dark Lord Company had killed in exchange. He wakened with his brother's face in his mind: Sam's eyes were closed, then they jerked open as Huebner awoke.

The two worlds didn't match. Inside the tank, he had precision and control. Outside was chaos. He had remembered what Colonel Agard had said to him when he'd tracked the Bedouins that first day on the ground in Saudi. Something about when tar-

gets came to life, about the difference between battlefield in a
tank and on the ground.

Sergeant Huebner's favorite poem was always the one by
Yeats, "the center cannot hold."

It was what he imagined of combat when it was still just a
concept. Inside the tank all the directions were laid out for him,
outside it was a mess; he had to give in to the animal he felt inside to see any kind of pattern.

Sergeant Huebner was the last one on the ground outside the
tank. The wind had stopped and everything was silent and stood
still. The whirring voice of the sand rubbing against the earth or
hissing in the wind ceased and everything that happened, stood
for that moment in relief, as if the moment would last forever. He
could leave, turn away for perhaps many years, but at any moment there it would be tapping on his shoulder, as big as life.
Something of all of them, the living and the dead, would always
be here, no matter the impersonal nature of the weaponry. He
had killed another man. The war might make it all right; it could
never make it not so. The wind came up again and blew a veil of
sand into the air and the thing, whatever it was, disappeared,
gone to whatever place there is, in the world, in himself, where
such things are kept.

Later that night Jobe called Sergeant Huebner aside.

Hey, dude, Let's talk.

Dude? Huebner said, and they laughed together.

That's what I wanted to ask you about.

Maxwell?

You read my mind. What do you think, Huebner?

What are you asking me, sir?

We could have him replaced. We could have a new man in for tomorrow.

We got backups for all of us, don't we? Maybe I'll take a pass myself. Go back to reserve, see how the view is from back there.

I could make a request, Sergeant.

I was just kidding, Jobe.

That's Captain to you. So what do you think? You want to go to war with Maxwell?

Huebner shook his head. I'm not sure I'd like to have dinner with him, he said.

Jobe shook his head, Roger that, he said.

But we're not having dinner. I think we should keep him. When do we get our orders for our objective?

I just got them.

Well?

Our company will lead the division. We're the first ones in. The mission stays the same, a zone recon to Phase Line Opus.

Then we wait for the rest?

Right, first we'll establish a screen. We occupy the opus until the rest of the task force is ready to attack.

What's our first objective, sir?

There's an airport west of the Euphrates River. Our orders are to dissemble the airport and push east to Basra.

Dissemble the airport . . .

Take it! Take the damn airport. You know what I mean. Don't worry, we won't be alone. We're going to have a lot of help.

I only got one thing to say, sir.

Shoot.

All those tanks following behind us, a long line of itchy trigger fingers, they'll have our ass in their thermals. What's to keep them from blowing us away?

Jobe smiled. Prayer, he said.

1 2

The night of the Independence Day parade was not the first time their mother did not come home. But no one had talked about it before. Zeke, Uncle Pete and their grandma and grandpa were drinking at the dinner table, scotch whiskey and Ballantine beer. Hours past dinnertime, cold spaghetti on the stove; no one felt like eating.

On the television the same footage from Vietnam that had played at six repeated at eleven. American forces had overrun a landing area in the northern sector. Casualties were low. The screen showed a Vietnamese with his arms splayed, facedown in a puddle on the dirt runway. An American GI walked away grimly, his eyes averted from the camera.

Zeke frowned and took a drink. She got out of the car and walked away? he asked.

It was at the traffic light, Grandma said. She ran off into the traffic. She wasn't even dressed properly.

It was a hundred degrees today.

Still, I don't like those short skirts.

Come on, Ma, you ought to go to bed. Let me take you upstairs.

I know where my wife is, Zeke said. No one has to tell me. I know what's going on.

A young mother doesn't just leave her husband and two kids and go live in Buccleuch Mansion. Bunch of hippies and drug pushers have taken it over.

Mother, don't.

Damned crazy son, Old Will said, turned and looked his oldest boy in the eye. You ought to look into it, he said to Zeke.

They were all still at the table, Smith and Sam still in the room, little kids sitting in the kitchen trying to do drawings and finish a bowl of Lucky Charms so they could get the 3-D baseball card from inside the box. Old Will made them wait for the prize. Don't want to spoil them kids, he'd said.

These young people, they're just scared, Old Will said.

These old people don't understand the world anymore, Pete said under his breath and swallowed down his glass.

Burning flags, I don't understand *that*. You're a soldier, son. That parade was for you.

Pete shook his head and refilled his glass.

Zeke came back down the stairs and said, I'm going home.

Pete walked him to the car. You want me to go over there and look for her? he asked.

Zeke sighed, lit a cigarette and pulled on it as he put the car in gear. Pete stood in the yard and watched the headlights careening through the dark trees as Zeke pulled the car into the street: lighting the house, the old maple trees where they played baseball as kids, blinding Pete, who was lighting a joint before he turned back to the old house where they had all grown up.

After Old Will's father stopped taking care of the mansion where he had worked for so many years, the funding was reduced and the services cut. The city did not hire a new watchman, just locked it up. The paint faded on the building and the once well-tended gardens became overgrown with weeds. The ivy went untrimmed and covered the house in green in season and hung limp, brown and scraggly in winter. Boards rotted on the porch; birds' nests hung from the gutters and the roof; rodents got the run of the crawl space under the house and gaps and holes showed in the stone foundation.

No one knew the hippies had moved in at first; they used it to party at night. Police patrols got complaints of loud noises and fires in the woods by the river, but the Buccleuch land was public park and set off from the city neighborhoods. The nights got longer and stretched into mornings, then days. On that July Fourth Pete heard them and saw the dim lights in the old soldiers' clubhouse on the back grounds of the Buccleuch Park. There was the mansion itself overlooking the Raritan River, the keeper's house where his parents still had a place to live as long as Old Will's father was still alive. The clubhouse was a quarter-mile away across the old marching field.

Pete shook his head and went back inside to drink with the old man. He could have stayed with his brother Zeke at his apartment downtown, but Old Will was better company right now.

It's just a parade. The Fourth of Goddamn July, Grandpa Will said to Pete when he came back in.

Zeke spent the night at his own kitchen table, in the cramped one-bedroom apartment on George Street in downtown New Brunswick. Zeke sat by the window, not even looking out, staring. He drank and smoked all night, like he was waiting for his wife to walk through the door and tell him what had happened.

She didn't have to tell; he didn't want to know. The men he

worked with at the construction site, who stopped talking and really dug into their bologna sandwiches when he walked up, told him enough, thank you.

What the hell you looking at? he had said to that loudmouth Joe Kelly.

Kelly did this licking thing with his tongue. Zeke rushed across a pile of boards, took a poke at him, then tripped and fell down. Everyone broke out laughing. Zeke let it go. It was a good job; he didn't want to lose it over a fight.

I heard they got the guns out and chased those hippies away, Smith told his brother when they were teenagers. This was one version: that Zeke just went over there one night, a bottle of Old Mill Stream in him, and tried to drag her out of a circle tripping out in front of the fireplace on the abandoned house's living-room floor.

Come on, Zeke. Have a drink. We're just having some fun.

This is trespassing. This is a historic place.

Try ancient history, buddy, some stoned longhair said. Leave her alone.

A woman had taken an old tapestry off the wall and wrapped herself in it for the chill. Zeke saw this, cursed and tried to take it away from her.

She screamed and looked at Zeke like he was someone to be afraid of.

Grandma told them that Zeke did go over there, but she wasn't even there. She never was there. She was gone, out on the street for a few days, and then she ended up in the psychiatric hospital in Princeton.

This jibed more with what Smith really did remember. Something was wrong in the house. Their mother was gone. Zeke had just given little brother Sam a bottle of milk, and when he went to the door, he pulled it out of Sam's mouth. Zeke must have been distracted, half-drunk at least. Sam cried and cried. Smith could still see his brother's tiny hands reaching for a missing bottle. If no one ever answers, a child eventually learns to stop asking.

Sam's always been really smart, maybe too smart. New York's a big city. It might take a while for him to get on his feet. Smith wondered if his younger brother had the patience for this. If he got in over his head, got a little scared, how would he react then?

In the early hours of that freezing February morning Sam was still out, walking around Tompkins Square Park when he heard some men cheering around a transistor radio.

What happened? Sam asked one of them.

We just invaded Iraq, the man told him. Sam drank Wild Irish Rose with some men gathered around a fire in a trash can and read an early edition of the *New York Post* with big four-inch war headlines: We Go To War!

The Marines were going into Kuwait City; the 1st Armored Brigade, the Big Red One, would back them up.

We will take the battle to them, a General Byrd was quoted as saying. If they run, we will catch them in the desert. They can run, but they can't hide.

The *Post* had a special war folio section, the first sixteen pages front and back of the paper. His brother's division had crossed the Iraqi border and was bearing down on Republican Guard positions south of the Tigris and Euphrates Rivers. The War for the Garden of Eden, one *Post* headline read.

Sam bought five bags of heroin down on Eldridge Street. He sniffed from the first with the dealer standing there. He shivered, then coughed when he felt the bite from the H in his nose.

Hey, watch it there, the dealer had said. The Five-O was out before. Sam smiled and stuffed the little bags of H into his jeans pocket.

As the sun rose, Sam walked back uptown to Forty-third Street to see if Clayton was awake. Clayton had a pot of coffee going. Sam could smell it in the hallway when he came around the corner. Sam took his boots off at the door. Clayton had a thing about cleanliness. He wore leather, black jeans and a T-shirt, but he was from Boston and one of the most articulate people Sam had ever met.

Clayton shook his head. Get some coffee, he said to Sam, you're fucking shivering.

I stayed out all night, Sam said.

Clayton looked at him. You could have stayed here, man.

Sam nodded and said, I wanted to walk around.

They hung out all day at Clayton's, then back in Tompkins Square with some activists staging a speak-out and at nightfall walked up to Times Square. Shivering in front of the old Army Recruiting Building, they joined the protesters at the corner of Forty-second Street and Seventh Avenue. It was a party with chanting, songs and signs. Everyone watched the war news in stunned excitement as it flashed in neon overhead on the Times Building.

After a couple hours, a march broke out. They made it twenty blocks before being dispersed by police on horseback and chased down Broadway.

Don't worry about the horses, Clayton yelled to Sam, they won't hurt you. They're as scared as you are, man.

Sam saw fear in one of the horse's eyes as the cop riding the animal pulled the reins. Sam was pinned in a corner. His brother's face flashed in Sam's head and then he was on the ground. Another cop helped him to his feet and Sam just said, Thanks, man.

The cop had his cuffs out. He gave Sam the once-over. You piss me off, he said. He was black, still in uniform approaching middle age, just a little frustrated at having to run after people like Sam.

Sam was ready to say, Fuck off, but the look on the cop's face softened him. What do you mean? Sam asked. It would be different if this war meant something, if it was about ideals. This war is about how much sports I can watch on how big a TV, this is about having a big, honking car.

I understand protest, the cop said. He took off his hat and brushed sweat off his forehead. But this isn't very patriotic.

Maybe this is our way of showing our patriotism. This is the wrong fight.

The cop shook his head. He hadn't shaved and he looked tired. Maybe that's right, he said, but still men are going to war tonight. Americans. In a foreign land they could die.

My brother's over there.

Maybe you should look at that, the cop said.

The officer turned away from Sam. G'wan, get out of here, you, he said.

Sam went around the corner to a pay phone, lit up a Newport and dialed Eleanor's number. They didn't see much of each other lately. When he last asked her if she was mad, she paused.

I'm disappointed, she said.

Sam flinched. He missed her.

Upon hearing her voice on the phone, he asked, Can I come by, tonight?

She hesitated before answering yes or no. That second brought Sam back to the way things were just a few months ago. Now he was scoring dope from guys who carried sawed-off baseball bats and wore gloves with no fingers so they could handle the little glassine bags in the cold. He told himself it was all part of the book he was writing in his head, but the war had started to rip real holes in the fabric of his fantasies.

Look, I know I fucked up before, Sam said. I'm getting clean now, I swear.

Sam?

What?

I miss the old Sam.

I do to, Ellie, I swear I do. I've been going to Narcotics Anonymous meetings.

What's that?

I don't know. It was pretty weird. But it's supposed to help with drug problems.

OK, Sam. I guess you can come over, Eleanor said. But don't keep me waiting, she said. Have you heard from your brother? she asked him.

Not lately, he said. I guess he's gone in.

You know what, Sam?

What?

I wish I could tie a rope around you and drag you off the street, put you somewhere.

I'm out of quarters. See ya, baby.

He gathered his coat around him, walked down to the F train and caught it into Brooklyn.

Sam didn't ring her bell or call; he thought surprising her would be a good thing. He didn't have a key, so he climbed up by the neighbors' window, almost slipped and fell, but he made it and tumbled down onto her second-floor balcony. The brick was hard and his hands were cold. When he opened her window and crawled through, she screamed.

Oh, God, Eleanor said. I heard everything, she said. I thought it was a burglar. You scared me to death.

He tried to smile.

She was in her nightgown. Eleanor drew him a hot bath, watched his every move and when he was in the bathtub, took her wallet out of her purse and hid it under the bed.

Ellie, he said. I'm really sorry about last time.

You really hurt me, Sam.

I'm sorry about the money.

It's not the money. I don't care about that. I just don't know who you are anymore.

I was high.

And you're not you anymore. Everything is all right now. I'm supposed to believe that?

Sam started to speak, but Eleanor shook her head and held up her hand.

No, don't lie anymore to me. Sam, I can't do this.

He got up. She saw he was crying and she took him into her

arms. She had sat down on the toilet and he put his head in her lap. She rubbed his head. Then she dried him off and took him to bed.

In the morning he left without waking her.

Every tank and truck gave off its own dark, hot stream of dust, smoke and sand. Waves and waves of them in V formation with the command vehicles in the center, waves that surged but never crashed or broke but kept building. The XVIII Airborne Corps front was fifty miles long with the tankers, infantrymen and engineers in the front followed by the support.

A helicopter pilot Sergeant Huebner talked to later said it was like a gigantic avalanche of boulders, raising dust hundreds of feet into the air, rolling across the wide desert with no beginning and no end, as if the center of the earth had opened and spit out some monstrous force.

The sandstorm followed them into Iraq. Black Hawks and Apaches flew low, like monster hornets, descending, in pairs, hardly visible at first, distorted by the sand and wind. Supply lines stretched out. Huebner started to hallucinate. He'd been at his station for three days, the twenty-fifth, twenty-sixth, twenty-seventh. He spent an hour trying to figure out something in his view sight. He felt paranoid, afraid to mention it to anyone until he had it figured out. A shadow of some kind, he thought maybe he'd broken the sight. Finally he realized it was a reflection of his own face.

A lane opened over the sand; he daydreamed that it was the dark path through the woods to his house back home when he was a child. They rumbled along in the darkness, Morrison with his shoulders out of his own turret or down with Huebner, going over the ammo supplies. Maxwell steering, cut off from the other three down in the hull, Jobe on watch from above. The wind and sand paused and the sight lines were perfect, but it only lasted a moment.

Y'know I'm going to be a father, Maxwell said quietly over the intercom to Huebner.

Huebner blinked. No kidding, he said. You did that girl back in supply?

Shh, Maxwell said. They sent her back home last week, Maxwell said.

Suddenly Captain Jobe was speaking.

We are timing our offensive so that they will have maybe just a few minutes between when the air attack has ended and when we hit them, Captain Jobe told them. Maybe they will be eating, or have gone out to take a shit. Maybe they will be trying to sleep. But they won't be ready.

The Marines would win the south and the VII Corps the east and now it was up to the XVIII Corps to get them in the north, in the valley of the Euphrates River. Iraq's command believed that the United Nations force was incapable of sweeping over and taking the rugged terrain south of the river. For this task the 66th Division had thirty-four battalions made up of twenty-six thousand troops, eighteen hundred tanks and other armed vehicles.

At just after midnight on the twenty-seventh, the 1st Brigade had reached their battle position. They were looking down Highway 8 less than one hundred miles from Basra. Their forces blockaded the road, taking over a thousand prisoners by dawn and destroying at least one hundred enemy vehicles with tank and TOW fire.

At their last fuel stop before their objective, Jobe called his crew to attention, knelt beside the tank and drew some lines in the sand.

This is where we fit in the larger plan, he told the men.

Isn't this a violation of orders to show us this? Maxwell asked.

That's right, Jobe said, and spat a glob of black snuff on the ground. You're not supposed to know, but I thought y'all should.

When they got back in, Jobe let Huebner ride in the turret for a few minutes. You go 'head and get some air. You're going to be down in the hole for a long time.

The Dark Lord Company kept a course north. They passed by a hill full of Bedouins sitting and watching the passing parade of firepower. They held their little ones up to see. Huebner saw their mouths open and they were clapping, capes billowing in the wake of the tank movement. Jobe jerked his shirt to take his place in the turret as they passed by a desert encampment. A man in a thoab had come out with cookies and biscuits.

It's a fucking silver tea service, he yelled down to Jobe.

I know, I saw it, the captain replied. Morrison gave Huebner the thumbs-up from his place in the other turret. The whole brigade passed by, kept up constant cruise speed of fifteen to twenty miles per hour, kicking up dust in the man's face. Five companies, hundreds of armored vehicles. Then Captain Jobe pulled on his leg and Huebner went back down into the hole.

Go to Red Con One, Captain Jobe said over the company net. Guidons, Jobe said, calling ahead to Lieutenant Holmes's Scout platoon, this is Black Six, bring your elements to Kill-4 battle formation and report when ready.

Each of the men had kept little pieces of nonregulation equipment, for luck and to remember who they had been before:

Morrison wore a black and red bandanna on his head. The colors were the same as his grandfather's minor-league baseball team, the Mockingbirds out of Macon, Georgia.

Maxwell wore a Superman watch.

Huebner had the photo of his brother and the ones he and Meg had taken at the Kmart before he left.

Captain Jobe carried a letter from his wife and a card his little girl had drawn with crayons and sent to him. He had a Nascar key chain, Bill Elliot's car, and also a packet of Goody's headache powders he said he was saving for when he really needed them.

Black Six, this is Red One, roger. Will go.

Black Six, this is White One, all elements report Red Con One, ready.

Black Six, this is Blue One, all elements report Red Con One, ready.

Oh-six-thirty hours: Red Con One, repeated Captain Jobe. Await orders. He hitched his latch in the turret open-protected position. Specialist Morrison, load sabot.

Sabot up, Morrison replied.

Rogue FSO, this is Rogue Six. Initiate preparatory fires. Time now, over. This was the order from the battalion commander Colonel Agard to begin the artillery and mortar assault on their objective.

Rogue Six, this is Rogue FSO. Preparatory fire is initiated. Time now.

Hold on to your freaking jockstraps, fellas, Jobe called out over the tank net, and Maxwell, Morrison and even Huebner whooped back.

The first round of concussions were loud and shook the tank. Over and over and over, the rounds were let go. Fifteen seconds later Huebner saw the flashes over the hill through his daylight sight. He was gripped by a sudden fear. He felt it in his hands. They trembled and shook. He took them off the controls in turn and flexed them. He still felt tight, but the trembling stopped.

They assaulted the Basra Airfield in full battalion strength. Their full arrow formation would sweep across the objective in waves and set up a hasty defense when they reached the far side. That was the plan. Huebner tried to picture them there, as if the future could be every bit as sure as the past. He heard Maxwell's nervous cackle over the tank net and it made him laugh. He checked targets and all the nervousness of the moments before was swept away.

Dark Lord Company came in from the northwest, pacing with a revived gale of wind. Rocky flats on both sides of a shallow dry basin, the bottom littered by a carpet of desert growth still green even now. Bare white, cracked, parched land. A single paved runway cut through the middle of the basin, a line of five hangars to the north side, planes and tanks set in formation on either side of the runway; some already hit by the artillery prep, a truck cut in half, black smoke pouring from the cab, a jet turned somehow on its side, with one wing cracked off and lying on the ground, the other sticking straight up in the air, a gasoline fire hissing orange and spitting black smoke.

It was hard for Huebner to breathe and his hands went numb. He did not take them off the main gun control from Jobe's first order to ready fire. Sweat dripped into his eyes. He tried not to blink, afraid he would miss something.

Maxwell closed to within one hundred meters of the lead platoon. He revved the engines and waited, humming the riff of some metal song over and over again under his breath. He brought the tank almost to a complete stop before a chain link fence that protected the perimeter of the airport. They paused in front of the first one to await the final word.

What are you waiting for! ? Colonel Agard shouted over the battalion net. All elements go!

Red, White and Blue. All elements, Captain Jobe echoed over the company net. Red Con One, go to Kill-4!

In the primary daylight sight, Iraqi soldiers tumbled out of a clamshell bunker, weapons drawn, rubbing their eyes, looking surprised. The first was pointing out the tanks to another man who was looking up in the sky for the assault. Then they seemed to look Huebner straight in the eyes.

Get the fuck out of the way, Huebner heard himself saying. Don't you know how to run?!

Right?! Maxwell answered, and Huebner felt like he was caught talking to himself. The Iraqi soldiers' expressions were like kids drinking in a parking lot, caught in the headlights of a cop's cruiser. One yelled, shook his fist and joined two more on their knees returning fire with their Kalashnikovs. Another just stood there. Others just turned and ran. They all looked wide-eyed, scared as hell.

Enemy troops, Huebner said to Captain Jobe.

Gunner, co-ax troops! Jobe commanded and Huebner hit the co-ax switch on his gunner's control panel. The captain had his .50-cal, more powerful but less accurate, the wrong gun for this situation.

Huebner switched his fire control. I can get him with the .30-cal, but I'm going to hit the tanks in front of us! What do you want me to do?

White One, this is Black Six, button up, repeat, button up.

Both hatches quickly closed in the tank in front of them.

Black Six, this is White One. Thanks for the heads-up.

Okay, gunner, fire when ready!

Huebner squeezed the trigger. An Iraqi started to run, but he was caught by the .30-cal and dropped in midstride. The second saw this, froze and held up his hands.

Huebner took a deep breath and lifted his finger off the trigger control. He actually had to stop himself. Their tank went right by the man, holding his weapon over his head, kicking dust in his face. If it was possible to die from fear, this man might, Huebner thought. He waved his weapon over his head, standing there in the middle of the battlefield, unable to run.

The Iraqis left to defend the airfield fired off mortars that bounced off the M-1's armor. Helicopters trying to take off were hit and exploded. On his thermal sight Huebner saw the outline of a plane, the engine dark, hot within a clamshell bunker.

Enemy plane on ground, he reported.

Load HEAT, Jobe replied.

Huebner sensed Morrison near him, changing the ammo load. HEAT up, Morrison called.

Fire, Jobe said.

Huebner switched his primary sight to daylight and saw the bunker explode into a mushroom cloud of fire and smoke.

Wow, look at that shit, he said, and breathed in.

Yeah, always wanted to do that, Jobe said in reply.

They were both shouting, to be heard over the noise of the battle. Huebner wanted to make sure he did everything right. He was trying to get his breathing in line with his fast-beating heart. The Iraqis fired machine guns and some light artillery. There was the constant ricochet of rounds hitting metal and zipping through the air, the smoky trails of RPG and antitank rockets. Fragments bounced off the heavy armor, got tangled in the camouflage netting and blew out taillights.

Amid the flying metal, more Iraqi soldiers appeared, their hands thrust up in the air, trying to surrender.

They look like they're coming out of the ground, Huebner said.

A lot of them are, Jobe confirmed, from bunkers.

Huebner still had on the daylight sight. He saw an Iraqi with his hands up, weapon held over his head, get shot and then crumple down onto the sand.

Oops, someone said over the tank intercom.

Huebner spotted an Iraqi with a scoped rifle, a Dragunov, firing at the platoon in front of them. He was crouched behind a wrecked car, a stream of smoke coming off it. If he got off the right shot, it looked like he could do some damage. The Iraqi's first shot had hit the Sponson box of the last tank in White platoon.

Enemy sniper on the ground.

I see him, Jobe said. Co-ax, can you get a shot?

Negative, Huebner replied. No clear shot.

White One, Jobe called the targeted tank, you see that? You've got a dismount in your element.

Black Six, this is White One. We can't see him, but we heard that ricochet shot. I almost shit my pants.

White One, this is Black Six. We'll get him.

Driver?

Roger, sir.

Maxwell, just run this sniper over. We can't get a shot on him.

Sir?

Repeat, run his ass over. Flatten that fucker!

Yeah?

Yes, fucking A! Go!

Roger, out.

On his daylight sight Huebner saw the Iraqi sniper's face, when he realized what was going to happen, go from disbelief to anger, then finally pure fear . . .

Huebner watched his screen until he was gone. It was like TV. They rode over the man and the car he hid behind. No noise, no bump, nothing, just an empty feeling in the pit of his stomach and the nervy jag of excitement that crackled through his veins.

Over the intercom Morrison whispered, Goddamn.

Whoo! Captain Jobe yelled.

Did you see that? Huebner called into his mouthpiece. Did you fucking see that? The look on that motherfucker's face!

We got 'em, didn't we! Jobe answered.

Ouch!

This is just like a movie, Maxwell shouted. He was nineteen years old. If he had not joined the Army, he would be a freshman at some state college, skipping classes, chasing girls, taking bong hits.

Colonel Agard's tank joined from the left. They jumped a hill together.

Check targets, Captain Jobe yelled into the headphones.

After the hills they ran the length of three football fields. The tank took fire from machine guns tucked in the wadis along the desert floor. The Iraqis shot off antiaircraft fire, but it just zipped over the tanks and exploded behind them, far off target.

It must be all they have, Captain Jobe commented as brightly colored tracers lit up the morning sky in surreal flashes of silver, yellow and blue.

Huebner sighted three Iraqi armored personnel carriers to the left, standing between two hangars. Two of them were on fire. One of the APCs started to come right at them, a BMP, an armored personnel carrier with a 76-mm main gun.

One of those BMPs ain't dead, Jobe said. You got it, gunner?

Target identified, Captain.

Morrison?

Sabot up.

Huebner saw the colonel's tank ahead of theirs, his helmet was sticking at least a foot out of the turret.

Sergeant Huebner, do you see what I see?

Colonel Agard's out of the turret. He's directing the show.

He's going to get his head blown off. You got that BMP?

Identified! Huebner yelled, and switched from the daylight to the thermal sight, lased and waited for the command.

Fire! Jobe commanded. Go!

Huebner released. The tank lurched. The range flashed in the gunner's primary sight; 750m, in digital numbers. The armed box illuminated white. On the sight it was one heat source to another. Huebner heard Jobe shout behind him in the turret.

Maxwell crashed the M-1 through another chain link fence and followed down the main runway. Sand blew so fierce that Huebner could see nothing at all through the daylight viewer, then it cleared: collapsed fuel tanks, an entire tank battalion destroyed, helicopters and fighter planes in flames.

Everyone all right? Everyone still here?

The platoons called in Red, White and Blue.

Over the radio, Jobe breathed out a sigh of relief and hollered, Who's your daddy now, Saddam?!

13

Zeke Huebner sent a postcard to his son Sam, plain white U.S. post office issue. On it was written that he'd be in Washington the next week. Could Sam meet him? Sam sent him one back and confirmed his plans to take the train down to Union Station.

The old man was still big, taller than Sam by a couple of inches. Zeke had broad shoulders, slim hips, hair cropped short now and sprinkled with gray. Sam saw him first at the station, waiting, smoking a cigarette by the trash can, looking at his watch and then off into the distance as if he had not come to meet anyone, like he was just someone who liked to go out to the station and watch the trains come in, like he was not attached to anyone. Some things never change.

Smith once said, He's always acted like he found us one night on his doorstep.

Yeah, and took us in because he thought we were the milk.

Or a six-pack of beer.

You look good, thinner, Sam said.

Look who's talking.

You remember this station? Zeke asked Sam when he walked up.

I brought you here when you were very young, with your mother, you and Smith. You always were the sentimental type, Zeke said, so I figure you'd remember.

Is sentimental bad?

Nah, course not. You were always more like your mother . . . that way.

His mother never had a name. Zeke never said it and the boys of course did not. He had never heard his grandparents say it either. Her name was Cassie, Cassidy, a family name. Sam had only heard his father say it once over the phone when he was a boy and he'd been struck by the sound, like his father was using a foreign language. His voice totally flat, without inflection.

You want some coffee? Zeke asked. Some breakfast? I saw a place.

A diner?

What else is there?

Something in his voice tugged at Sam's heart. Thank God he'd gotten good and high on the train.

On the walk over Zeke started to speak a couple of times, then caught himself. He would wait until they'd gotten the food. There was always a code of behavior with Zeke.

Zeke picked up a laminated menu. He put on glasses to see the menu in the diner and laughed at himself. Sam patted him on the back. There were times when he and Smith were little kids when they didn't dare to move without an eye on Zeke. Was he watching? Would he smack them? Even now it was like a ghost followed his every move, the ghost of the scared little child he had once been.

Let me guess, ham and eggs? Sam joked.

Of course. How could a self-respecting ham and egger not have ham and eggs? He means bacon, Sam said to the waitress. I'll have mine on a hard roll and he'll have his with home fries, over easy.

Oh for Chrissakes, she knows what I mean. Zeke rapped his knuckles on the Formica counter. That's quite a suit, Zeke said.

Got it at an Army-Navy store, Sam said. They both had on jackets; Sam's was military Air Force blue with a pair of dungarees and a button-down shirt.

Someone might ask me to dinner, Sam said back.

If you're lucky.

We could go on like this all day.

Zeke blinked. What would you like to talk about?

You wrote me, Sam said.

Zeke laughed and they both clammed up as the waitress brought their food over. Zeke smiled at her and Sam took a big bite from his sandwich.

So you turned fifty this year? he said after he swallowed.

The big five-oh, Zeke said.

Smith would have liked this place. I got a letter from him the other day, Sam finally said.

Zeke looked over and scratched his head. What did it say?

Army talk. Getting pretty hot there, but will get hotter when we go north. Say hello to the folks back home.

I guess he couldn't really tell his location.

They must have left Saudi by now, Sam said, and felt himself tiptoeing over the reality of Smith in combat, like it was some sort of minefield and they both kept careful watch over their instruments to avoid the danger spots.

Yeah, I guess, Zeke said, and took a thoughtful bite from his sandwich.

Have you heard from him? Sam asked.

He wrote to me at the outset, when he left. He was just letting me know they were going. I sent him a card then and then a couple of weeks ago.

On his birthday?

Right.

Sam saw that Zeke probably didn't even remember the birthday, then he saw too that he was probably wrong, that his father did remember, that he was wrong all along. He saw it in the gesture Zeke made, looking to wipe some grains of salt off the Formica surface of the table.

It's funny, he said. That we're here.

It's good to see you.

It's good to see you too, son. No, I meant in Washington, that your brother's in Iraq and we are meeting in Washington. We're the ones who are against war.

I never thought you were against it.

You never think anyone's as smart as you, Zeke said, laughing so hard he almost lost the last bite of his potatoes. He coughed and then swallowed, tapped his chest with his fist in a showman-like gesture.

Sam laughed. Naw, he said. I figured you thought it was silly or something. You never struck me as the political type.

I went to protests with your mother.

What's her name? Sam asked. He said it before he had a chance to think. He felt like he had stepped off a cliff and found there was a bridge there.

Zeke cringed, then softened. You know what your mother's name is, he said.

I've never heard you say it.

Cassidy, Cassie, he said and looked out the window. I deserved that, I guess, You were so young . . . Zeke started to say, but trailed off.

You did love her.

Of course I did, son. Zeke gave him a look that said, Don't be a sucker, don't be soft, don't be taken in.

Can I have one of those smokes? Sam asked.

Zeke handed him one and the book of matches.

When did you go to a protest? Sam asked.

It was with your uncle.

After he was out of the Army?

No, Pete was still in. He had come home on a pass. His commander, a West Pointer he looked up to, got killed. Pete came home with his body on the transport. When the plane landed in Washington, your mother and I met him there. We took Pete all the way out to Culpeper, Virginia.

It was a gray October day, early in the morning, the sun a deep blue promise that never broke from the clouds. Hollis's family lived in a small white house, with a stone walk. There was a weeping willow tree that leaned over the front door. The wind picked up and turned the little leaf petals over to white. A flock of blackbirds lit up for the sky from the uppermost branches. A pretty young woman with red hair and green eyes opened the door, rubbing sleep from her eyes.

She started whimpering and walking backward when she saw Pete standing on the porch in his dress greens. He wished he was there for a different reason. When he reached to hug her, she glared back at him. He had meant it as a gesture of comfort. It was just a bad moment. He knew the captain so well. To her he was just a stranger bringing bad news.

At the funeral in Arlington National Cemetery the wife hugged her two blond daughters close to her. Pete stood in the back.

Pete, Zeke and Cassidy got a pint, Pete still in uniform, and walked the streets of the nation's capital. One hundred fifty thousand people were in town that weekend for a protest against the war he had just come from. Pete wanted to talk to them. They walked around the edges of the crowds, sipping from the bottle and listening to the speeches. Pete was looking for the face that would unlock the words he wished so badly to say. Some spat on him; others shook his hand; still more just stared. To all he held up his hand and forefinger like John the Baptist, but the words never came.

The three of them stayed in Washington that weekend, crashing in the parks and on the great mall. One morning they woke up and someone had draped the stars and stripes over Pete. He folded the flag properly and took it with him. Pete got on another plane, went back, volunteered for reconnaissance patrols and got into killing. It felt like the right thing.

Your uncle was never the same after that, Zeke said. When he came home for good there was something different about him.

Do you hear from Uncle Pete now?

Zeke looked at Sam and shook his head. There was never anything anyone could do for him, Zeke said.

Do you know where he is?

He disappeared. I guess he's living on the street somewhere, if he's alive, Zeke said quietly. He paused, shook his head and speaking up a little said, I never stood with my brother, back then, during the war. I never tried to understand what he'd been through. You got to stand with your brother, son. Not against him.

Zeke looked at Sam, who was looking away, thinking of something.

You know something, I loved your mother, Zeke said. Maybe all you've heard is the bad, but there was good too.

Sam looked up. I haven't really heard much at all, he said. Did she leave, or . . . ?

She might have left me. I fucked up.

Sam let it go. They left the diner and started walking through the streets.

By and by, they had reached the Washington Monument. Sam stopped and just looked for a few moments. Shades of gray: tall stone structure, wet in a foggy, intermittent rain, the cloud-rent sky, even the grass, robbed of color by the winter season. Sam felt chilly; his nose was raw and hurt from the coke and the wind. A wet flag flapped and rang its rope and rigging against a pole.

Let's go look at this thing, Zeke said.

You want to?

Sure.

You get in line. I have to go find a men's room, Sam answered. He snuck some more dope in one of the stalls. His dad had waited by the door for him. The stairway felt damp and close inside and Sam was gasping for breath and got a little sick by the time they reached the top.

A little too high? Zeke asked, watching a flock of birds far off.

Sam realized he knew. He had to know and what he said

completely sealed it. Of course he must know, after the story he had told about Pete and all he had seen Pete go through. Sam always thought his father was a drunk, a drinker, that he didn't know what a drug was, wouldn't know reefer or anything like that. How silly was that?

They were on the way, with all those people around. Hey, I just thought of something, Zeke said.

What's that?

You owe your father some congratulations. He said it like he was talking about someone else. I haven't had a drink in seventeen years, Zeke said.

Is that right? Sam said. I was never around when you quit for good. I thought it would have been later.

I didn't become a saint, just sober.

When they got down, Sam said to Zeke, I went to a meeting. He braced for a speech, but it didn't come.

Easy does it, Zeke said to him. Of course he knew. Sometimes it takes a while, Zeke said.

You mean like with you.

Zeke winked, but he did not smile. Sure, son, he said. That's what I mean. They were both silent for a beat and then Zeke said, Here's something for you. Remember the Barracuda?

Sure, that was a bad-ass ride. You wrecked it.

Yeah, I did it on purpose.

Really?

Yes, sir. I did not want to be on this earth. I thought I'd lost my manhood. She loved you kids, Zeke said. She really did. I felt like I drove her away.

Smith said you used to hit her.

He would be the one to remember. You were too young and I

was in a blackout most of that time. My beautiful young wife, I hit her. Everything is not contained in one moment, son. But sometimes you have to pay for it like it is.

Zeke shook his head and looked away. He cracked his knuckles and rapped them on a park bench they were standing by. Let's walk back, he said.

Sam nodded. He had not signed up for all of this. He was already planning his escape. He had just enough coke left for the ride back and he was thinking of that now. Though he was walking with his dad and feeling something of what he imagined anyone would at such a moment, Sam's mind was already in the bathroom of the train, with the door locked and a nice big line laid out before him on the counter.

When his father shook his hand and said, I love you, Sam didn't hear it.

The Iraqis came walking out with their hands up, through the clearing smoke, with dirty, blood-smeared faces. By 1000 hours the infantry started taking prisoners, some from dugout bunkers, and others who were hiding out in the hangars. The bunkers were holes in the ground, with plywood thrown over the top and sandbags to weigh down the wood. The hangars were clamshell-shaped concrete structures, with holes at either end, built to withstand an air attack but not one from the ground.

That's a motley crew, Maxwell said, and the way he said it, straight out and dry, made everyone laugh.

So true, Morrison replied. After the battle, the tankers had pulled their vehicles into a pool for reloading fuel and maintenance.

The Americans led the prisoners away from the airfield, toward the middle of the desert. One man held up his hands, defiant, disgusted, looking forward, too proud to look at the ground. Another sucked on the shreds of his uniform shirt, now draped over his head like a shroud. His eyes flickered, open and shut. He held up a piece of paper, a cartooned leaflet depicting an Iraqi soldier surrendering to an American. He waved it in front of his face.

OK, buddy. We get the message, Morrison said to him.

Sergeant Huebner, Specialist Morrison and Private Maxwell walked among the parade of prisoners, weapons in hand. The soldiers had soaked bandannas in canteens and wore them under their kevlar helmets. Sweat rolled down Huebner's nose onto his lips; it dripped down the small of his back. The air smelled of things burning: gaseous, toxic fumes, mixed with the earthy natural mineral oxides of iron, tires, metal, other unnamed solids breaking down, crude oil and jet fuel, piss, sweat and fear.

Dogs barked and whimpered over something in a dune. They were curs, brown, yellow, and some spotted white. An Iraqi, uniform almost completely torn off by the dogs, lay there. The American soldiers yelled and squeezed off rounds to scare away the dogs.

Must have been hit in the air strike, one of the Americans said.

Hey, I think he's breathing.

But he's in pieces, Huebner yelled. There's nothing left.

Call for a medic, a soldier hollered back. We got a severely wounded raghead here.

Wounded hell, he's dying.

Yeah, another said. His head and chest is still together.

This soldier aimed his 9-mm pistol and shot two of the dogs barking around the dying man.

There's nothing we can do for him, said Captain Jobe. They've called the medics. We sent a runner down to the aid station. C'mon, Captain Jobe said. Let's hustle up and rejoin the march.

Sun glittered off the tiny crystals of sand sharply enough to cut Huebner's eyes. The heat lay heavy on his tongue. Hard to breathe. The ground shook beneath them and an M-1 came over a hill with two Iraqi prisoners riding shotgun to join the captured.

What the hell are y'all doing? Captain Jobe yelled at them, spitting snuff all over the sand. That ain't real smart, he said. He walked right up to get them off himself.

Wait! said a corporal who stuck his head from the turret of the M-1. Sir, hold on a minute, he said.

Giving up on the captain, this man looked at Huebner, Morrison and Maxwell when he said this. He blushed and held up his hands, helpless.

Bullshit, Captain Jobe yelled, and spat.

He pulled off the Iraqis and both took a couple steps, swaying as if impossibly drunk, wincing in pain. Each of them had one bad leg, the right one where the bottom of their pants were stained brown, like they'd walked in mud up to the ankle and the boot was caked with dried dirt. But it was blood. Their right Achilles tendons had been cut.

Captain Jobe drank from his canteen and wiped a sheet of grimy sweat from his eyes.

They tried to desert, the corporal said. The Republican Guard did that to them. He had red hair under his desert floppy hat, blotchy pale white skin.

Jobe waved his arm. The two prisoners struggled back to the Bradley and half-slid, half-pulled themselves up onto the armor.

Huebner had a pack of Marlboros; he walked up and gave cigarettes to each of the wounded soldiers. One of them smiled and offered his black beret for trade. Huebner hesitated, took it and put it in his pocket.

Thanks, he said and nodded his head.

An old man came up and Huebner gave him a cigarette. The company had gotten a shipment and he had been carrying his around for the right time.

Huebner, the captain called out. What the hell are you doing? Get back in line.

The old man said in English, Thank you, thank you.

Huebner was embarrassed. The old man deserved better. Huebner walked on and dropped the cigarettes on the ground as if the pack were empty. When he turned back, the old man had stooped to pick up the pack.

Engineers had hastily set up a temporary fence. They had rolls of concertina razor wire and the prisoners were herded inside. Morrison took guard duty with the prisoners and Captain Jobe went to meet with command.

Sam rented a room in the Sherman, a cheap hotel off Eighth Avenue near Times Square. The desk clerk had on a dirty T-shirt, sweat-stained yellow under his arms. The dingy lobby smelled like disinfectant.

You're lucky, the man said, laughing, when Sam involuntarily wrinkled his nose. We just had the place deloused.

Great, Sam said.

You a vet?

Uh no. Why do you ask?

No reason. Vets get a discount is all.

Missing floorboards, cockroaches crawling, piss-smell in the bathroom.

Clayton's friend, the actor Delancey, came in wiping sweat from his forehead, looking pale and sick, looking to score.

Delancey said, It's dark in here.

It's light enough, Sam told him.

Delancey said, Fuck, I got a problem up in my room.

What kind?

Guy shot himself.

Where?

In the head.

Dead?

Delancey nodded.

You shoot him?

He shot himself, Delancey said.

Nah . . .

Yes, sir. We were smoking some dope. He was playing with a gun and he shot himself in the face. It was nasty, Delancey said, and tried to spit, but couldn't. He pulled out a smoke and Sam had to light it for him.

Sam lit one for himself and took a long draw.

Who was he?

Nobody. He had a bunch of H, needed somewhere to smoke it. So I said, Let's go to my place.

Delancey stood up. He was big, a menace. Delancey worked

a lot in Hollywood because he was scary and darkly handsome. He looked like someone who might do anything and not look back.

Where do you find them? Sam wondered. At the bus stop? In some shot-out, abandoned building? You're a peach, Sam said. Do you know his name?

I think it was Charlie. Let's call him that.

It's your call. Whose gun was it?

Hunh?

The gun. Whose gun?

It was my gun. I just got it. It's a sweet gun.

You better get rid of it.

I don't want to. It's a .38. Police issue.

Where is it?

I got it in my pocket.

Great, Sam said, and turned to the window. This is crazy. This is a crazy fucking story. You sure you're not making this up? he said, turning back to Delancey.

You want to see him? You can help me. I called my father.

What did he say?

He said to cut him up.

Your dad did?

Said to cut him up and get rid of him.

Fuck that.

Yeah, my dad's crazy, Delancey said.

And you are?

Me, I'm a successful Hollywood commodity, Delancey said with a rueful laugh.

You *are* in the movies.

That doesn't change where we are or what we're doing, Delancey said. So I get paid to be a piece of shit. That doesn't change the smell.

He took Sam upstairs. Delancey had the body covered up with a newspaper. Stuck to his head with the blood.

Sam looked away quickly, feeling the bile rise in his throat. He looked back. The man's hand hung limp over the side of the bed. It was the same hue, pale, drained of color, as the paper. Though up by the man's face the blood had darkened it. Sam just stood there, losing track of time. He could hear Delancey's heavy breaths behind him. He had never seen anyone dead before. It was exciting: it quickened the beating of his heart. But it was also banal as yesterday's papers. Sam recognized the front page of the *New York Post* from the day before.

For a second he got a creepy feeling that he had been in the room before and stood before the dead man. Everything else went away, Delancey's breathing and the sounds of the city streets coming in through the open window. The moment seemed like it would never end, like Sam could go back to it and it would always be there, waiting somewhere inside him. He felt responsible, just standing and looking. The dope he had done before Delancey came to get him dulled his feelings, but nothing made it all right.

Y'know what, Sam said, and turned around to face Delancey, I lied. I got some dope.

Delancey smiled. His lips were gray; his skin looked waxen. You been holding out, he said.

Sam laughed uneasily and Delancey laughed too. Sam took a couple bags of dope out of the breast pocket of his shirt.

Delancey pulled a set of works from his sock.

If I wanted to score some weight, do you know anyone I could look up?

Delancey laughed. He pulled a card from his wallet and wrote down an address. Try Fat Tony. Tell him I'm with you.

Thanks, Sam said. He looked over at the couch. You want to go back to my room to do this? Sam asked.

Delancey said, Naw, we can do it right here. I got everything we need. He looked over at the dead man and shook his head. We don't have to look at him.

14

The wind died as the American soldiers ate, but the sky didn't clear. Medics gathered by the Bradleys that had been hit by friendly fire. Great gouges had been ripped out of the earth, so that it looked exposed, angry. Water had seeped in from some unknown place; oily chemicals made rainbows of color on the surface of the viscous liquid. Everson and Williamson killed and five more wounded. The infantry had been clearing up the crippled machinery along with the dead since the afternoon.

The engineers and artillery support took over. Captured T-62 and T-72 enemy tanks were cleared of enemy survivors and secured.

Two medics called over to Morrison. He talked to them and then rejoined Huebner on the perimeter of the holding area.

What's going on? Huebner asked.

Something ugly.

Huebner laughed, his throat full of sand.

Morrison told Huebner a couple of the prisoners had gotten into a fight.

After we marched them down, two of them were fighting for

food. These two started throwing punches, and everyone just stood around and watched. It was pathetic. Both of the Iraqis yelled at each other and spat. Some matter of honor. One was an officer and the other an enlisted man. The enlisted man insulted the officer. He used the Arab word for disgrace, the worst possible insult. Said that he had been scared the whole time, the whole three weeks of the Amriiki blitz. Or at least that's how the guy who knew some English made it seem.

Morrison said he ran inside the fence and helped break it up. The other Iraqis just watched, too dazed from the bombing, or just bone-tired. There were so many. They had been bombed for days now. They were out of their heads. Others just didn't care.

When they started fighting again, Morrison just let them go at it. They looked like a couple of fighters in the fifteenth round just holding each other up for the bell. The enlisted man got a couple good socks in. Then the officer went down and the enlisted man stomped him with his boot.

The man on the ground had stopped moving. He lay prone, with his head lolled at an odd angle, blood running from his mouth. He was breathing still. Morrison got his canteen from his belt and gently poured water on his head.

Captain Jobe volunteered a squad of ten soldiers with Sergeant Huebner in charge to help.

Y'all be careful, he said, This ain't like those movies where they all give up at once. A lot of this place is still hot.

Huebner nodded and looked at Maxwell. Maxwell was chewing on a piece of gum, singing something to himself. Some song with the word "love" in the chorus.

You're sure you don't want to go with us, sir?

That ain't funny, Jobe said. I have to attend to the company. Just don't take any chances, boys. We got a helluva lot of help here. Don't try to win the whole war by yourself, he said and poked Huebner in the chest, maybe a little harder than he meant to.

Is this a war or what? he asked Maxwell.

I guess they'll decide what to call it later, sir.

Huebner and Maxwell walked away from the prisoners' compound to the ruined runway. Their boots crunched over the graveled sandstone.

This all looks familiar, Maxwell said.

What do you mean?

This is our kill, Maxwell said, and he pointed. See that APC there? From when we saved the colonel's ass?

I think you're right, Huebner said.

Through a veil of smoke and blowing sand, they watched a couple of infantrymen pull three bodies out of the carrier they had hit. The tank round had blown a crater in the ground and the armored personnel carrier had slipped into the soft sand.

The infantrymen were pulling the bodies out with shovels.

Humpty-Dumpty had a great fall, said a young soldier whose tag read Gonzalez.

Humpty-fucking-Dumpty's in pieces, a black soldier whose tag read Tucker said, and wiped sweat from his eyes. He was laughing. It was like he couldn't help it.

Huebner and Maxwell watched as they laid out the dead.

That's a gruesome fucking job, Maxwell said. Is that the infantry too?

Attached to infantry, yeah. But I hear there's a special squad. They carry the body bags.

The death squad.

That's catchy. I thought I was in that group, Huebner joked, but neither laughed. The afternoon was gloomy, the sandstorm and all the smoke brought with it a premature twilight.

Gonzalez was waist-deep in the crater now. There was the sound of something, a crack.

These got it pretty good, Gonzalez said.

This is ours, Maxwell said.

Gonzalez held his breath to avoid the smell.

I think this is our kill, Huebner said, and Gonzalez grimaced. His face was covered with brown freckles that went down his neck and mixed with the sand that dotted his face. He had found a part of a man, a boot with a bloody leg stuck in it. He quickly put it on the ground.

Huebner nodded and they walked on. There were a couple of cars, their chassis burned to black, tires gone, on their rims in the sand.

They look like Chevy Cavaliers, Maxwell said. One of my sisters has one back home. I'd know that body anywhere.

Sergeant Huebner and Specialist Maxwell spread out with their weapons drawn.

The Iraqi soldier came out of the gray light. He had no helmet or shoes; his features were outlined in the smoke, like a halo around him. He had been through a different war. His eyes looked like his soul had flown out of them. He had been through the air bombardment, the artillery barrage and now the ground attack. He breathed in short quick bursts, pursing his lips, sucking at the smoky air like a man trying to draw clean water from a dirty pond. He held up an empty mortar tube.

A sheen of sweat glazed the Iraqi's forehead. He had stringy, greasy hair pulled back on top and falling into long black tendril curls in back. The sand stuck in his hair made it look gray. His uniform shirt was torn, and his breastbone poked through a hole in his chest, like his flesh had been scraped off with a trowel. He had a caterpillar-thick mustache.

I love George Bush, the Iraqi said.

Sit, Huebner said, and waved his M-16. They were by the carcass of a fighter plane, with one wing shorn off and lying in a big, gaping hole, bare metal with the paint flaked off in slivers the size of the sergeant's hand. Smoke trailed off in the wind. The breeze picked up and made it hard to see Maxwell, twenty-five yards to Huebner's left.

The Iraqi looked like he needed to sit down. I love George Bush, he said again.

I heard you the first time, Huebner said. He wished the whole thing was more efficient. This wasn't a battle; it was a mess. These soldiers weren't an opponent; they looked like they needed their mother. He wished the Iraqi didn't look so scared. You speak English? Huebner asked.

Yes, the Iraqi said. He held his cupped hand over his mouth, like it was a secret, like someone might smack him for saying it. I learned in university, he said.

A smoky breeze blew back a patch of weeds at their feet. The Iraqi soldier winced, hyperventilating, bringing his hand to his breastbone like just now it suddenly hurt, like that part of his nerves finally caught up to where the shock had sent the rest of him.

The Iraqi looked at him, raised his eyebrows and sipped again at the swirling air.

There are more of me, he said.

What? Huebner asked. You speak English, then speak it right, asshole.

The Iraqi held the mortar tube above his head for a moment, then he let his arms fall and moaned softly. He looked so tired, even this simple gesture of surrender was exhausting for him.

Maxwell! Huebner called. Get over here. Come quick!

The Iraqi soldier flinched.

You all right? Maxwell said, hurrying to Huebner's side.

This one's not dead.

You want to shoot him? So let's shoot him. What the fuck? Maxwell raised his pistol and walked toward the prisoner. When the Iraqi threw the empty mortar tube on the ground, Maxwell slowly lowered his pistol. The Iraqi pointed at a piece of sheet metal on the ground.

Sarge? Maxwell asked. What's he pointing at?

He's out of his mind. We should give him up to the infantry or take him in ourselves.

He's just scared to death.

I don't care if he's pissing in his pants.

He's already done that, man.

Huebner felt dizzy. Something in Maxwell's voice was strange, not so much in what he was saying, Maxwell was always strange and getting stranger by the minute. But what hit Huebner was how he heard his comrade. Something had changed. He had felt completely in charge of the situation up until now. Suddenly, Huebner felt exhausted and wanted to sit down. He was having trouble breathing and he was worried about his hands trembling. He looked at them again now. Not too bad. He wondered if he would know if he started to lose it. He wished he could have a nap.

It would be nice to have a beer, he said out loud to Maxwell.

No kidding, Maxwell said. Then he turned and looked back at Huebner. Sergeant, he said. Sit down a minute?

I think I will, Huebner said. He took off his helmet, scratched his head. He looked at the prisoner, who had started to crouch down with him, keeping a good ten feet away.

Not you, buddy, Maxwell said and grabbed the Iraqi's arm and pulled him back up to his feet. Keep a gun on him, Sarge. Would you? I'm going to see what he's pointing at.

I got him, Huebner called back.

The metal was just scrap, and when Maxwell kicked at it with his boot he was able to move it out of the way pretty easily. He stood there looking down at his boot. From where he was, twenty yards away, Huebner could not tell what Maxwell was looking at.

Hey, Max, he called out. What you got? What is it?

It's a bunker. Maxwell ducked then and rolled on the ground. He took out a grenade and threw it into the hole. A muffled explosion sounded down below. The prisoner jumped up and ran toward Maxwell and the bunker. Huebner shot him in the leg. The Iraqi tripped, lost his footing and fell to the sand. He grabbed at his thigh, writhing there and calling out.

What the fuck was that? he called to Maxwell.

Don't know, sir, Maxwell called out. But something's moving down there. Huebner had jumped to his feet. As he ran over there, he kept his weapon trained on the wounded prisoner. He heard something moaning in the bunker.

Hear that? Maxwell asked. Let's go check it out, Sarge.

Wait a goddamn minute! Huebner shouted. We should call for backup. He took a couple deep breaths. He needed to think. He wished that the procedure was as clear now as when he was in the tank, doing the job he was trained to do.

For now Maxwell was on his feet again and walking toward the bunker. He held his gun out before him. Huebner looked back to check on the wounded prisoner. He was in an almost fetal position, a darkening splotch of blood spreading across the leg of his pants.

He's not going anywhere.

What was that? Maxwell asked.

Just talking to myself.

Don't do that, Maxwell said. You got a flare? he asked.

Why?

I think there are some kind of steps, here.

You got your PVS-7? We can use those.

Huebner watched Maxwell pull the vision equipment over his eyes and secure it with straps over his head like a catcher's mask.

You ready?

Right behind you, buddy.

A sort of primitive stairway carved into the dirt led down into the dark. Everything was colored green from the mask and light and dark took on different shades. Huebner pulled his radio out.

This is Dark Lord Six, grounded, he said.

Dark Lord Six, this is Blue One.

What company?

Charlie Blue.

Charlie Blue, we got a live bunker, coordinates 456222. You got someone nearby?

Dark Lord Six, this is Charlie Blue on the way. You got a sit rep?

We got a disabled raghead, maybe some more in the bunker. Requesting backup to sweep and secure the area.

Roger, Dark Lord Six. This is Charlie Blue, out. We are on the way.

Roger, Huebner said. He had paused on the stairway. He could still see Maxwell a few steps below.

The bunker opened up as they went down. The steps formed a passageway into a cavelike large room. When he reached the floor level, he saw Maxwell standing in the middle of the large dark space.

Look at this shit, he said.

Huebner nodded. Then he flinched and said, Hey, watch your back.

Fuck, Maxwell said, turning around.

Huebner had seen something moving toward Maxwell, something dark, on the ground. It took a while to recognize what things were, with the mask on. There was a tiny time lapse between sight and recognition to deal with the changed value of light and dark.

The man on the ground had a chain around his ankle. He was unarmed and looked like he could hardly move. He looked weak and near death.

What the fuck? Huebner said.

Look at them all.

One, two, three . . . Huebner got up to seven and then stopped counting, let his hand fall. It felt like the wrong thing to do. Huebner shook his head. Thirty minutes ago he was in command and when he faltered, Maxwell had picked it up. There was nothing wrong with that. He wasn't sure who was calling the plays now. This was the test he had been trained for. A soldier had to endure beyond the fatigue. Even when he was scared and disoriented, these were temporary conditions he could control.

Are you thinking what I'm thinking? Maxwell asked.

Let's get the fuck out of here and meet the backup.

This is bigger than we thought.

Some of the men moaned on the ground and reached out with their hands as Maxwell and Huebner walked away, back toward the opening of the tunnel.

This is fucking ugly, Maxwell said.

Just keep walking toward the opening, Huebner said. We'll be out of here in a moment.

That's not soon enough for me. Did you notice how many of them were dead?

I didn't get a count. You?

No.

Huebner and Maxwell sprawled on the sand and gasped for air, watching as the soldiers they had sent for walked the prisoners out of the hole.

The sun hurt the sergeant's eyes as he took his mask off. He watched Maxwell biting off his fingernail. There was a bit of blood and still he kept worrying it.

You know your planes, Huebner said. Maxwell?

What? What plane, Sarge?

The one burning over there.

Sorry, sir, Maxwell said, grimacing in pain. I just don't give a shit.

Maxwell, don't.

Don't what, sir? Maxwell yelled and stood up and started walking in a circle.

Maxwell, I would have done the same thing, Huebner said, getting to his feet.

What? Would you of? Maxwell asked.

Sure, Huebner said. Sure I would have.

You started to call for backup. That's what we should have done, Maxwell said, a pleading tone to his voice. He looked away from Huebner, away from the men, at the gently smoking plane. I just wanted to do the right thing. I was just following my instincts, Maxwell said. You know what I mean? he asked, and sucked at the bleeding place on his finger.

I get it, Huebner said. He looked at Maxwell long enough to catch his eyes, then looked back to the American troops still gathered around the hole.

The wrecked plane, it's called a Fulcrum, MiG-29, Maxwell said.

Huebner nodded. Oh, yeah, right, he said.

What do you think those soldiers were doing down there?

They must have tried to desert. I guess they chained them up and left them down there to die.

I guess so, Maxwell.

You don't blame me, sir. You don't think . . .

Maxwell, please. If I did, I would report you.

Really?

I'd turn you in. No kidding.

All right then, Maxwell said. He brushed his finger on his pants. Neither of them had anything more to say.

The other soldiers kept their guns on the Iraqi troops and

walked them back through the field to the control area. One of the Iraqis looked hard at another bunker where some more infantrymen were finishing up, at their faces in the moonlight and at the black body bags laid out on the sand. He did not pause; he kept walking. His country had become theirs. It was better to walk slowly. They walked over some rough earth, a place where the wind had whisked the sand away from the earth's surface, as cleanly as a broom might, baring striations and stretched places in the rock, imperfections and marks that had been covered and clothed in uniform sand for time beyond human conception, like the marks left by the roots of long-exterminated forests, marks left by the bones of long-forgotten civilizations.

Huebner picked up a stone off the ground. It was flat and felt good in his hand. It would have been a good skimming rock if there were any water around. Maybe if he were back home in Georgia with his brother and they were sixteen again, down at the pond behind Old Man Baker's house with a couple of fishing poles and maybe a six-pack of cheap beer to split. Huebner reared back and threw the rock as far as he could. Then he turned away. He didn't wait to look where the rock landed.

At three o'clock in the afternoon Sam finished teaching his introduction to literature class down on Chambers Street. It was a Friday, the first pay week of the spring semester. Sam felt flush. He'd cashed his check from another job in one of the narrow storefront check-cashing places nearby, and this somehow made him feel like a man of the people. Cash in the pocket.

He had scored earlier that day, six bags of dope at dawn, and did a couple before class. His basic lesson veered off into a lecture on something he called The Outlaw Tradition of American Literature, drawing a line from Melville to Kerouac. The students tried to keep their heads off their desks. Near the end, a Greek student raised his hand and asked him to explain the difference between "there" and "their" again. Sam went back to the men's room after class and did another bag. Now he was going back for more. He had three bags in his shirt pocket and what he could still scrape out of the empty glassine envelope of cheap blow in his wallet.

He walked across to the east, past City Hall and the courthouses, through the crowded sidewalks of Chinatown and Sarah Delano Roosevelt Park where ragged men shared pints of cheap wine and always seemed to need a quarter. On Stanton Street was a bodega where he could sometimes score. He didn't really need any more, but he had money and if he stopped and sat still he might have to think about what he was doing: how little money he had left, how much time he spent scoring or getting high. Most things were out of his control: he could not bring his brother back alive from Iraq. He could not seem to finish his novel; he could not see Ellie without hurting her. But he could cop any time he wanted.

No mas, the man behind the counter told him.

B-but I need it, Sam said. It's okay. Sam put down a fifty-dollar bill.

The counterman looked at it, twitched his mustache like a rabbit, raised his eyebrows, but wouldn't touch the money.

Uh, dude, somebody said behind Sam. It was a balding long-hair wearing a jeans jacket. The cops are right outside, he said. You see that brown car sitting right there. That's the cops.

The counterman nodded.

It doesn't matter, Sam said. Give it to me.

They can see everything we're doing in here, the man in the T-shirt said. A little boy came out from behind him and looked at Sam. He had spiked blond hair. He was drinking from a plastic container of blue sugar water. The way he' stared at Sam made him nervous.

Sam pushed the money across the counter a little farther.

You junkies are funny, the longhair said. You could just walk around the block and score somewhere else, but you can't. You're under the grips.

Excuse me?

Yeah right, you're a tourist.

You know what, Sam said. You should mind your own business.

It is my business. I got a kid here.

Yeah?

You think you get a pass? Because you're so smart. Because you're white. You're just a fucking junkie.

I am not a junkie, Sam said, and pointed at his money.

The counterman's nose twitched again. He shook his head and put his hand on Sam's money. He shrugged his shoulders, reached under the counter and replaced the money with two little blue plastic envelopes of cocaine.

Sam picked the bags up, then went in the back by the potato chips to hide them. He slipped one in the tag of his tie and stuck the other down in the tiny change pocket of his slacks. Sam selected a bag of chips from the stand and a soda from the cold case and quickly exited the store. The cops let him turn the corner onto Attorney Street before two of them came up behind him.

Where do you think you're going?

The police found the heroin in his shirt pocket and the cocaine in his tie.

Twelve hours later he was down in the Tombs below the courthouse at 50 Centre Street.

Five hundred men were crowded inside a steel mesh cell the size of a tennis court. Hundred-watt light bulbs in wire cages hung from the ceiling. Hard wooden benches with steel railings spaced to prevent a man from stretching out completely to sleep. Vermin darted to and from grime-caked cracks and corners of the dirty, cold concrete floor.

No belts, shoelaces or keys allowed. Twenty-five policemen with billy clubs and revolvers. The corrections officers threw sandwiches over the top of the cage and laughed as the prisoners grabbed and fought after them. If the prisoners weren't hungry, they could be sold for money, thin processed ham with mayonnaise on stale white bread.

I don't really like mayonnaise, Sam told a cop.

Give it to me, the one handing out the food, an officer with a name tag that read Santorini, said in an accent from Queens. He had hunched shoulders and Sam told him he looked a little like the movie star Al Pacino.

They say I look like him in *Dog Day Afternoon,* he said to Sam. That was twenty years ago. Keep your hands to yourself. Remember, we win. We got the sticks and the guns.

And oh yeah, by the way, he went on. This one says he doesn't like mayo. Anyone want to eat his sandwich for him? There was a murmur and a few of the prisoners raised their hands.

The officer threw the sandwich back at Sam. It came apart in the air, hit him in the chest, smeared mayonnaise on his jacket, and fell on the dirty floor. Sam picked the pieces up, put the sandwich back together and ate it. He asked someone in a blue gang bandanna for a cigarette.

He must have been all of nineteen. Let me get this straight, he said, blowing smoke in Sam's face. You're not asking to buy a cigarette. You expect me to just give your lame ass one.

You could put it like that, Sam said. I don't have any small change, he whispered to him. I want to get high when I walk out of here.

Yo man, don't tell nobody you got money here. You got balls or you're really stupid. You lucky, I got money. Have a cigarette. Take two and then go over there. Get the fuck away from me.

Sam thanked him, offered his hand.

The guy shook his head. Move along, he said. You're one of maybe three white boys here. I wasn't put here to watch your ass.

Sam slipped the second cigarette into his coat pocket and walked away.

Hours passed. The prisoners were called out by name, chained together twenty at a time and trucked from the central booking cage to another jail beneath the basement of the criminal courthouse building. They waited down there to go and face the judge. They got bigger bologna sandwiches with cheese and four packets of sugar down here in the Tombs; the last was supposed to help with the heroin cravings. Sam sat down on the bench against the wall, crashing. When he woke up, he was sitting next to a man with gym shorts and a T-shirt. He had old sneakers that looked like he had found them, tongues hanging open and his feet coming out.

What are you wearing shorts for? Sam asked him.

The man just looked at Sam. Sam asked again and the man waved his hand at a fly.

They took my pants, the man told Sam.

How long have you been here?

The man looked both ways. Three weeks, he told Sam.

But they're supposed to call our names after a few hours. That's what the cop said.

They don't know my name, the man said to Sam.

Sam called Eleanor from the precinct and left a message that he'd gotten in a little trouble. He couldn't think of what else to say and tried to make it cute.

You'll never guess where I am . . . it's kind of cool, really . . . and I'll tell you all about it later, baby.

When Eleanor got the message at home, she brushed it off. Sam had really hurt her. Recently, she had actually met a cute guy from the neighborhood. He had asked her out that night for a couple of drinks after work. She kept her date and he was nice, but she told him she was sort of seeing someone. Later that night, when she came home with a little buzz on, it was dark and she was alone and Eleanor began to worry about Sam. She started calling hospitals.

Try the police stations, they said, so she did.

Try central booking, they said and gave her the number.

Once she got started, it was hard to stop. By three-thirty she had a piece of paper with fifty different scrawled numbers. She called Clayton. Eleanor finally fell asleep on the couch with the lights on.

Sam called the next morning from the new Angelika Film Center on West Houston Street. He said he had been in jail all weekend. He was raving; he talked about dying, about his parents, his brother, the war. She told him to wait there for her. She called a hospital and spoke with a mental ward social worker. They could send someone, but it was still Sunday. They would have to keep him for a certain amount of time if they took him in.

Are you with him now? a nice woman asked Eleanor.

No, I spoke with him over the phone. Eleanor told the woman what she knew.

Is he on drugs now?

Probably.

When Eleanor put down the phone, she looked out the window at a flock of pigeons banking against the sun. She tried to remember the last time she had seen Sam when she was sure he wasn't high.

Command had set up a protection perimeter and released a lot of soldiers from duty for sleep, but most of them were still too keyed up. They had lined the tanks up in a temporary motor pool. There were at least fifty and a half-dozen of the M-88 maintenance vehicles with great booms sticking up into the sky like grasshopper legs, twice that number of M-1s and howitzers.

A soldier said he'd heard the war was over. They haven't announced it yet. But they will.

Maxwell handed Morrison and Huebner each a can of nonalcoholic San Miguel beer to drink. He'd kept a case hidden down in the driver's compartment of the M-1. He put his forefinger to his lips, for quiet. He looked excited, giddy, a child who hadn't slept, a pure source of energy with redness edging from his eyes like the sun.

It tastes like it's real, he said. I got it from the Filipino at Mukmhar's. He choked, burped, then gurgled down a long swallow.

I can smell it, Huebner said.

Maxwell handed him another can.

Wow, Huebner said, it tastes exactly like warm, skunked, nonalcoholic beer.

Maxwell frowned and turned back to Morrison, who was staring at the can.

All the gathered soldiers wanted to talk about CENTCOM and the possibility of pushing farther into Iraq. Were they going to cross the Euphrates? Were they still shooting? Maxwell just wanted to tell everyone the story of how he became President of The Country of the Near Beer.

Huebner felt drained: the prisoners, hemmed in a quarter-mile away, a murmuring presence like a vacuum that sucked away any elation he felt from the victory.

Come on, Morrison said to him. Look alive, soldier. You're alive. You faced action with bravery.

I was trained to do that.

So, you can take pride in it.

Huebner wasn't moved. He took a drink and swallowed. I expected an opposition, not a scared enemy begging to give up. It was like the Iraqis were caught in between Saddam and the U.S. Army; they didn't have a chance.

They were fighting back, weren't they?

They were fighting for their lives.

Same difference.

I shot a man in the leg today.

Did he have a weapon?

Yeah.

That's all that matters to us.

But now the captain says we're not going to Baghdad. So I don't get it, why did we come here?

We're here to liberate Kuwait, not Iraq.

Huebner gulped the beer and opened another one. Someone from the quartermaster crew had a big Hefty bag. He was walking around taking everyone's empties.

Huebner said, The desert's littered with broken planes, spent shells, and he's worried about beer cans.

He doesn't want to leave the wrong impression, Maxwell said.

He's an ass, said Morrison.

The sun came out for a moment, then it was gray and dark again. As darkness began to fall, a low ceiling of clouds blocked light from the moon. A light rain fell and drifts of wet fog that came down from the high dunes to the north in the direction of the Euphrates. The feeling, the fog and everything in the air became like a being unto itself that Huebner could feel sitting next to him, looking at him like he should say something, like his grandmother when he had done something wrong as a child.

She had raised them. Sergeant Smith Huebner remembered when they went those three times with their father to the hospital ward in Trenton to see his mother. They rode in Zeke's 1968 Barracuda sucking lollipops. When they arrived at the hospital, their mother looked at the boys like they were going to explain why she was there.

This is where they take people who take too much acid, their father told them.

Smith didn't know what Zeke meant then, but he remembered the words and the jumble of scenes and feelings they evoked. When he was older, he thought doing drugs helped Sam feel closer to what his mom must have been like before she was lost, when she was pretty and young and wanted to have fun.

Captain Jobe woke Huebner later that night and said they were heading out.

We've been ordered toward Basra. Once we secure the area and the 6th Cav gets up here, we'll follow the highway to the border.

And then?

And then I guess we go back home.

What they were saying is true, then. No Baghdad.

That's right, Sergeant. The war part of this is over.

We can only hope, sir.

They were first in line, at the head of the arrow formation of tanks. Black spotlets of moisture dotted the metal of the tank. The rain wasn't strictly black; it contained all the things that were in the air, the gray metal, streaks of cordite. A battalion of fifty-eight tanks rambling through at cruise speed cannot be good for either the air or the land. The air they breathed was heavy, even at the top cruise speed of about fifty miles per hour, the turret and all the vents open. The sky looked like a piece of burned tin, turning to red, purple and gray. A flock of black birds flew out of the sky like they were trying to get away. The wind blew folds in the sand that wrinkled back toward the horizon like old skin.

When they stopped for a break in the morning, Captain Jobe

noticed some letters one of the tanks in Charlie Company had written on their turret.

What kind of a name for a tank is that?

It's an acronym.

D-C-F-S-Y? That doesn't spell anything.

It stands for, Dick Cheney Says Fuck Y'all.

The Iraqis, right?

Them too.

Come again?

Cheney said we'd be rotated out originally. Well, did it happen?

No.

There you go.

Jobe laughed and saluted. We did fuck them good, he said.

We fuck them all good, Maxwell piped up. We're America.

Everyone laughed at that. They all needed to.

Sam ended up at a dope spot on East Sixth Street. He called the number Delancey had given him and was given a password to get by the nickel and dimers in the street. He went upstairs and asked for Fat Tony.

You come from Delancey? a voice asked through a chained door.

What? Delancey?

You said you knew Delancey.

That's right. Sorry, Sam whispered through the door. I spaced.

The chain fell, the door opened and the man there said, Have a seat.

From the next room, Sam heard a dog barking. Someone kept opening the door, then it would slam shut. It was like someone was trying to escape. There was a man's shout followed by a woman's scream that was quickly muffled, like a towel stuffed down her throat.

Tony kept working, unaffected. We make films here, he said.

Is that how you know Delancey?

Tony laughed. Yeah, that's funny, he said. We're in the same business.

At one point the door to the video room flew open and the knob smacked against the wall next to Fat Tony's head.

Motherfucker, he said. He kept counting and sorting.

Behind Fat Tony's shaggy head, Sam saw the flash of a girl in the other room. He saw her lips and throat and she looked at him. Sam was not there. It was like she was already on a screen somewhere in someone else's apartment across the alley. The door slammed shut again.

So? Tony said.

Excuse me?

You didn't come here to watch the Jets game. Can I help you?

Delancey said you could front us a few bundles' worth.

Cocksucker. He never pays in advance.

Sam shrugged.

You're just the bag man, Tony mocked, and laughed.

I guess.

Tony sighed and snorted a big fat line. You all right, bro?

Uh, thanks. Sam said. He leaned over and took one himself. It was dope-fiend ethics, which could mean nothing one minute, then everything the next.

Fat Tony laid the drugs out on the table. Delancey said to

watch him; he was psycho, but harmless. He wasn't dangerous when he didn't need to be, an old biker with long greasy hair shot with gray, red eyes. He wore a dirty baseball cap with half the bill torn off.

All right, here's what I can do for you. Count it and be ready to pay me the five hundred bucks in two weeks. You get a free bag for each bundle of ten.

Looks good to me, Sam said. He took the paper bag and stuffed it into the crotch of his pants.

The door opened again and someone came out pulling up his trousers. He looked familiar, so Sam nodded. Black, with a nice build. Sam laid a couple of lines on the table. Fat Tony gave him a straw. When Sam looked up, rubbing his nose, the black fellow was gone.

Once in a while the buzzer rang, for the street business. No one was supposed to come upstairs, so it pissed Fat Tony off.

This is not good, Fat Tony said. This is a pain in my fucking ass.

Must be a big fucking pain, Sam said.

Fat Tony huffed and faked blowing Sam's lines off the table. Not funny, he said. It's supposed to ring at the place across the hall. No one's supposed to know this place.

Right, Sam said, and did the lines left.

Up at the sink, he washed out his nose with water. Fat Tony had a bowl and his hands stuck wrist-deep in the mix. Now and then he patted his hands together, held a finger to his nose, licked it and showed his teeth.

Sam sat down again, leaned back, lit a cigarette and thought of Eleanor. The dog barked again from the other room, then this strange howl, like a bird dog after something wild. The door started to open, then slammed shut. Someone knocked at the front door.

Do you hear the bell? Fat Tony asked. I don't hear the bell.

Sam was thinking, Let the fat man worry about it. If fucking Jesus came up to him and offered the keys to the universe, Sam would let him wait.

Fat Tony coughed, wiped his hands and headed for the front door. He bent and looked through the keyhole.

Fucking hell, he said. No one's supposed to come here.

Fat Tony hitched up his pants and opened the door. The first punch hit him on the forehead, the second square in the nose. Even before Fat Tony hit the floor, this Spanish kid was inside, kicking the fat man in the gut.

Everything seemed to happen in slow motion. Fat Tony writhed on the floor and the Spanish kid waved his pistol. He was pudgy and had a goatee.

He walked over to the video room door, rapped on it with his gun, then waved everyone into the kitchen: a couple of dazed girls, half-dressed, and some guy with a beard holding a video camera, its red light still blinking.

The Spanish kid laughed and moved everyone against the wall. He gathered up Fat Tony's dope and the money. When he pointed the gun at Sam, his hand darted to his pants where he'd stashed the dope. Sam couldn't help it.

Never looked down the barrel of a gun before, have you, white boy? the kid taunted. What you got in your pants?

Nothing.

The man laughed. That's right, he said, and took off back through the front door.

The whole thing lasted three minutes. Sam put on his hat and left. All he could think about was whether the dope was double-sealed. He'd pissed his pants when the kid shook the gun in his face, but the dope was cool. He sighed, cracked a bag and sniffed it down. He lit a cigarette. The sky above the alley showed a line of clear night sky, no stars or moon. He guessed he might need another place to crash that night.

15

The road north from Basra was paved and rode straight as an arrow from the outskirts of town, marked by the carcass of a dead camel no one had bothered to dispose of. Three klicks past the camel, the road climbed a hill and wound along the ridge top to the west for two hundred yards, and then descended down in a straight line and again headed due north. Jobe's company, the Dark Lords, set up their blockade at the bottom of the north crest.

We can't see what's on the other side, Huebner said to Jobe. We have to keep in close radio contact.

Their orders were to set up a cordon around Basra to block entry and departure. Jobe split the four platoons, with one on either side of the crest, one on top and one on break in reserve, grinding gears of the machines treading terrain into dust, erasing the marks of the earth into a smooth path.

Red, White and Blue, this is Dark Lord Six, over.

Red.

White.

Blue.

Okay fellas, listen up, Jobe said into the radio. Let's go over the rules of engagement: Individual Iraqis can leave, but without weapons. No combat systems are to leave on trucks or otherwise. Roger?

Roger, Red.

Roger, Blue.

Roger, White.

As for nonmilitary vehicles, we search those too. Confiscate weapons.

Dark Lord Six, this is Red One. Do we have a prisoners' policy?

Depends on how much trouble they give us, Jobe cracked.

Sir?

If they're dangerous, they're prisoners. If they have uniforms, they're prisoners. Officers should be segregated from enlisted men. If they talk any shit at all, they're ours. We'll set up a fence. If they're Bedouins, if they have goats, set them free, roger out?

Jobe's orders were answered by a chorus of baas and other animal sounds.

All of the platoons took position and waited for orders. The detail proceeded through the late afternoon of the arrival into the evening. A prisoners' cordon was organized a quarter-mile from the road; an infantry detachment set up a chain link fence and kept guard.

By nine o'clock they had collected over one hundred prisoners. The parade never stopped on the highway, mostly nonmilitary, cars of various makes, often filled to capacity, stuffed with rugs, chairs and other sundries in the trunk. Drivers coming to a careening stop and smiling at the checkpoint soldiers, pulling out handfuls of soiled money.

If they don't pose a threat, let them go, Jobe ordered, and Sergeant Huebner repeated it later when Jobe let him take over the platoon command net to get some sleep. A couple of the platoon leaders were concerned about soldiers confiscating souvenirs.

If you have to take something, then do it, he told the various platoon lieutenants and their subordinates who called in. Don't pack your tanks too full with booty. We still have a job to do, here.

Soldiers took weapons, bayonets and items from the intermittent caravan, but when exhaustion caught up with them, they got bored with this. The road became quiet for several hours during a long descending dusk, this prolonged by heavy cloud cover and smoke blowing north from the oil fires around Kuwait. Huebner called in to each platoon for reports every quarter-hour, and it was exactly at midnight, and dark as pitch, when the Blue Platoon, on the south side of the crest, reported movement.

They don't have their lights on, sir.

Blue, how many are there?

We can't tell from here.

Blue, at what speed are they proceeding?

Pretty fast, sir.

All right, Blue, if they don't stop, let the Red Platoon know on top of the hill. I'll hear it over the platoon command net.

Roger, sir.

Huebner took a deep breath and waited, sitting up in the captain's command space in the turret. Their tank was placed directly at the spot where the slope met level ground at the nearest north position. Suddenly the radio crackled with voices.

Here they come, Red! Repeat, here—they—come!

Roger, Blue, we're ready for them!

Huebner turned his attention toward Morrison coming out of his turret, stretching his arms.

Battle stations, Huebner whispered to him.

Specialist James Morrison heard a ping and felt a tightness in his chest. He had been singing softly in the turret.

Maxwell and the captain were dozing. Jobe had been listening to Morrison; he wanted to imagine it was a radio, in a car. It wasn't really a song, something between a whistle and a hum, a Smokey Robinson melody. The captain's wife liked this song. Morrison's voice was that good, Jobe would remember later when he heard the singing stop.

Sergeant Huebner heard Morrison gurgle, like something caught in his throat, a cough.

Are you all right? Huebner whispered.

Yeah, Morrison said. He touched the bandanna around his neck and it was wet, but he didn't think much of it. He had been drinking water. It helped him to stay awake on watch.

Maxwell heard the whispering between the sergeant and Morrison. Maxwell had his head down at his station and he shifted. He was in the deeper sleep and tried to get back to it.

The captain, waking a little, asked Huebner what was going on.

We got some locals passing by, Huebner said. Went through the first checkpoint and Red's got them now up top.

They went through the first checkpoint? Jobe repeated and rubbed his eyes. Where's that coming from? Can you see anything? Jobe asked Huebner. The captain rubbed his eyes, jerked fully awake. That was gunfire?

Yes sir, said Huebner.

Get on the command net, see if there are any friendlies around, just to be safe. Rogue TOC, this is Dark Lord Six, Sergeant Huebner said, switching his radio to the battalion command frequency. Any friendly activity in the area? Coordinates 345987, contact with unidentified enemy vehicle.

Dark Lord Six, this is Rogue TOC. Not known. The 6th Armored Cavalry is in that area. Will check with them.

Unidentified vehicle, Huebner said. Coming over the ridge.

We're getting more fire, Morrison said. Let's shut the hatches, Sergeant!

Huebner, take your place at the gun, Jobe shouted. Battle ready! Let's go!

Jobe called into the radio, Rogue TOC, this is Dark Lord Six. We are taking small-arms fire . . . possibly enemy activity, coordinates 345987. What are the rules of engagement here?

Respond with minimum necessary force.

Morrison?

Yes, sir?

Load HEAT and prepare to fire.

Morrison reached into ammo reserve for a HEAT round and slammed it into the breech. Pain made him grab his arm under his shoulder, coming away with blood on his hand.

HEAT up, Morrison rasped.

Morrison, are you all right, you got it?

HEAT up, sir. Yes, sir, go.

Jobe checked his scope. Fire! he yelled.

Huebner let go the HEAT round. He switched on his daylight sight. A stream of pure heat shot across the black space, impact, then flames and black smoke.

Red, White, Blue, Jobe called the rest of the company. We took fire and returned it. What's going on up there, Red?

Dark Lord Six, this is Red. Nice shot! We got a vehicle on fire. They were on their way down the hill to you. They are significantly disabled and we are on our way to check it out.

Any resistance?

No, sir, vehicle is on fire. Y'all fucking got them good, sir.

Roger out, Jobe said, and called to the other platoons.

Anyone else report suspicious activity? he asked. He got back two negatives from Blue and White.

Black Six, this is Blue One. There's a caravan of vehicles cresting the ridge.

Have they stopped?

Yes, sir.

All right, proceed with a search and detain status. Proceed with extreme caution. We still don't know where that resistance came from.

Captain, Huebner called out. Troops on the ground. There appears to be a line of vehicles.

Morrison, ready fire, the captain commanded. Rogue TOC, this is Dark Lord Six, with an updated sit rep. Identified troops on the ground, possible enemy prisoners of war. Any word on the 6th, please advise.

Dark Lord Six, this is Rogue TOC, we are on higher's net right now trying to find out the 6th Cavalry's exact location. They should not be far away from you.

Roger, Jobe said. He switched to intercom only. Morrison, Jobe called out again. Ready on ammo?

There was no answer. A deep rasping sounded from Morrison's mouthpiece.

Sergeant! Jobe called out. Check on Morrison! See if he's all right!

Huebner crawled over and saw Morrison with his eyes closed, leaning back away from the gun breech. The glow from the sight yellowed Morrison's skin. Huebner saw the blood and reached for his friend.

James! Huebner yelled. Are you all right?

Morrison opened his eyes, a strange look on his face. I must have got shot, he said. Then he coughed and spat blood.

Where? Dammit? Where?! Sergeant Huebner untied his own bandanna and tried to wipe the blood away. There was too much. He tied the cloth around the corporal's neck.

That won't help! Captain Jobe yelled. He had come down the hatch to help. Look at his arm. His arm! Let's get him out of here! the captain yelled, and then in a regular command voice, Sergeant! he yelled. Get the aid bag!

Huebner found the bag at Morrison's feet. He knelt over Morrison as Captain Jobe struggled with the corporal's clothing.

Where is it, James? Where is it?

Morrison gasped as Huebner tore off his clothing and pressed the place under his arm. Then Morrison went under.

Maxwell! Jobe called out. Take the radio! Call us some medics and get them here. They should be attached to Blue Platoon with the infantry reserve tending to prisoners.

Got it, sir, Maxwell said, and climbed into the captain's hatch.

Tell them to keep their heads down. Now! We'll meet them on the top of the tank. Bring your weapons!

Yes, sir, Maxwell shouted.

Dark Lord Six, this is Red on the hill. Situation is under control. No resistance.

The vehicle on fire was at the front of the line. The flames leaped high and lit up their tank when Jobe and Huebner dragged their fallen comrade out into the open air.

Maxwell was shouting frantically into the radio: Band-Aid, this is Black Six. We need a Medevac. Man down with possible life-threatening injuries! The radio started humming with what sounded like a hot mike. Maxwell relayed the order but couldn't hear the reply. Loud feedback and static. He had to take off his earphones.

Huebner took Morrison under his arms.

C'mon, Morrison, come on, the captain said.

He's gone under, sir, Huebner said.

No, dammit! Jobe shouted. Don't let him!

Band-Aid, this is Black Six, Maxwell repeated into the radio. We need a Medevac. Over.

The medics arrived in two minutes and took over.

Sergeant, one of the medics said to Huebner, and tapped his shoulder. Sergeant, he said and motioned for Huebner to move away, but Jobe intervened.

Sergeant Huebner, he said, you and Maxwell secure the area. Head toward the vehicle on fire and keep this area clear for the helicopter to take off.

The bullet must have entered under his arm, just above his vest, the medic said. It's the only place not protected.

Go now, Jobe said to Huebner.

Maxwell poked his head out. The radio's jammed, someone has a hot mike on at battalion command, he said.

Jobe nodded. Maxwell, he said, take—I mean go with Sergeant Huebner and help secure the area.

The medics were still working on Morrison. When Huebner looked at Morrison laid out on the ground by the tank, he noticed his head was at an odd angle. Huebner walked over, straightened his fallen friend's neck and said, Let's go.

Maxwell handed him his weapon and they walked away. The fire was still burning about one hundred yards up the road toward the crest of the ridge.

As Maxwell and Huebner trudged up the hill through deep sand toward the burning vehicle, there were other American soldiers out there. Dark shadows, the outline of their helmets. Huebner got sick for the first time. His vomiting was like a punch in the chest. It tasted of blood. He had to fight to breathe, wondered for a fleeting second if it was possible to die from it. Maxwell just watched and didn't say anything.

They saw the bus just before it was hit. A screaming came over the sky that lit up the darkness: written in English on its side was Kuwait City and Suburban Transit. The round came in from beyond the other side of the hill, a direct hit. The door had been open for what breeze the desert night might offer. The round entered there and for a moment the hull of the bus expanded from the intensity of the heat. The bus swelled up like a heat blister, then all at once popped, with an audible rush, and exploded into flames. The thin metal of the outer layer melted, oxidized into burning sheets that laid onto the skin of the human occupants like blankets of pure molten heat. The night was filled with the sound of the glass windows shattering, the horrible screams of the occupants burned alive, running from the burning bus and rolling hysterically on the sand.

*   *   *

There were both Iraqi soldiers and civilians; the ones that had survived and had guns, surrendered. Infantry medics swarmed over the area near the still-burning bus. Huebner and Maxwell joined other soldiers from Dark Lord Company and a couple of Bradley crews had started to set up a perimeter to guard the prisoners.

There was a caravan of vehicles behind the bus. Some military vehicles and some not. They could see it now, coming over the ridge, illuminated by the bus they had fired upon.

There was another flash in the darkness. The whole scene flared up for that instant. Everyone dove for the ground and then something else in the caravan was hit.

Shit! Maxwell said. What was that?

Artillery fire. We're in the middle of some kind of firefight, Huebner said, and spat to clear his mouth.

It's ours, Maxwell said. It's got to be ours.

Who else could it be? No one else is firing.

They were among a squad of infantry. One of them had a radio.

Cease fire! he yelled, and nodded to Huebner and Maxwell. Americans on the ground. Repeat, this area is secured, he said. We're taking prisoners. He looked at Huebner and Maxwell, shook his head and cursed. The 6th Armored Cavalry is on the other side of that ridge, he said to them. They don't know we're here!

They sure as hell don't, Maxwell said. Huebner tapped his shoulder, nodded back at the radioman and led Maxwell on.

Give me the radio! Sergeant Huebner commanded.

Rogue TOC, this is Dark Lord Six. We need a sit rep on the 6th Cav. We are receiving fire and we don't know its origin.

Dark Lord Six, this is Cav Six Command. We have orders to proceed to the Euphrates Bridge and break up any resistance on the way.

Cav Six, this area is in the process of being secured. We don't need any backup. Will call if we do.

Got it, Dark Lord Six. We'll tighten up our lines.

Yeah, do that, would you! Maxwell cracked.

Roger, out, Huebner said. He handed the radio back to the infantryman and thanked him. He saw an enemy soldier lying spread-eagled. He had on dirty brown boots and green desert fatigues. His helmet lay by his head. His skin, burned black, tight on the bones of his face. Beside him there was a carpet of perfect green grass, like a golf course green, lit up by the fires.

He looks like an officer, Maxwell said.

Yeah, Huebner finally said, he's got the stripes.

Maxwell walked ahead. Huebner let him go. His head felt light. Huebner saw another man. This one was older. His head was dirty and mucked with wet sand. It could have been Huebner's dad. His helmet had come off and landed a few feet away. A piece of his head, where his brow should have been, was gone. Huebner took a gulp of water from a bottle he kept in the pocket in the side of his pants. He couldn't hold it down. The water hit the back of his throat and then flew back out, speckling his boots. He wiped his mouth. Huebner heard a gunshot, then he saw Maxwell walking toward him through the darkness.

In the land of the blind, Maxwell said, the man with the biggest gun is king. He looked wired.

Maxwell? Huebner asked, What's going on?

I just got one, he said. He came really close. Maxwell sounded excited; his eyes were crystalline.

Huebner pushed him away and Maxwell slipped in the sand, lost his balance and fell on his backside, right next to the old man on the ground.

Hey, Maxwell said, waving his arms. What the fuck you do that for? His helmet had fallen down over his eyes and he flailed his arms.

The wind blew sand all around them. For a minute, Huebner could not see him, even though Maxwell was right at his feet. There were a lot of civilian Iraqis around.

A few had gathered around the corpse. Two Iraqi men looked at Huebner, at his weapon, and at Maxwell lying on the sand. Huebner returned the look and the Iraqis averted their eyes. Rags of smoke rose from the wreckage by a row of dunes at the side of the road that was perpendicular to the ridge.

Maxwell tried to get up. One of them wasn't dead, he said. I had to do it.

What do you mean? Huebner asked, and looked back at Maxwell. Then he took his hand and helped him to his feet.

I swear to God he had his hands on his rifle, Maxwell said.

What the hell are you talking about? Huebner asked.

He had a gun, I swear.

Did he fire at you? Huebner asked.

No, I had my weapon and I shot him, Maxwell said. He had a wound in his chest. I could see his ribs.

You shot him because he had a gun? Or because he was dying? Which?

They got Morrison, Maxwell said. They got one of ours and now we got one of theirs. A tear welled in his eye and he wiped it away.

Fuck, Huebner said. Show me.

They moved toward the head of the line and as they did, the Iraqis moved away, all but one of the two men that had been looking at them.

What the hell you looking at? Maxwell said to him.

Huebner looked at Maxwell, then at the man. C'mon, Huebner said to Maxwell, put an arm around his shoulder and pulled him away.

Huebner saw the body and the man's face. He was swarthy and dark-skinned with a few days' growth of beard. One eye was closed and there was a grimace on his face.

I don't know if he's dead, Huebner said.

I shot him, Maxwell said now. He was alive and I shot him.

Huebner took the man's Kalashnikov. It had fallen out of his grasp, half-covered in the sand. He held the weapon up to Maxwell's chest as if to bar his path.

We should call a medic, Huebner said.

You mean a coroner, Maxwell said.

Huebner knelt down. The Iraqi wasn't dead but would be soon. There was another explosion then and everything turned to brown.

Sergeant Huebner came to and saw dark shapes bursting into bright burning stars on the ground. He watched in awe for a minute, not understanding what he was seeing: they were people on fire. Trails came off them. They were like stars bursting and rolling on the sand. Huebner, for the first time, thought that it was entirely possible that he would die here.

One of the burning people was running toward him. Huebner saw the shadow of a man's features. He had his thoab around him, just the white sheet, but that burned away as he ran and then he was naked. Other people rolled on the ground, but this man came toward Huebner. He was screaming, frantic with agony.

It was like this man wanted to show him something. Huebner took a few steps back. The man slowed down in the sand, then just stopped running and fell. He crumpled into the sand and the outline of a human became a little fire, like someone had built a campfire in the sand.

Huebner wasn't hit, but the explosion had sent him tumbling down the road into a ditch. His pants were torn and when he first got up, his knee buckled.

A few yards away an Iraqi soldier lay, burnt to black, hands and arms shrunken from the heat and pulled up close to his body as if in a last-ditch, desperate effort to defend himself against an indomitable enemy.

Huebner must have been still staring at the dead Iraqi when Captain Jobe walked up. He had Maxwell with him.

Looks like you got the best of him, Maxwell said.

Huebner winced, turned toward the dead man, and knelt down.

You all right, Sarge?

Yes, sir. That bus just blew up, Huebner said. He picked up the dead Iraqi's weapon, held it for a few seconds, feeling the heft of it. He ejected the ammo, then threw it into the still-burning bus.

I guess he won't be needing that, Jobe commented.

Yes, sir, Huebner said, and looked at Jobe. We were getting shot at by our own men, weren't we, Captain? Huebner asked.

Not ours, the 6th Armored Cavalry. Honest mistake, Jobe

said. He looked up and tugged at Huebner's shoulder. The thing that pisses me off is that they're ten miles away.

Ten miles?

At least. They get a fucking bleep on their radar and fire. Fucking pussies, Jobe said, and spat. Sergeant, he said meeting Huebner's eyes, they took Morrison away.

Huebner nodded. His knee hurt; that was all. With a stiff-legged gait, he walked ten steps away and stared off to where the fires burned, clenching and unclenching his left fist.

It was a pleasant false spring morning in early March. The sunshine and church bells Sam woke up listening to made him feel lonely. He decided to visit his grandmother. Short of money for the bus fare, he rode his bicycle over the Brooklyn and out to the Verrazano Bridge. There was no bike lane so once he got on the bridge he was in the traffic. Cars beeped and swerved, then sped by, going sixty and seventy miles per hour. It was a harrowing ride. After Staten Island he had to take Route 1 through Jersey because bikes were not allowed on the Turnpike. It took all day and he didn't make it to New Brunswick until it was almost dark. He was tired and hungry. He had not thought this out very well.

He figured he could get her some flowers. She would be glad to see him, would feed him and treat him like it was nothing out of the ordinary. She always offered him money; maybe this time he would bring himself to take it. The last time he had seen her, he'd brought Eleanor and Grandma told stories about her own romance with his grandfather. She was frail and her voice wavered, but her eyes shone with gratitude that they'd come. She told them the story of how Grandpa been shot down over Germany, killed a couple of Nazis, stole a car and was a hero for that.

That morning, Clayton had called to ask Sam if he wanted to join him at a protest at a parade for some of the soldiers who were returning. Sam said he didn't want to go. Clayton asked him if he was all right.

Sam told Clayton how he was worried about his brother. About him having to kill people. About what that would do to him and how he would come back. He talked about his uncle Pete. He admitted again that he had felt the urge to go over there himself, to be with his brother if he was getting shot at.

Maybe you were just worried you were going to lose him, Clayton said. I would be.

Sam didn't say much then, but he could stop thinking about this now. His brother was his best friend. What had his dad said? You'll never have anyone as close as your brother. You have got to be on his side.

Clayton didn't say anything about how often Sam had been getting high, but the implication was clear. Sam thought about what he had heard at the twelve-step meetings.

I didn't get clean at first either, one man had said to Sam. But coming to these meetings sure did spoil my get-high, he said.

Sam told himself he wanted to see his grandma, that he just wanted to get out of the city and try to stay clean for a single day. He could not remember the last time he had spent an entire day without getting high. Did jail count? Had it really been since the summer and now it was what, April? That's nine months. He had always smoked a lot of reefer; for years he had gotten high almost daily. But the white powders were different.

He crossed into New Jersey and on Route 1 he saw a Channel lumber store and it reminded him of his father, the smell of the lumber. There was a market next door with fruit and vegetables. Sam had virtually no money. He had not eaten. All the fruit was out of season and expensive. There were some plums and Sam was able to get a half dozen of them for the dollar in nickels and dimes he counted out. He put them bulging in his pockets and ate as he rode on past the old places like the lumber yard that he remembered going to with his dad, being bored and playing games with his brother, running and hiding in the stacks. He always loved the smell of the wood, even though it also reminded him of his father's temper and the times he had smacked him and Smith around.

The taste of the first plum reminded him, however, of his mother, when she was young and he was maybe four, before school, when he was first allowed to walk around by himself and play with his friends. He would run as fast as he could and sometimes fall down. And he would go to his mother. She would sit him down on the toilet, kneel before him and kiss the scrape. Often he would already have a Band-Aid there that he had torn in half in the fall. She sprayed it with Bactine.

She said, Hold on, Sam. This will make it better.

He did not always trust his father; he was scary, he didn't always know what he was doing, prone to rages and drunkenness, but his mother at that age, he trusted her. Then she was gone. All he had then was his brother, Smith. Maybe Clayton was right.

I would sure be scared if it was my brother, he had said.

Scared of what? Sam asked.

And he was surprised by the answer. He had expected something else.

I would be scared that he was going to die.

He had started to ask him to say it again, like he didn't hear Clayton right. But he did and he didn't want to hear it again.

He glided off the highway and through South Plainfield. This was where his mother had been born and where she was buried. He went to her grave, in the cemetery yard behind the golf course where he had ridden sleds with Smith and come home with numb feet, that his mother rubbed by the baseboard heaters. Sam had found baseball cards lost by another kid in the space between the heater and the wall. There had been a plum tree in the yard of the apartment house where they lived when he was very young. He had gone with his mother with his Easter basket full of ripe plums. His mother had a paper bag and Smith had his own Easter basket full of them. There was a lady down the street who had a yard full of flowers and plants and fruit trees. She was very old; Sam remembered the white hair and the ropy veins in her leathery tanned skin. She showed his mother how to make jam from the plums and they ate it with their peanut butter in sandwiches. It was a time when his father's drinking was at its worst, when he had looked up maybe and realized that he was married at twenty-five with two kids.

Before he went to war Smith had told Sam he had done the math.

The math? What are you talking about?

I was born just six months after they were married. Mom was pregnant when they got married. I was an accident, Smith said.

Fuck, we're all accidents, Sam told him.

In the cemetery, the trees were just beginning to bud; Sam recognized the dank smell as he rode by the pond where they had caught tadpoles as kids. They had put them in an aquarium on the porch because his mother wouldn't let them bring them into the house. Mom and Dad had a fight. She opened the door quickly, there was a crash, a flow of water onto her feet and then slimy things on her skin and then dozens of tadpoles on the dirt beside the porch, dying there, thirsty. Sam wanted to go and save them. He had heard the crash and he knew what it was, but he was scared. He imagined all this when he heard his mother's reaction.

There's nothing we can do. They will die anyway, Smith said to him.

Sam sat on his bike there in the cemetery where his mother was buried and he threw some of the plum pits there in the dirt by her grave. He remembered the time of the plums as the last time before she had started to go away from the house, leave the yard all the way, when she had sat gazing at the dust by the window in the sunlight and Sam would call to her and she would not answer, but just sit and stare.

There was a bridge under an overpass as he passed the back way toward the Buccleuch Mansion park. It was busier here, with constant traffic on the bridge up above and also on the road Sam was on. He went under the bridge and for a moment with the noise and the shade of the bridge way, he could not see or hear anything. He rode blindly and held on to the handlebars. He had a feeling that he was being carried in someone's hands; he had a feeling of grace. It felt something like what he had always wanted to reach getting high, that moment of weightlessness when he could just disappear.

He had also heard someone speaking of something like this at one of the meetings. Of grace replacing the high.

You can call it whatever you want, said a longhaired woman with a tattoo on her shoulder. Call it God if you want to.

Sam had never believed in anything really, not since he lost his mother, he guessed. He believed in his brother and now he was going to war and could die.

Sam had a pack of cigarettes and he smoked one when he finally got to the mansion. He had hated cigarettes his whole life and never smoked them because they reminded him of his father and it felt half like treachery and half like a conciliation with his father. Now he always had a pack, though when people asked him he said he was not a smoker. Just like when he was confronted, he said he was not an addict. The cigarette made him feel dizzy and he felt the lack of drugs in his legs and arms. He thought of what he had heard a guy named Craig say at one of the meetings:

I didn't want to get high anymore. I would do all my drugs the night before planning to quit the next day, but then I would get up in the morning and against my own will I would be going off to get high.

Sam had approached the man who said this. He was older and looked like some kind of Irish mob guy, broken nose, roughly handsome. He was from Hell's Kitchen and had run with the Westies, but now he had been clean for five years. He had the most clean time of anyone Sam had met. Sam had asked for his phone number and asked him to be his sponsor. But Sam had never had the nerve to call him. He looked in his wallet now and the number was there on a little piece of pink paper he had torn off a flyer for somebody's band. When he put out the cigarette, he thought of what Craig had said after to him specifically.

When you want to get high, man, call me. There's no shame in that.

Now was the time Sam should call him. But he was in Jersey

and he had no money. He could call collect and the guy would probably meet him somewhere and buy him a cup of coffee and something to eat. That's what they did for each other at those meetings. But Sam didn't call. There was a moment when he lit another cigarette, when he thought he might actually do it. There was a pay phone in the park by the swings, but he turned and walked in the other direction.

Behind him the old Buccleuch Mansion loomed up on the hill over the river. Grandma's house, the converted carriage house, was closed. Sam tried all the doors, thought for a moment that she was dead in there. But when he looked in a window everything was gone; the house was empty. He pushed in the cellar window that had been without a sure latch since he was a kid, went up the dark stairs and walked around empty rooms that smelled of dust, mothballs and emptiness. There were a few light spaces on the wall between the windows where pictures of the family had been. He watched a police car go by with the sirens on. The lights came in through the windows and went all around the room. It reminded Sam of how he had sat up watching the cars pass in the dark this way as a child. This was the house where he had been first brought home from the hospital as a baby.

He said hello to a neighbor who surprised him walking up. She was a middle-aged woman fresh from the beauty shop wearing Madras shorts and a supercilious grin. The neighbor told him his grandmother had been moved into a nursing home by his father, Zeke.

Didn't he tell you? the neighbor asked.

I've been away, Sam said.

Are you the one in the Army? the neighbor asked. Zeke said he had a son in the Army.

No, that's not me, Sam said, and he left it at that.

Sam followed the winding trail that led away from the Buccleuch Mansion through the tall grass down to the river. There by the dirt bank that fell away into the water by a tuft of earth, a couple of old wooden chairs were still there from his childhood. When they were young he and Smith would go down there with an elder, usually Grandma. For Sam the sounds of the river, the unseen crickets chirping in the grass, the coursing flow of the water, the wind through the leaves and the creaking branches of the oaks and the hickory trees that lined the waterside, would always be associated with his grandmother's voice, with these family stories, of country and duty for the men and for the women.

Sam had never come alone before; he thought of the last time the family was together, the death of his grandfather, the funeral held here when he was thirteen. Grandpa had surely loved this home; it was truly a beautiful piece of land, but he had been ambivalent about its history and what that meant to *his* father. Old Will's father, the boy's great-grandfather, had taken the job as caretaker for the mansion in 1910. He taught the boys the history of the place, the place where Washington met with his army sometime around their crossing of the Delaware. He showed the boys the marks the soldiers' swords had made on the banisters as they'd passed up and down the stairway. And Sam remembered the Fourth of July days when Great Grandpa gave Smith and Sam flags to wave at the parade; he remembered the burning flag and when Grandma was sick that day.

Grandma's stories went all the way back to Great Grandpa's father, the one named August who had immigrated from Germany and fought out West in the Indian wars. She guessed he had witnessed or survived something terrible out there and come back no longer the same.

Your great-grandfather is a very patriotic man, she told them. Character skips a generation, she said, and Sam knew she was speaking of her own husband. Every son goes against the father. Sam had come here looking for something, someone to talk to, something that would remind him of who he was and maybe what that had meant to him once. This house, this place had always done that for him before, but now it was empty.

He felt hurt that his father had not told him about his grandma. He had always been close to her as a child, but he guessed he wasn't trustworthy just now and his father had left it out, or maybe he just didn't want any lip about having to put her away. It must have hurt Zeke to have to do it. Grandma had been the first one to listen to him and Smith and to talk to them about what they wanted to do with their lives, even as children, and as they got older when Smith joined the Army and when Sam moved to New York to write.

Smith had gone to the war and become a soldier. He had taken up the family legacy. Sam felt the same patriotism as his brother. But where Smith was a fighter, Sam had never been. It wasn't that he was afraid. It was true that he had never liked physical contact. He had not been in a fight since he was a boy. Once he had choked a schoolmate and had been horrified by the sound of his friend trying to get his breath back. After that he had been punched a few times, but he never punched back.

While Smith was fascinated by the military legacy, Sam was just as fascinated by the stories that Grandma had told of Pete rebelling against the war and related to the ambivalence that his grandpa Will expressed about this patriotic legacy of their family. He knew that there was a connection to his brother going to war and his own losing his way. It tore him apart to think of the killing. He and his brother had both come of age in the aftermath of Vietnam. Both of them wanted to be like their uncle Pete—Smith wanted to be a hero and serve his country; Sam wanted to have his voice heard, to change the world—neither wanted to end up like him.

For Smith it was duty, right or wrong, the old patriotic standard; for Sam it was something different. His own father had said he was too sensitive, that he was like his mother, that he felt too much. And look what happened to her was the implication.

Maybe there was nothing wrong with that. Maybe there was nothing wrong with who he was. He just needed to find his own way to make a life for himself. Drugs had once been a sign of rebellion to Sam; now they were just an escape. Some people think that once you realize how bad drugs are for you, then you will stop. Right. But if you could do that, Sam thought, then you weren't an addict. Sam knew he was now. He didn't get high because he wanted to anymore; he did because he had to. It had happened so quickly. He had reached the point where he knew he had to stop. But he had not found the way to do it yet. What was it going to take?

16

Sergeant Huebner dreamed they were going home. It was the
early morning hours after Morrison had been taken away. The
air was humid, with no wind and the air harsh and filled with
smoke from a munitions fire the infantry had set with confiscated weapons a half-mile off. He stretched out on the rear of
the tank. He had not intended to sleep. It was Jobe's watch and
Maxwell had gone below. As Huebner drifted off, he could hear
Jobe talking quietly on the radio. He was gossiping with other
officers, going over the last few days' events, keeping an ear to
the company net for new developments. The area north of
Kuwait was filled with Iraqis fleeing the capital city. Activity was
heavy in every sector. There was talk of air strikes to control the
situation.

Huebner dreamed they were in a last caravan, headed back
down through Saudi toward the port in Dammam. Captain Jobe
was talking on the radio in the dream. There was a problem and
Jobe was laughing. One of the platoons had found a dead Iraqi
and used parts of his corpse to decorate their tank. It wasn't
anyone in their company. Jobe could laugh about it. It was a

fucked-up thing to do. It made Huebner think about what he'd been through. Parts of his dream were surreal and other parts were clear. This was one of the second parts. How much of the war had he seen? How could he judge another soldier's experience? It was terrible to do such a thing to another human being, surely, but every soldier's war was different. Huebner had killed and had seen death. He had come to the war expecting, what? It was hard to remember how he had pictured it beforehand.

We can't let them just drive the tank in like that, Jobe was saying, laughing. With some burned, dead sand nigger hanging on to the main gun. They would be court-martialed for sure. Or would they?

What each soldier sees never adds up to a whole story. Huebner could not forget the look on the face of the Iraqi soldier he'd taken prisoner, the one who'd been through the air war. The Iraqi had been through life and death and back again. Most of the war was just little snapshots that did not add up to any coherent narrative.

Huebner woke up with the sun in his eyes and the smell of gunpowder tickling his nostrils. The radio blared static, then stopped, and he could hear Jobe's high-pitched, exasperated voice and other random officers reporting in from different sectors.

What are our orders now? Huebner asked.

Jobe turned to Huebner and mouthed, Good morning, with a sarcastic smile. He waved at a buzzing horsefly and slapped the back of his neck. I can't believe this fucking shit, he said to himself, under his breath. Jobe raised his eyebrows and put his hand over the radio mike. I've been trying to send in sit rep for the last two hours. The frequencies are jammed like Kennedy Airport at rush hour.

Huebner nodded and stretched while Jobe went back to work on the radio.

A voice broke in, If they are just on the road sitting there or standing around without weapons, if they maintain a nonaggressive attitude, don't attack. If there is a crescent, that's the sign for medics. The voice was suddenly lost in static, then seconds later broke in again clearly. Repeat, Do not engage them.

There's no crescent, said another voice in reply.

Use your judgment then, came the answer back.

What?

Exactly!

Jobe switched frequencies and the radio went back to static. It's been like this for two hours now. We're not the only ones who are busy this morning, Jobe said, and sighed. Huebner, yawning, reached into the Sponson box on the back of the tank for a bottle of water. He looked around.

He turned to the sound of Maxwell's voice. You think it's so hot because of all those burning oil wells we keep hearing about on the radio? Maxwell asked. He had come out and was doing light calisthenics on the sand ten feet away from the tank. Jumping jacks and now dropping for pushups.

The oxygenless heat, the awful glare of the sun and the suffocating suck of the wind seemed to stop the movement of life itself, so that seeing things moving was strange: a lone Bedouin with three mangy sheep picking through the carnage of the caravan battlefield, a couple cur dogs barking at his heels, or the scrub pinelike scraps of tree life that dotted the wadi, the choked to gray grass and withered weeds; everything seemed to be utterly without vitality or godly purpose, like survivors of some awful vengeance for man-hubris, evidence of terrible transgressions.

Smoke wafted amidst the other bad smells of things burning all around them. The 6th Cavalry's bombardment of the area had ceased and the Dark Lord Company had things under tenuous control. As the situation had deteriorated under fire from their own forces, they fell back to their lines until the area was completely secured. In the confusion some of the company's ranks had fired on and taken out whatever vehicles in the line had aggressive capabilities. There were reports that some of these vehicles had exchanged fire with the American forces.

The dark night had given way to this hot, airless morning. The nightmare of last night left everyone uneasy. Everyone in the company, to a man, was exhausted and on edge. At least five Iraqi T-72s had been destroyed and two of their APCs. More prisoners had been taken and gathered in the chain link fence compound off from the road. They were given water and MREs. A few of them were scared and crying. They had to be reassured that they wouldn't be executed.

Jobe pulled on Huebner's shirt and held up one finger to wait. There was static again and Jobe sighed.

If I can't get through, Jobe said, I want you to go down and check on the S-2, the officer in charge of intelligence. He's going through some interrogations. He's trying to get a clear idea of what we've got here to follow up my report. I'd like to know what he finds out too.

Roger, sir. Huebner nodded. Should I go now?

Let me see if I can join you. Give me five more minutes here.

Roger, sir, Huebner said, and walked off behind the tank to find a place to piss.

Once dawn had come, more and more Iraqis came streaming out of the desert to surrender, in cars, in small trucks and on foot.

Most of these were not military and just wanted to be assured of safe passage.

If they're not dangerous, just send them on their way, Captain Jobe finally said. He wiped his brow and shook his head in frustration. I don't know what they're so fucking scared of. Then he laughed and looked around at the tanks gathered around the ridge. Forget what I just said, fellas.

Weapons confiscated from the enemy were hastily thrown into a big pile. Some of the soldiers were going through and taking off the bayonets for souvenirs until Lieutenant Holmes ordered them to quit. Someone called him a hard-ass, but the order was obeyed. When Jobe got an order off the command net to destroy the whole cache, Holmes turned out to be the company demolition expert. His platoon loaded the weapons onto an Iraqi truck, which was then booby-trapped with three charges of C4 plastic explosive.

Those who were injured on either side had been attended to, the serious ones evacuated. All that was left was for Jobe to report to command what had happened.

Static again interrupted Jobe's radio transmission. As he buttoned his pants, Huebner watched a wrecked T-72, with its turret exploded off, gone, nowhere in sight, smoke curling out of the hole where it had been. Its tracks were unhinged from the body and the tank's nose was buried in deep wet sand.

Jobe rapped his hand on the metal casing of the turret and cursed. All that came from the radio for a few moments was static, then suddenly it broke and a voice was shouting:

Your orders are to shoot anything that runs!

Anything with a gun?

Anything that runs.

Is that people? Or tanks . . . more static and then another, unidentified voice on the radio broke in and Jobe threw up his hands in exasperation. They were waving a fucking white bed-sheet, a voice was shouting. On a freaking broomstick? It was the same conversation as earlier. Would you call that a fucking atti-tude of aggression?

Jobe turned and looked at Huebner, waving his arm toward the prisoners' compound.

Who should I report to? Huebner called out.

Captain Mickey Kross, Jobe answered, and turned back to the radio, saying over his shoulder, he's an old friend of mine.

Huebner suspected Jobe was trying to keep him busy, after Morrison's death. He didn't mind. He felt numb. The prisoners' compound was three hundred yards away through deep sand. He took it at a slow jog just to clear his head. Most of the men were awake, but they were still lying in the sand, a few standing and talking. The thought flashed in Huebner's mind that the man who had killed Morrison could be there, lying on the sand, look-ing up at the sky now. He tried to put it out of his mind, but it would not go away.

There were sentries along the outside of the chain link fence that had been hastily put up. He found Captain Mickey Kross talking to a prisoner. He stood by the open gateway of the fence with his arms behind his back, erect. He was a short man and his ears stuck out. Kross had a squeaky voice and penetrating dead-on blue eyes that twinkled.

Jobe sent you? he asked.

Yes, sir.

I guess you guys will be pulling out soon. You haven't got your new orders?

No, sir.

Yep, Kross said, and flashed a goofy smile. He blinked once but never took his eyes off Huebner's face.

Huebner had to look away and he was glad when a couple of sentries walked up. He felt exposed. The sentries had a prisoner with them, an officer.

This one speaks pretty good English, one of them spoke up.

Just leave him with me and the sergeant, Kross said, nodding at Huebner.

The prisoner's hands were bound in front of him with a plastic tie. Kross turned his steel blues toward this man, looking him up and down.

You speak English? Kross asked.

The prisoner nodded, squinting in the harsh sun, sweat breaking out on his bare forehead.

What kind of unit are you with?

I am the leader of a rifle brigade, the Iraqi said.

Sniper?

The Iraqi nodded.

Huebner tensed and he rubbed his weapon's stock. He had brought Morrison's M-16 with him. This man could have killed his best buddy. There was no way of being sure, but something about the way the man returned his look now, proud, defiant and direct, made the hair on the back of his neck prickle. He had not expected anything like this. It was an irrational line of thinking, but he could not stop himself. His heart started beating really fast and he felt a sudden hunger pang, realizing he had not had anything to eat since dinner the night before, since everything had happened. He felt a wave of nausea. He opened up his mouth to try to breathe deep.

Kross went on with the questioning. Kross asked the man what he was doing here, and the strength of his unit.

Do you have any special equipment? Kross asked.

You have confiscated all of our weapons, the Iraqi said, and then looked at Huebner and raised an eyebrow.

Answer the fucking question! Huebner said harshly, and Kross put up his hand Huebner had surprised even himself. He took a step back, still self-consciously cradling Morrison's weapon in his hands. It was an A2 from the M-16 family, with a longer, thicker barrel, brown hand guards, standard issue, with a thirty-round magazine. A good marksman of Special Forces rank can hit a target at five hundred meters. Huebner could pull the trigger, hold it for just three seconds, the time it took this man to breathe once, maybe twice, and he would be dead before he fell. Huebner looked at the prisoner. He had a thick mustache, high cheekbones, his face streaked with black oily grease and smudges of dirt.

Kross's voice brought Huebner back to the moment.

They don't tell us much, Kross said. They were all given the wrong information. Some of them did not even know of the cease-fire, Kross said.

You are from the Republican Guard? Kross asked.

That's right.

Why did you break the cease-fire?

We defended ourselves. We had many civilians, many scared people. Our orders were to back travel to Baghdad. We are to protect Saddam, he said. He orders us not to fight, to come back to Baghdad and protect him from attack. We must go back, the Iraqi said, and wiped his forehead.

Kross asked him if he had directly exchanged fire yesterday

and the man nodded. We shot at the American tanks with our rifles, he said.

Huebner swallowed, watching intently. He looked at the man's hands and his neck, his Adam's apple when he spoke. He pictured the man's neck under his boot, the Iraqi gagging.

The Iraqi looked at Kross, then at Huebner, and he smiled. Just the one corner of his mouth. Huebner would swear he did. Huebner, very self-consciously, took a breath. He didn't feel angry. He felt sociopathic. He felt no feelings at all toward this man. He just wanted him dead, now. Huebner wanted to kill him.

Huebner actually made a step forward and flexed his left hand. The Iraqi officer blinked his eyes and there was the subtlest flinch to this movement. He covered it up, but Huebner had seen it, sensed like an animal of prey, the fear. His chance had been there and now it was gone. The sun went behind a cloud and a belch of smoke from a Hummer someone had started up passed between them. Huebner held himself back.

It was a very long second. He had never felt anything like this before. He wanted to kill this man so badly it sickened him. He took a step back and had to catch his breath. Another tiny hint of a smile appeared again at the corner of the man's mouth. He had noticed; he knew that Huebner would do nothing.

Kross had waved for the sentries, meanwhile, and they walked up and they took the man away, each leading him by an arm. As he walked away, back to his place among the faceless others, the man never took his eyes off Huebner until Huebner turned away.

Kross started talking in his squeaky voice. He didn't look at Huebner now. He told Huebner there was no clear picture of what had happened yesterday except the obvious things he already knew.

You can tell Jobe my report will be basically the same as his, Kross said, and when Huebner did not answer, Kross spoke up. Sergeant, he said.

Uh, yes, sir. I will tell Captain Jobe, sir.

Walking away, back through the deep sand, the sun had come out and it was hot again. Someone handed Huebner a canteen; he took a drink. He wanted to explain everything to Kross, but he was more grateful he didn't have to. What he had thought was irrational, was random. It was just as likely that Morrison was killed by friendly fire as by the enemy. There was no way that this man could have done it. If he had, there was no way of knowing. Still there was no denying what he had just felt and what had passed between them. If he had killed him or tried to, it would have been wrong. It would have been murder.

Huebner wished it all made more sense. The one thing he had expected of war was that it would be demonstrative, that one thing would lead to another, but it was nothing like that. That was the last thing it was. Maybe this man had killed Morrison. He could not be sure about anything.

The tanks in his company were taking their positions in formation. The incredible, heart-pounding loudness of the engines enveloped Huebner. It was numbing, and comforting somehow. Huebner knew it well and he was glad to be lost in it again. He saw Jobe in the turret in their place behind the point in the arrow formation. He ran through the deep sand toward Jobe. They were finally leaving this place behind.

Sam found a back door of the Buccleuch Mansion unlocked and went inside. It smelled of dust, mildewed wood and old family memories from his childhood. He took a nap there, woke up and stole a collection of pocket watches. It was a stained wood box, darkened with age, six by eight inches, that closed with a clasp. He slipped it into his jacket pocket and headed for a pawn shop in town. It was just closing. He made up some unnecessary story about his grandfather dying.

I hear a lot of stories, this old man said.

He offered Sam a drink of cheap whiskey and Sam drank it down gratefully.

Y'know, some of these are pretty old. They are souvenirs of military service from the inscriptions.

Sam shrugged his shoulders.

The man gave him $126. This was what it amounted to, the whole family legacy of service to country. He had heard his grandfather talk about these pocket watches: there was one that his own grandfather had gotten at a reunion of veterans of the Indian wars. There were others from different wars, donated by the local VFW chapter for the permanent collection at the Buccleuch Mansion museum. Smith loved to hear these stories growing up; something in his eyes would shine. Sam never got it. He wanted to think taking the collection was like an upturned middle finger, a big fuck-off. But what he defaced was not his family legacy but himself. He knew this.

He spat on the ground, waiting for the New York bus on the corner. He counted the money five times. He got on the bus, left his bike there on the corner, lying in the little median of grass near the parking lot of a Pizza Hut franchise. He had caught this same bus to New York since he was young, with his grandma, with Uncle Pete, with Zeke and Smith. He remembered going to a Yankees twinight doubleheader the year they played at Shea

Stadium. Thurman Munson hit a home run to win the first game in the fourteenth inning.

What is this word, effigy? the man sitting next to Sam asked.

Sam ignored him. It wasn't crowded. Sam had checked him out and the man had seen him and put up the paper real fast, like he didn't like to be seen.

He spoke to Sam from behind the paper. The whole thing was strange. The headline had to do with United Nations forces routing the Iraqis and chasing them down.

This word effigy, it's in the news. They're burning President Bush.

No, I think it means more than that. You burn something, like a dummy.

A burning dummy, the man said and rattled the paper. I don't think so. He lowered the paper and looked across at Sam, who shook his head. You burn something in effigy. You don't burn the effigy.

So? Sam asked.

It could be a flag or a country, or the grass.

The grass?

The Indians, the man next to Sam insisted. They burned the grass as they left when they were being chased by the cavalry.

The Indians?

Yes. The man nodded.

Are you talking to me? Sam smiled.

Are you laughing?

Yeah, I am, Sam said.

Good. The man smiled back.

Didn't they burn the grass so the cavalry's horses didn't have it to eat? Isn't that different? Sam asked.

I don't know.

The man had on an old-fashioned fedora, gray. It seemed out of keeping with the rest of him. It was an immaculate hat. There was a feather in the band. He had on a soiled white shirt. And an ill-fitting suit jacket, worn at the cuffs. They were going past the swamplands, soon in the Lincoln Tunnel, then Port Authority. When the door opened, the wind came in and smelled of diesel. He looked for the man to say good-bye, but he had vanished. The bus driver was staring at him from down the aisle. Sam was the only one left on the bus.

When Sam got back to the Sherman Hotel, Fat Tony was there waiting for him.

What are you doing here? Sam asked.

Delancey told us you would be here. What ya think? You got the money you owe me?

Sam walked to the closet and reached into a coat pocket.

I got half, he said.

I'll make you a deal, Fat said, and took the money.

What?

You do me this favor, I'll give you ten bags.

A bundle free. And forget what I owe?

Don't be fucking silly.

Okay, Sam said.

You haven't even asked what I need from you.

You got anything on you? Sam asked.

Fat Tony smiled and tossed him a bag. So, you get to borrow the car, Tony said. It's downstairs. Chico's in there waiting for you.

Who's Chico?

Unh, unh, unh, Fat said, and waved his forefinger in front of his face.

So Sam went and drove Chico up to Harlem. They talked about basketball, the Knicks and Ewing's knees. Weren't the Nets looking a lot better these days with Fitch as the coach? Sam asked.

Right, Chico said, and laughed. The Nets. White boys always wantin' to talk about the fucking Nets. The Nets fucking suck and they always will.

Sam drove him to 143rd Street off Amsterdam. A shabby apartment house with windows broken out, a lot of scary characters shifted around. Chico got out and said, Wait here. Sam locked the doors all around, sniffed the rest of the dope Fat Tony had given him. He smoked a cigarette and fell into a nod.

Chico came running back out, had to bang on the window to rouse Sam.

Open the fucking door, he said.

Chico threw a gun into the backseat. Sam saw it and Chico gave him a look and said, Go!

Sam took off, banging fenders with the car in front.

Chico laughed.

By Chico's order Sam stopped in the middle of the Harlem River Bridge where Chico got out and tossed the gun into the water. With no traffic, Sam heard the sound it made. He waited there, but Chico waved him to drive on, so Sam went.

Later, he dropped the car off at Fat's place downtown. The police were there; the place had been turned upside down. Sam walked in and was arrested. He spent the night in a holding cell waiting to be questioned, staring at the four walls, reading a paperback he had with him that a cop let him keep, *The Disenchanted* by Budd Schulberg, a novel of the last days of F. Scott

Fitzgerald. Sam was glad he had left his stash at home, but was left to jones all night until the cops brought him in sometime after dawn. There was a detective named Officer Riley.

So what do you do? he asked Sam when he sat down, a hardwood chair behind a painted green metal table, the same paint as on the caged windows. The day outside was rainy and windswept, April.

I'm a writer and a college professor.

Don't bullshit me, kid, I'm tired, Officer Riley said. He indeed had the biggest bags under his eyes Sam had ever seen and was drinking coffee that smelled burned. You want some coffee? he asked Sam, but Sam said, No, and pulled out his faculty ID to show the man.

So what the fuck happened to you? Riley asked, and his manner jarred Sam.

What do you mean?

Says here on your sheet you got picked up just last week and now you're pulled in on possible connection to a drug and murder one rap.

Uh, c'mon, I hardly know these guys, Sam said, shivering a little when the cop got up, opened the window and spat a mouthful of the bad coffee down into the alley.

You're going to have to do better than that, Riley said.

I swear, Sam said. He looked around then at the pitiless look on the detective's face and suddenly he was hit by a wave of sadness. He looked down at his shoes to hide the tears welling in his eyes. It took him by surprise.

It's all right, kid, Riley said. Spill it. What else you got to lose?

Sam sniffed, then just started telling the truth. I did it the first time just about six months ago.

Did what?

Heroin, Sam said.

And now you got a habit.

Uh, yeah, I guess I do, Sam said, and took the tissue Riley handed him, embarrassed, looking down at the grimy floorboards.

Look at me, Mr. Huebner, the detective said, checking over Sam's record. We get people like you all the time. Wanna take a walk on the wild side. You know how many like you I've seen bleeding on some floor or six days cold blue in some shooting gallery with a needle hanging out of their arm? For music, for fun, for a little wild fucking cherry. You want to be a writer, then be a writer. This is not the way.

Yes, sir.

Where you from, kid?

I grew up in Georgia.

Riley looked Sam over and scratched his whiskery chin. You ever read *Crime and Punishment?*

Excuse me?

Riley laughed hoarsely. You think cops don't read. You junkies all think you're so smart.

I read it, Sam said.

He was smart too, that guy. He thought he was going to get away with it. Everybody thinks they're going to get away with it. But no one gets away with anything.

Sam winced, but didn't say anything. Riley liked to hear himself talk.

You're playing it to the fucking bust.

I don't even know what that means, Sam said with irritation.

You're waiting for the hammer to fall. You say, I'll stop when

X happens. When I lose my girlfriend, when I steal from her, when I borrow from my brother, when you go to jail. You know what most guys do when they get out of jail? You think their girlfriend is waiting for them?

Sam looked at the floor and was quiet again.

Tell me quickly, no bullshit, what connection you got with this case?

I got a little dope from Fat Tony. I planned to sell it, but . . .

You did it all.

Not all of—Sam started to say, and cut himself off when he looked at Riley, who was shaking his head, No—that's right, Sam said. I did it all.

Riley laughed sadly. And Fat Tony came to collect his money. Go on.

He told me to drive this car to this place in Harlem. I had to do what he said.

I guess you did. Riley nodded. And you picked up a guy.

Sam just looked at him, he didn't nod yes or no.

And he went in the house and killed somebody. You waited and drove him back downtown. He got out. Did he toss the gun?

Again Sam just returned Riley's look.

Riley laughed his sad laugh. I'll take those both as yeses, he said. Well, today's your lucky day. I got bigger fish to fry. If I say you're free to go, how quickly you think you can get out of here?

Uh, real fast, sir.

You get popped again, I'll hear, and you'll write your own fucking ticket, you hear?

Yes, sir.

Now Fat Tony and Chico have already been arrested. You won't have to pay them back. When I turn around I never want to see you again. You can look at this as junkie luck and keep going the way you are. Or you can figure out a way to get your shit together. You look like a smart guy, Mr. College Professor, you decide.

With that Detective Riley shook his head, lit a cigarette and turned back to the coffeemaker.

Sam got to his feet quickly and left.

In the daylight sight, Sergeant Huebner saw what looked like Iraqi soldiers.

Troops on the ground, front, he reported.

Got them, Jobe said, .50-cal. Hold your fire.

Huebner clicked on ten power for a closer view.

Sweat poured down the face of the burdened man.

The man he carried had passed out, tongue hanging from his mouth. One of his boots was gone, just a blackened, charred stump.

What should we do with him, sir?

Leave 'em for the infantry. He won't get far that way. We've been ordered out of the area, Jobe said. We've been ordered to move east along this road. It crosses the Basra highway. We turn southwest to the border, then back through Saudi to the port of Dammam. We're going home, Jobe said in a soft voice.

Since they'd lost Morrison, they all doubled up. Jobe refused another man and Colonel Agard let it go. He owed them. In a different situation, maybe it would have mattered, but it didn't now.

What's the travel plan? Maxwell asked over the headset. Down in the hull, driving, he had followed their conversation over the radio.

Straight down beside the highway, Captain Jobe said. Huebner looked at Jobe and they exchanged grim smiles.

As they rode on, Jobe and Huebner switched places. Jobe
said he wanted to get out of the sun, though there wasn't any.
They took turns riding in the turret and manning the main gun.
Reports came over the command net of more oil fields set afire.
The oily smoke clung to everything, the tank, his skin, and what-
ever refuse of the war was on the ground.

This is it, fellas, Captain Jobe said over the company net to all
platoons. This is Kuwait City to Basra highway. The road
stretched from Kuwait City to Basra and on to the Tigris and Euphrates River Basin. Blackened burned-out cars, blown-out windows, bits of glass scattered, glittering in the sun amidst the sand
and corpses.

Maxwell slowed the tank to a crawl. The tanks rode single file
now in a long line snaking down the length of the highway. A pris-
tine orange Chevrolet Impala station wagon had been pulled up
sideways across to the edge of the road, the back door sprung
open, footprints leading off in the sand.

The highway led to the crest of a valley and then cut down
through the middle. Captain Jobe called over the radio and they
stopped there at the edge. Little scrub trees sprouted from the
sand; their long fronds swayed in the wind.

Let's establish a laager, Jobe said. Minimal security.

He was tired. All of them were; no one talked about Morri-
son, but it was like they all were carrying sandbags on their backs.
The three of them got down from the M-1 and stood looking.
They had the company in line behind them. Alpha, Bronco and

Charlie were sweeping down through other sectors of the desert. The Dark Lords had been assigned the highway, with the others near if they needed assistance.

Cars, trucks, everything faced in a different direction: a gray Isuzu flatbed, windows broken out; a dusty black Caprice, police-car style, covered with a film of blackened red silt that glowed in the eerie twilight; hundreds more. Afternoon sun broke through the oil clouds. The road gave way to chaos, the remnants of what must have been a fierce air attack.

The fleeing Iraqis were driving up the road in a long convoy when they came to this canyon. A woman with three small children driving a truck for the first time. She had her dead husband's father with her, newly married, taking care of an old man she hardly knew. He cursed the planes as abominations from another world. Then the sky darkened; a storm of fire turned the caravan into a frenzy of fear, smoke and fire. A-10 Warthogs spat sudden death from above; their cannons sounded like the very earth itself ripped apart by chain saws from hell.

Pieces of paper still fluttered in the air, a lampshade with most of the papery covering burned away, a family album, smiling pictures, the plastic pages melted together into a one inch-thick mass, a teddy bear with one arm torn away, old newspaper stuffing leaking out, kitchen pots, blankets for children with little images of tomatoes, a cheap hydraulic fan with bright blue petal-shaped rotors. Behind it was another truck, a Toyota, in front, a car blown apart. Here, parallel to the road, a rock face had been cleaved by an explosion.

The twilight sky was like a bulb with a bad connection, flickering on and off. Everything seemed to be smoldering, still burning. The heat of the summer and fall had given way to black smoke that smothered the wind and fires that would never go out, fed by gasoline, by molten metal and ordnance, explosive charges, by chemicals and nuclear experiments, the black sky, the foul-smelling wind, unnameable pools of liquid lying by the road, portents that promised no end, no God and his benevolence, but only the truth before them. The soldiers stood and stared as pilgrims at a forethought of apocalypse flashing before their eyes. They stood and listened to the stories from the blackened lips of the burned corpses in the cars.

Suddenly an explosion a mile off shook the ground beneath their feet and sucked away the wind. Great columns of smoke rose from the opposite side of the valley and turned the sky dark. Sand churned upward in an immense vacuum, swept clean the floor of the desert, funneling into a great mushroom-shaped explosion of flames at the top.

Captain? Maxwell shouted. What the hell was that?

Huebner looked at Jobe.

Did you feel that? Maxwell said. Did you fucking feel that?

Huebner nodded.

Swirling clouds of gray and yellow smoke had reached across the valley to where the American soldiers stood. The captain wrinkled his nose and spoke calmly into his mouthpiece. He wiped the sweat from his brow, listened for a moment, said something the gathered soldiers could not catch, then dropped the handset.

Jobe lost it, just for a moment. Huebner was close enough to see it.

Jobe cracked his mouthpiece on the turret and the plastic

splintered onto the ground. He climbed down from the tank and stood beside the gathered soldiers.

Well, Maxwell said.

Engineer Corps destroying ammunition, the captain hissed.

The radio reported a weapons depot demolition in progress.

Right, Jobe said. Nice, if they would have told us they were going to blow up a bunker.

Is this some special place or something? Maxwell asked.

Captain Jobe looked at his map, checked the coordinates and laughed.

What's so funny, sir?

This is the Iraqi border. We top that ridge on the other side and we're in Kuwait, fellas.

The border, Maxwell said, you think it would be marked better.

Huebner tapped his shoulder and waved once around the whole scene with his hand. They made their mark sure enough, he said.

Jobe ordered all the men back in the tanks.

Red, White and Blue, this is Dark Lord Six. Let's take it straight through the valley. We'll meet you on the other side.

Roger that, came the reply, and they headed down into the valley at top speed. It was a release. There was nothing left alive, nothing they had to kill. Maxwell ran their tank right up over the cars or bashed them out of the way. The Dark Lord Company rode in a diamond formation through the valley of death and back up over the far ridge. They flattened everything in their path. Captain Jobe ordered it. Fuck it, he said. Let's ride, gentlemen.

At the top of the opposite ridge, Maxwell turned the tank south and skirted the edges of the exploded ammo dump. Gray smoke churned outward from the epicenter in a plume that kept them a half-mile from the source. Heavy dark clouds, no sun, like God pulled down a shade. They were beyond the border now. The tanks followed their course south, back toward Saudi Arabia, and left the war behind.

When they stopped to camp that night, Huebner slept under the gun and dreamed someone was in the tank, started it up, and he was run over. When he got up, he checked ammo and waited for the fuel trucks. When the trucks came down at dawn, Huebner was ready for them. He made a humble breakfast of T-ration oatmeal they all called Drano, and two packets of instant coffee. It was seven and a half months now since he and Meg conceived their child, since he had come to the desert. He wondered how Meg and the baby were doing. For the first time in weeks the thought of his wife and their child-to-be seemed real to him.

17

The doctor called an ambulance to take Meg to the hospital.

I feel great, Meg said.

The doctor had blazing red, bushy hair and her name was Sally. She said she was concerned about Meg's blood pressure.

There are just some tests they can do at the hospital that I can't do here, Sally said.

I really do, I feel great, Meg told Dr. Sally, who nodded at a nurse as a wheelchair was produced upon their arrival at the emergency-room entrance of Hinesville General Hospital.

Of course you do, dear. This is just a precaution.

But I'm only seven months, Meg said.

Seven and a half, the nurse answered, an older woman with a helmet of black hair and gray roots.

Dr. Sally had taken Meg's blood pressure at her own office and then said, We're going to the hospital right now.

For what? Meg asked.

The doctor just laughed. She was a tall woman who radiated authority. Meg didn't listen to what she was saying until she heard something about "inducing birth."

Did you say what I thought you said? Meg asked. I can't go to the hospital, I have to go home and clean my house. My husband is going to be coming home soon.

You will do no such thing. You have preeclampsia, rising blood pressure. You feel great because your blood pressure is so high.

I want to clean my house, Meg said.

You will stay at this hospital until you have your baby.

But I'm not due for weeks, Meg said.

Yes, as long as it takes.

Meg spent the night and the next day lying on her left side, attached to a machine that monitored her blood pressure every fifteen minutes. The doctor inserted a sponge doused with a solution to soften her cervix muscle.

This should bring junior out, the doctor said. If not, we'll have to try something else.

He looks like he doesn't know what to do with his hands, Meg said, and sighed deeply.

What? the doctor said.

Meg pointed up at the television. She was watching the news with the sound off. President Bush, Meg said.

Cecily Morrison and Nancy Jobe came in.

He looks handled, is what he looks like, Cecily said, and shook her head.

Meg smiled and gazed at the sun, just a knife of light cutting through the plastic curtains and crossing over her hospital bed.

Meg fell asleep and woke up alone. She thought only fifteen minutes had gone by, but it was dark. The doctor said if she could sleep, they should let her. Cecily and Nancy had been taking shifts. Meg dozed and dreamed that her husband, Smith, was

there in the room. She dreamed he confessed to her everything
that he had done in the war. She dreamed she had told him that
everything would be all right. She woke up again and saw the
chair was empty, and thought, He's gone.

I'm going to have the baby and he's still gone.

Around midnight, the doctor came in and checked all her vitals.

How'm I doing? she asked.

You're doing great.

I feel like I'm flying, Meg said.

That's the blood pressure and the muscle relaxer.

The doctor laughed. Oh, by the way, I called your mother.
She sounded mad that you were not coming home to have the
baby, but I told her: Doctor's orders.

That sounds like my mommy, Meg said.

The next day she still lay there. When once she turned over in
her sleep and lay on her back, the nurse woke her up. The doctor
came in the next morning, wiping sleep out of her eyes.

Did you sleep here? Meg said, waving her finger at her.

Don't worry about me, honey, the doctor said.

Why is this happening? Meg asked. Doc, I feel fine. I feel
great.

Cecily called her that morning, sounding tense.

Meg had gotten home from the hospital with the baby a week
and a half ago. Her mother had been there and every single day
James Morrison's wife checked on Meg. Meg just assumed Cecily had left something at her house. But the timbre of Cecily's
voice woke Meg up. She sat right up in bed.

I'll come and get you.

I just can't move, but I have to go there right away. I have to do something, but I can't move.

I'm on my way, Meg said.

She called to the baby. She had taken to announcing to her everything they were doing at any given moment, as in: Now we're getting dressed. Okay baby, let's put on our hat.

She was a very good-tempered baby too. Even when she cried, she seemed to be happy somehow, like she was thrilled to find she was capable of so much noise.

It was a windy morning, with the leaves dancing around way up in the trees and once in a while rain coming down like one of the gods had just thrown a bucket of water, for fun. Meg got out of the car in the rain, but by the time she reached the porch she had walked right out of the storm.

Little Jay was sitting on the porch with his baby-blue blanket, leaning his head on his shoulder, eyes languid and waiting. He stood up on the porch and poked a finger into Emma's little hand. He was going to be just fine, this one.

Cecily said her folks were on the way. She had called them, but it was a four-hour trip from Dillon, South Carolina.

They didn't talk much on the way to the post. A high school band brass section, two trumpets, three trombones, one clarinet and a girl with a bass drum and cymbals, were practicing in the gym on post that Saturday. The father of one of the trombone players worked in the office there. The band has no place to prac-tice, he said to Meg, and shook his head. He looked at the bath-room door where Cecily had excused herself. The desperate way he started talking to Meg about whatever was there made her feel sympathetic. Meg nodded and stroked Emma's head.

Cecily came out of the bathroom and followed the man into

his office. He had on perfectly pressed desert BDUs and horn-rimmed glasses.

Sergeant James Morrison's son hadn't combed his hair that day.

It's nappy, he said to Meg. She touched his cheek. You're a brave boy, she said. Be brave for your mother. When she comes out of that door there, I want you to go up and give her a big hug. You hold your mama's hand.

My daddy is killed, little Jay said.

We don't know that, Meg said. Jay looked at her, curiously, and Meg patted his head, picking at a piece of baby-blue cotton lint stuck in his hair.

There is nothing more beautiful than the hair of a child, Meg thought to herself. It helped a little to pronounce things like this to herself and keep her mind off what was happening. She tugged at her own child, nestled in the carry bag across her chest, with a little sailor's hat, sleeping, blowing a little bubble out of her adorable mouth, not disturbed by the keening, sometimes out-of-tune music coming from the other side of the gym.

She could see Cecily through the little glass window to the office.

Why were they doing it here? she wondered. Why does the Army do anything?

The Army is really good at one thing, Smith said to her once. They were parking for a family picnic on post the year before. A muddy mess, on a hot, humid day.

It could have been Smith. Whenever she let her mind wander anywhere near that thought, even in the same vicinity, she lost her breath. It just went away, like the wind just before a tornado hits, when the air turns that sickly green and everyone stands there waiting for the boom and crash and knows there isn't anything at all they can do at that moment to stop it.

The brass section marched in a circle. They played a version of "Take Five," the jazzy Dave Brubeck tune. Meg knew it from her old days in the band. She had spent a couple years as third chair in the clarinet section until she filled out and felt comfortable enough in her own body to go out for cheerleading.

Now Cecily was coming out of the office. The band stopped for a moment as if on cue and there was a fragile silence there in the dusty gym. Little Jay got up, took his mother's hand and that's when she started crying, soft at first and then slowly collapsing into real tears at the touch of her son's hand.

The formation stretched out over miles across the desert. At night, the Dark Lord Company camped in a great circle, the soldiers out in the open by their tanks. Sergeant Huebner was numbed by fatigue and everything else, almost too tired to stand and piss. He drank three bottles of water, then passed out in the sand. When he woke up there was the pungent, fresh smell of onions and a man yelling at them.

Hold on there, Captain Jobe was saying.

Maxwell had the M-16, but the captain stood in front of him.

Huebner walked up to the Kuwaiti. They communicated by making signs with their hands.

This is his land, Maxwell said. A farm.

What does he grow? Huebner asked.

Onions, the captain and Maxwell said at once.

That's right, Huebner said, and smiled. He doesn't want us to run over his land.

The man smiled. He had a perfectly starched white thoab, a pair of dress slacks and sandals. The man spread his arms, gesturing over all of his land. A hundred goats milled around the tanks.

What should we do, Captain? Maxwell asked.

Go around, Captain Jobe said.

They gave the farmer a short ride in the tank. He rode with his head out of the hatch, in Morrison's place, pointing the way around his crops. The farmer seemed to offer to cook up a goat for the Americans, but the captain said no.

Another time, Jobe said.

They spent a couple of weeks back at the port in Dammam. Soldiers came in from the war and were shipped home. Huebner and the others spent a lot of the time washing the tanks and accounting for equipment. All the tanks in D Company had to pass inspection of the U.S. Department of Agriculture before they could be sent stateside.

A mile's walk into the tiny old fishing town, there were a lot of old boats, wooden fishing rigs, old crusty captains. It reminded Huebner a little of the docks in Georgia. The second day they were there, the black water started to wash in and by that evening the water was the color of tea. Huebner stood on the dock and watched a sea bird swoop down toward the water.

No, don't, he shouted at it, futilely.

There was no splash when the seabird entered the oil-clogged Gulf water. It was almost sucked in from the sky. The bird came up once, choking, Huebner could see it from fifteen feet away, then it was gone into the black.

Another kill, thanks to the absurdity of modern warfare, Captain Jobe commented.

They held a memorial for Morrison and the two others who had died at the Basra airport. Full battle dress, with a twenty-one-gun salute, a chaplain. Colonel Agard said a few proud words, quoting from President Lincoln's Gettysburg Address.

On the street one day Huebner walked into a raucous victory parade. It didn't cheer him, though. He was almost run over by a honking car. The Mercedes convertible pulled over and a chubby man got out and handed Huebner a cheap Kuwaiti flag on a wooden stick. He held up a picture of the emir.

No thanks, Huebner said, and smiled. You keep it.

The man bowed, got back into his car.

Can I give you a ride? he asked.

Huebner smiled and got in. What the hell! he thought.

They exchanged hollered pleasantries as the man sped through the streets, past wrecked buildings, with looted and abandoned possessions: couches, bicycles, refrigerators and washing machines, scattered on the sidewalks. The sky was dark from the oil fires and F-15s streaked loudly overhead in tight arrow formation, fireworks in a storm.

This has been quite a war, the man said to Huebner when the man dropped him off at the port.

You said it. Huebner shook his head and thanked him for the ride.

Nice car, Maxwell said. He was standing at the gate talking to the sentries as Huebner showed ID and walked through.

On a clear day in April at dawn, Sergeant Smith Huebner finally got back on one of the DC-10s and rode to a connection in Germany. Thirty minutes before the plane landed in New York, word was passed that the connecting flight would not be until 1200 hours, nearly seven hours after their landing.

Groans went up. Fucking Army, hurry up and wait, Maxwell said.

Huebner sought out Captain Jobe. The seat next to the captain was empty. Jobe's eyes were closed, so Huebner was surprised by the captain's greeting.

What is it, Sergeant?

Huebner sat down and asked him if he could sneak away to see his brother in the city.

Are you joking?

Huebner didn't answer. The captain opened his eyes and saw the look on Smith's face.

You tell no one.

I'm sure I can slip away, sir.

I don't want to hear. Climb out the bathroom window for all I care. If anyone asks, I don't know where you are. If you're late, you're AWOL.

Thanks, Captain.

You heard what I said.

18

Smith had the name of the hotel scrawled on his hand. Everything had come together quickly. His body was in New York on his way to visit his brother, his mind and soul were still in the war and his heart was being pulled by his wife, Meg, in Georgia just eight hundred miles away. In a few hours he would see his new daughter for the first time.

Smith walked west on Forty-second Street to Eighth Avenue then north to Forty-seventh. The Sherman was on the southwest corner. The front door of the hotel was open and Smith walked right in. He even had Sam's room number from the last letter he'd gotten in the desert, 301. Smith walked up the stairs and knocked on the door.

Oh, shit! Sam whispered when he opened the door and saw his brother. Sam stood there for a few seconds like he didn't know what to do. Wait a minute, what are we doing here?

I'm your brother. That's what we're doing, Smith said. Sorry to come so early.

I haven't been sleeping.

Aren't you going to ask me in?

Sure, I mean yeah, come on.

Smith hugged his brother, but Sam was stiff, distracted, so it was awkward. Sam waved his hands in the air and went over and opened up the window.

Let's sit down, Sam said. The room was tiny, close and smelled of smoke. They took seats at a small card table. There were two chairs, both kitchen chairs, hard, with the cushions just pieces of cardboard covered by linoleum. There was a little wooden rocking horse, a dime-store American flag on one windowsill over the street, and bloody handprints on one of the dirty walls. Outside the window hung a sign with the name of the hotel.

You have a fire in here or something? Smith asked.

What? Sam said. No, must have come in through the window.

But you just opened it, Smith said, then regretted that he had.

Right, Sam said. So, how long are you here? he asked.

Six hours.

And you're going home tomorrow?

That's right.

I bet you can't wait to see Meg.

You know it.

Has she had the baby, yet?

She had Emma, two weeks ago, Smith said, checking his watch.

Wow, isn't that a fucking trip? Sam said, and ran his hand through his hair. Hey, wait a minute, Meg sent me a picture, he said. I wasn't thinking straight. I have a picture of your baby. Have you seen it?

No, my last mail won't catch up to me for months probably.

But you've talked to her.

Just for a minute, when I heard we were flying home.

Of course, Sam said. He jumped up to find the baby picture of Emma, like he knew right where it was. He looked under some strewn newspapers on the floor, picked a book from a stack and pulled the photograph out and handed it to his brother.

She's got Meg's eyes, Sam said.

Smith said, Oh, yeah, like he'd forgotten that his wife had blue eyes after eight months in the desert away from her.

Why are you in New York?

Just a stopover, Smith said. You got coffee?

I got beer.

All right, what the hell.

Sure, let me see, Sam said, and went over to the refrigerator. It's Beck's, he said. Wasn't that your favorite in college?

Yeah, when we couldn't get Red, White and Blue.

That was piss, wasn't it, Sam said, and looked at the one he'd gotten out for himself, Miller High Life. He shook his head like what the hell and drank almost half of it in one long pull.

You were thirsty, Smith said.

You must be too, Sam said. Just off the plane from the desert and all. He looked edgy, kept patting his jacket pocket.

Go ahead, Smith said. It's not like I called ahead.

Sam laughed uneasily. He reached into his coat pocket, took out a bag and laid a couple of lines out on the tabletop.

Smith started to stay something, but thought better of it. He took his beer and went to look out the window.

Sam nodded out at the table fifteen minutes after he did the lines. Smith helped him over to his bed.

I guess I'll go for a walk, he said, and Sam nodded. I'll get you some groceries, Smith said, but Sam was already out.

Darkness was falling when he went outside. He felt strange to be in the city. The noise of the traffic made him flinch when he crossed the street. This made him laugh at himself. All the lights seemed too bright. When he stared at a woman in a red dress for too long, she frowned at him and looked his uniform up and down. There was a bodega open on the corner. He spent a long time just staring at the rows and rows of brightly colored packages.

Can I help you find something, buddy? the counterman asked.

Smith bought juices and pasta, sauce, and lots of fruits and vegetables. Smith bought cans of black beans and some Luck's black-eyed peas that were the same brand they had down in Georgia. He took his time and an hour had passed when he went back up to Sam's. On the corner down the street from his brother's hotel, he saw a homeless man with a sign that said: Vietnam vet, Hungry and Need Work.

Smith dropped a few coins into the man's box and walked on. When the man called, Thanks, Smith didn't look back. He felt awkward and there wasn't anything he could think of to say.

Smith found his brother Sam awake again, at the kitchen table, staring out the window.

When Smith walked into the kitchenette area with the bag of groceries, Sam excused himself to go to the bathroom. Smith put the groceries away. After a half-hour he went down the hallway to the bathroom. He knocked once lightly and then opened the door. Sam was sitting on the toilet. He had a foil pipe in his hand. Sam took a deep breath and said, Don't.

Then something gave in him. He walked past Smith, back to his room. There was someone at the door, with dark sunglasses and a faded black T-shirt. The T-shirt said "Death With Dignity Hospice" on it.

Who the fuck are you? Smith asked him.

Charlie, he said.

That's Charlie, his brother Sam echoed.

Charlie scratched himself all over and drank from a little plastic bottle of orange liquid.

What the hell are you doing? Smith asked.

The man looked Smith over, took in his uniform.

Doing? he said. Ahh, he shook his shaggy graying head. He looked to be in his forties. This is just methadone. He said it like Smith should know. Then he said to Smith, Your brother owes me money.

You're not getting it from me, Smith said.

If he has drugs, I don't have to go, Charlie said.

Smith moved toward him.

Hey, don't get violent, Mr. Soldier-man.

Boo! Smith said, and stopped about an inch from the guy's face.

Awright, fine, I'm leaving, Charlie said, looking over at Sam as he walked away down the dark hallway.

Whatever you have to do, just do it here, Smith said to his brother.

He watched Sam smoke. Smith had smoked pot growing up. Everybody had. He used to smoke and laugh and smile. He had never seen anyone smoke heroin before. He had read about stuff like this in books and in the papers and, Yeah, he thought, this is it. The smoke smelled sweet and toxic at the same time, like something metal was on fire. It made Smith think of the airport at Basra.

Smith closed the door and Charlie knocked after a few minutes and called out to Sam.

He can smell it, Sam said. I owe him a buzz.

Fuck him, Smith said. He's not coming in.

Smith got up and stood by the door and yelled, Go the fuck away!

What did you get at the store? Sam asked.

Some beans, Smith said. Black-eyed peas, juice, pasta, stuff like that.

Thanks.

Haven't you had enough of that? Smith said. I can make us something to eat.

Sam's jaw quivered. He took a hit and held it. No, that's okay, he said, and coughed. You go ahead. I just want to finish this. Sam took a drink and another hit off his pipe. His eyes glazed over and when he looked at his brother, he seemed surprised to see he was there.

Smith, he said.

What is it, Sam?

I always thought that war was just wrong.

War isn't just wrong. It just is.

Did you kill anyone over there? Sam asked.

Smith nodded. He reached into his breast pocket and found the belt buckle he had kept there since Maxwell had picked it up and given it to him in the desert. He felt an immeasurable surge of anger well up for his brother, but he swallowed it. He put the buckle down on the table. Sam looked at it and then at Smith.

What was that like?

Smith looked at his brother to make sure he wasn't being fucked with, but Sam was the brother he once knew again. He was open. Why do you want to know that? Smith asked. Don't worry, I didn't do anything you have to be ashamed about.

Sam took a drink, then put his beer on the table.

That's not what I meant, he said. So you did it. Did you see what happened to the other guy?

There wasn't much left of them, Smith said.

That must have sucked.

It got easier after the first time, Smith said, looking away.

Yeah, for me too, Sam said.

What are you talking about? You didn't . . . don't try to tell me protesting was like the war, Smith said, and felt his anger rise again. He looked away and took a breath.

Sam said, I'm not talking about that. It's not the same. Nothing's the same. Just fucking up, getting high, lying to you, to Eleanor, to Meg. Things you'd never thought you'd do, they get easy after the first time. That's all I meant. I'm not trying to compete with you.

Don't start that, Sam. I'm not judging you. You want to get high, get high. What the fuck do I care? Smith said, and realized he was almost shouting.

Smith lowered his voice, and said, I mean, of course I care.

I know, it's cool, Sam said, his own voice almost too low to be heard as he finished his beer. I won't ask you about it anymore. I just, y'know, had to know.

You understand why I protested the war, right?

Smith sighed deeply and said, I admire my brother for standing up for his beliefs.

Thanks.

I don't get this, though.

When you went away, at first I was angry. Then maybe I got scared.

Of what?

Scared you wouldn't come back. Or that you wouldn't understand, that you'd be angry.

At what? Smith asked softly.

That I protested against the war you fought in.

Sam, I'm the soldier, not the war. I believe that it's the Army's job to protect freedom. I know it sounds hokey. I also believe in a country that lets me fight a war while you protest it.

I guess we both have something to prove.

I guess so. Smith nodded.

It was intense over there, hunh?

It was nothing you or I could have imagined.

Sam put down his pipe and took a long drink from his beer.

I talked to Dad, he said.

So.

He watched the war a lot. He seemed worried about you.

You think you're going to get something from him, if you keep trying.

I know I won't if I don't.

I don't need anything from him. He had his chance. He blew it.

I asked him about Mom.

Why'd you do that? Was he drunk? I heard he was drinking again.

He had a heart attack, Smith. He might have been on medication. Anyway he told me things. He talked to me like an adult.

Smith started to speak, then didn't. He looked at his brother and held up his hand for his brother to stop.

Sam went on anyway. He said it wasn't his fault, that he'd realized it finally.

Isn't that convenient, Smith said, and hit the table with his fist. Not his fault.

He said it wasn't our fault, wasn't anybody's fault. He said it wasn't Mom's fault.

He said that. Dad did.

Sam nodded.

Must have been a pretty good heart attack, Smith said, and cracked a smile.

Yeah, a real earth-shaker, Sam said, and they both laughed.

What else did Mr. Sphinx tell you? Smith asked.

About what it was like for him when she left.

He was plastered the whole time. What would he remember? Smith asked. He was a young drunk, trying to take care of two little ones. Sometimes Pete and Grandpa would come over and they would all drink together. Feed you your baby food, get a bottle of whatever, all of them fucking three sheets to the wind. But you wouldn't remember any of that, would you? Smith said. You were too young.

Once he tried to kill himself.

Smith was now standing at the window. He looked at his brother, ran a finger across his throat.

Sam couldn't tell if his brother meant quit talking or was just mocking their father. He didn't ask. It was in the car, Sam said. He went out, got really drunk and ran the car into the tree. You remember that?

Sure I do, it was right after he took us to see Mom in the hospital, Smith said. I never saw her after that.

Really?

You know I never did.

Well, I wasn't sure.

Smith frowned. It scared me. Did it get worse?

Sam nodded his head. Yeah, he said. She didn't even know me the last few times I went.

When was that? Smith asked. I always envied you for having the guts to go see her.

Before she died. Maybe two, three years ago. It was up here.

It's funny, Smith said. For me she was dead years ago.

She asked for you, Sam said. She called me by your name.

You said she was crazy.

Sometimes she was. Sometimes she wasn't. Sometimes in the same few moments. You couldn't always tell.

Smith checked his watch. Oh, shit, he said. He reached for his wallet. Look, here's fifty bucks.

Sam looked at his brother.

Smith took out the money and laid it on the table. He reached for his brother's hand. Come down and see us, he said. Bring your girlfriend. How is she?

Eleanor, she is all right, Sam said, and managed a smile.

Don't be a stranger.

Really?

Yeah. When you feel up to it, Smith said, and looked pointedly over at the kitchen table and the pipe lying there beside the belt buckle.

Sam looked at his brother. He walked Smith to the door and said, Good-bye.

After his brother left, Sam took a shower. He padded with his feet wet back to his room and stood by the table. The belt buckle was there where his brother had left it. Sam picked it up. When he turned it over, there was something written in Arabic on the back, maybe a man's name or a message, he couldn't know. He sat down at the table and cried for a long time. He wiped his eyes, went through his pockets, started to count all the money he had.

Sam thought of Eleanor. He found a clean pair of pants, a shirt, his jeans jacket and a suit jacket. This was the way he had dressed in the winter when they were first together. At the corner deli he bought a bouquet of flowers for her.

It took forty minutes to get to Brooklyn. He got off the train at Bergen Street, the stop before Eleanor's place. He wanted time to call her and tell her he was there. He did this right away from the corner.

Oh, she said. I've got a few minutes.

She came down and met him on the street. Eleanor giggled when she saw him. I'm not laughing at you, she said. I'm laughing at myself.

Are you in a hurry? Sam asked. Are you going somewhere?

She looked at him and said, Sam. In a soft voice.

What? he said.

Don't. I made a phone call, she said. It's okay. We have an hour.

Sam took a deep breath. I got you these flowers, he said.

He had them behind his back. Before this would be a joke with them. He always loved to buy her flowers. It was a nice memory he had from his mother. Eleanor made him feel like his mother had then, when she would open the door and smile. Sam would be standing there with the flowers behind his back.

She would mock trying to look behind his back and he might kiss her and it was fun.

Now she just smiled.

Aren't you going to take them upstairs? Sam asked.

She looked at him like he had said something odd.

Let's go to the café, she said. There's a café here that's new.

She said the word café as if she went there all the time. Sam didn't know of any café.

Sam felt like he had been away for a long time, like a convalescent. He felt sensitive, without any protective skin. He imagined the woman at the café looked at him kind of embarrassed and wary, like he had done something wrong. The way the woman took Eleanor's order too; she was angry or a little disappointed.

It's good to see you, Sam, Eleanor said.

You look really great, he told her.

Eleanor smiled and looked to the window of the café. She had laid the bouquet of flowers on the table like she didn't know what to do with them.

The woman came back with the coffee and they both took a sip at the same time. It was funny and they laughed. Sam felt a little better.

Do you remember when I left the Bronx and stayed with you? Do you remember what you said?

Sam, Eleanor said, and looked up from her hands at Sam.

You really look great, baby, he said.

She recoiled slightly.

I'm sorry, he said. I didn't mean . . .

She reached out and took his hand. Sam, she said. I know you didn't mean it. You didn't mean for any of this to happen.

Do you remember what you said?

I told you if you wanted to live with me, you had to do it. You had to make a decision. It wouldn't just happen.

I want to now, he said. I need you. I made a mistake.

Sam said it all in a rush. When she didn't answer right away, he looked out the window, then back at her. Their hands had fallen away from each other.

I took you for granted, he said. I'm going to get clean now.
Really?

I swear. I decided today. My brother came by.

Your brother did?

Back from the war. I have realized a lot of things. It's not just
that I need your help to get straight. I want to be with you. I
never realized how you really cared for me, Eleanor. I need that.

As Sam talked, he watched her face and something in it,
something sad, made him trail off until at the end his voice was
barely a whisper.

Eleanor sighed deeply, looked at her hands and then back at
Sam.

You don't know how sick you are, she said. Of course I care
about you. Sam, she said. I don't blame you. But I have to say it.
You threw it all away. It's . . . sweet that you still think that . . .

That what? he said.

That there's still a chance for that, she said.

It was his turn to look like he'd been struck.

I'm not trying to be sweet! he said. Is it because of some guy?

Oh, Sam, she said. I beg you not to be mean. We've never
been mean to each other, she said.

Sam swallowed and reached for his coffee, but it was gone.
He looked in the bottom of the little cup and there were a couple of drops there. He looked around for the waitress, but she
had gone into the back. She had left them alone. He started to
say something but then caught himself.

Of course, it's not about someone else, she said. I am not going to lie, she said. I am seeing someone.

When did you want me to leave? Sam asked.

Sam, I never wanted you to leave.

But I did.

Sam, she said.

He looked at her and it hurt, very specific,.like a bee sting.

Please, she said. You can always ask me for anything, she said.

Anything else, Sam said.

That's a bitter thing to say.

It's just hard for me to act like this is not happening.

Sam, where have you been? Eleanor asked, and then looked away.

You're not afraid to take a chance, Sam. That's your best quality. You care too much. And you're not afraid to show it. You're like the boy you want to walk to school to make sure he gets there.

Thanks . . . first, you chase me away, now it's like you don't want me to go, he said.

Sam, I always knew. You did the best you could.

Thanks, Eleanor, he said. Someday . . . he said, but he didn't finish the sentence and she shook her head like she understood.

He realized that she expected him to make it out of this, but it would have to be on his own. She couldn't wait for him. This was something, anyway.

They both got up awkwardly and she hugged him, with her shoulders, not with her hips. When he started to pull her close, she gave him a kiss on the cheek and held herself away from him.

Sam stayed straight for a few hours after that. He got back on the subway, but instead of paying, he squeezed through the turnstile. The attendant noticed and said something into the microphone just to embarrass him. He felt a hot flush of shame. And suddenly he knew he would get high again soon. He had created a whole scenario in his head before. He would go to Eleanor; she would open her arms and her heart to him and he would get clean. When he had taken the shower and his brother had left, something had touched him deep inside. Now it had vanished again. Did he ever really want to go back to Eleanor? What would he have done if she said yes? His mind raced.

Did he expect the world would stand still for him?

That Eleanor would wait for him, put her life on hold for the last months, waiting for him to get up the guts to take responsibility for his life and the impact that he had on other people?

Sam could see all of it as he stood there on the train platform. He stepped past the yellow line and leaned over to look down the tunnel. For a moment, he lost his balance and he wondered what it would be like to jump. But he knew he never would; he wasn't the type.

He counted how much money he had. He had the money his brother had given him and his rent money for the week. He knew it was over $350, almost $400.

When he was talking to his brother, that's what he had meant to say. He was betraying himself. Smith had not said it, but it was in the air. Sam suspected it was different for Smith. He really believed in what he did. Sam had always envied his brother for this quality. It was up to Sam to find something for himself. He knew that now.

Smith had the strength of his own beliefs. He had that and Sam never did.

Meg watched another woman with a newborn and wondered if she was thinking the same thing. Meg was worried that she would look at Smith a different way, wondering, what has he done with those hands? What if he reached for the baby and he could read her thoughts the way she knew he sometimes could?

Meg worried about how she would feel when she looked into her husband's eyes, how he would look at her and about the baby, how would that be? Would she and Smith connect in the way they always had before he'd gone away to the war, before they had a baby between them?

She watched the old classic movie with Fredric March from World War II called *The Best Years of Our Lives* and wondered how the wives could do it, for the men to be away so long. There was the older banker's wife and the girlfriend who'd waited chastely for her man to come home a cripple. The movie made Meg's heart weep. She could hear it inside herself, like one of the sounds that the baby made.

The soldiers came in on buses direct from the airfield. Meg saw Captain Jobe come out and watched his wife run across the open field of grass. Meg wished Cecily was here. She wished James Morrison was alive and felt that so hard for just a second that it hurt. Then she heard Jobe's wife shouting so loud and so long that the captain had put his hands up to his ears, laughingly enjoying it, standing there. Meg saw him wipe a tear from his eyes as he looked around at all the people and the yellow ribbons and the signs that said: Welcome Home Soldiers.

The wives had spent the whole day before tying ribbons onto the chain link fence and had filled every available space; every tree that ringed the field had one tied around it. Maxwell was met by his parents and what looked like his two little brothers. There must have been fifteen family members there for him. Maxwell saw her and came over.

You're looking for Smith, he said.

Her throat caught. Had she not heard something, was it possible?

Maxwell saw the look in her eye and started to say something.

No, was all that came out, and then she heard Smith's voice. He always had a very low voice and she could feel it somewhere between her stomach and her heart.

I was on a different plane, he said. He had his dress uniform on. Meg handed the baby to Maxwell, and Smith and she buried each other in a hug. They pulled apart and he reached with one finger and traced the path of a tear on her face, then kissed her again.

Oh, Smith, I've got our little girl here. I want you to meet Emma. Cross your arms on your chest, Meg said.

Smith did as he was told and Meg laughed.

What? he asked.

You look so serious, she told him. Relax, she said. Relax. She looked into his eyes and smiled and he took a breath and did relax. She could see it. Now put your arms out in front of you, she said. Just like that, keep them crossed.

When Smith took his daughter from Meg, he kept his arms extended from his body.

Meg laughed at him and teased, You can pull her a little closer, Daddy.

Smith did it like he was following orders.

It was only when little Emma opened her eyes for a minute and looked at her father that he felt the tug in his heart.

There, see, Meg said to Emma, and poked her belly, he's got it. He's all right. He's going to be a good daddy.

They said good-bye to the others, walked across the grass together under the puffs of blue clouds as the bright sun went down behind the parade stands and the last light glittered off the green leaves.

At home, everything was new again to Smith, from an electric can opener to the toilet. He made Meg come into the bathroom with him when he got up from a nap to take a shower. Meg came in and sat on the toilet with the baby and listened to her husband talk.

Some of us had to come through New York, Smith said.

Did you talk to your brother?

Yeah, I saw him, Smith said.

How is Sam?

Not too good. He's been a lot better, he said, and looked away. Meg, do you think it's all right to have the baby in here?

Why?

I don't know, he said. Because of the water?

Oh, Smith, you're so cute. You're not worried about the water. You're worried because you're a modest guy.

Well? Is it?

All right? Sure. Smith, she said, are you glad it turned out this way?

Yeah, he said.

She smiled and looked at the baby.

Meg put Emma in her crib, then Smith and his wife went for a short walk down to the water together. He told her about the weather in the desert, about camels and all the bad food they had to eat. He told her what it was like to live out of a tank for six months. She listened and did not ask any questions. She listened to her husband talk to her and felt a sort of wonder. He was back safe from the war. Smith told her about when Morrison died, what it was like and how confusing it was and how much it hurt. He talked a little about his brother and what he had seen yesterday.

Sam's at war with the world. He doesn't even know what's happening. He might act like he does, but I could see it in his eyes, he really doesn't.

Smith went for a drive in the old Plymouth Satellite for a few hours on the old country roads by the Canoochee River swamps. When he got back home that afternoon, they sat down together in the living room of their house.

When I was a little girl, Meg said, I'm not sure if I remember this or if I just remember being told about it. Maybe I was three.

She laid Emma down on a blanket on the couch as she spoke. There were no lights on in the room and outside the sun was almost gone over the bay, turning the blue water a silvery red, and the room was almost dark.

My father took me out shopping, Meg said. And I saw some wings in a store window.

You wanted them.

That's right. I wanted the wings.

Did your father buy them for you?

Of course he did.

That's great, Smith said.

No, that's not it, Meg said. We got them home. I put them on and started running across the yard. I ran and I ran and then I fell down and I cried. I cried like I never had before.

You hurt yourself?

I wanted to fly. I cried because I thought the wings would help me to fly.

What did your father do?

He told me all sorts of silly reasons why I couldn't have wings. He said I wouldn't be able to wear my favorite sweater. He said

I couldn't sleep on my back. He made it all right. He did the best he could, Smith.

Meg pulled her hair back from her eyes. She looked at Emma, asleep on the couch, then she walked over and gave him the keys to the car.

We need milk, for our baby, she said.

When he got home, the door opened and Meg came out. It was dark now, the stars were out over the trees, leaves scratching in the breeze. Smith had parked the car by the woods before their yard. Smith wondered if he'd scared her. It was very dark in Georgia at night, by the ocean, under the canopy of trees that shelter the coast. A breath of wind came up and swirled her hair around her face.

Meg went back inside for a moment and came back on the porch with Emma in her arms. The only light was way down at the pier and that was more than five hundred yards away. There were just the stars, and the moon on the water. Smith opened the car door and watched his wife move with the sound. She didn't look startled. She looked straight into the darkness. He walked away from the car and followed her eyes.

She shifted her hip and the baby with it. Emma was wrapped in a blanket. There was the tawny gold lace of her hair and the glow of her tiny face. Meg gave him a lightness that was like the moonlight that seemed to penetrate below the surface of the bay into the depths, when the stars and the moon hit the water just down the dirt road from their house.

He stood there in the yard for a moment. He looked up at the trees and what he could see of the navy and gray sky.

I thought I'd scared you.

You don't scare us.

ACKNOWLEDGMENTS

The author would like to thank Geoff Kloske; Simon Green; Dan Green; Caroline Bruce; Peter Pavia; William Georgiades; Jim Coleman; Mark Kemp; Joe Andoe; Nicole Graev; Jackson Taylor; Brian Keener; and the houses, Hubner and Smith, Graham and Hayes; The Desert Rogues, First Battalion, Sixty-Fourth Armor; Nicholas Edelson; Rob Holmes; Howie Sanders; Richard Greene; Craig Smyth; David Rosenthal and Muhammed Taki Ebrahegen.

ABOUT THE AUTHOR

Andrew Huebner lives in New York City. He is the author of *American by Blood*.